It Started With Flowers

A PORTHGARRION STORY

by

Suzie Peters

Copyright © Suzie Peters, 2022.

The right of Suzie Peters as the Author of the Work has been asserted by her in accordance with the Copyright, Designs and Patents Act, 1988.

First Published in 2022
by GWL Publishing
an imprint of Great War Literature Publishing LLP

Produced in United Kingdom

Apart from any use permitted under UK copyright law, this publication may only be reproduced, stored or transmitted, in any form, or by any means, with prior permission in writing of the publishers or, in the case of reprographic production, in accordance with the terms of licences issued by the Copyright Licensing Agency.

All characters in this publication, with the exception of any obvious historical characters, are fictitious and any resemblance to real persons, either living or dead, is purely coincidental.

ISBN 978-1-915109-00-2 Paperback Edition

GWL Publishing
2 Little Breach
Chichester
PO19 5TX

www.gwlpublishing.co.uk

Dedication

For S.

Chapter One

Gemma

"I might be a bit late home tonight…" Dad looks at me across the kitchen table, his teacup poised halfway to his lips.

"Oh?" I finish my toast, licking the last of the butter from my fingers, and stare at him.

He rolls his brown eyes heavenwards, and shakes his head. "I've got this new man starting today," he says, with barely disguised disdain. I remember him telling me now about a new police constable who's come down here from London. Dad doesn't seem to be very impressed with the idea, but this isn't the first time it's happened. I think this will be the third Metropolitan Police transfer he's had in two years. And none of them have worked out. I hope this one does though, because it means that Dad will be able to share the load a bit. He's not the only police officer in the village, but he is in charge, and he takes his role seriously… sometimes too seriously, if you ask me. That's why I would have thought having someone come in from the Metropolitan Police, with all their modern ways and methods, would only be a good thing. Still, what do I know? Clearly not very much if recent history is anything to go by. The last two Met

Police recruits have only lasted two and four months, respectively. If I remember rightly, there was another one, before them… about five or six years ago, who only stayed for a short while, before he left too. So I suppose Dad's reticence is easy to understand.

"I'm sure it'll be fine, Dad." I try to sound reassuring, and he smiles, before he drains his teacup and puts it back down on the saucer, getting to his feet and stretching his arms above his head. At just over six feet tall, he's quite an imposing character, even out of uniform. In it, I wonder why anyone in the village would ever want to break the law, and a slight smile crosses my lips.

"What's wrong?" he asks, noticing my expression, no doubt.

I get up and walk around the table to him, putting my arms around his waist. "Nothing, Dad." He hugs me, and I nestle into him, feeling safe, just like I always do when he's around. "Have a good day and try not to be an ogre…"

I feel his chest vibrate slightly as he chuckles. "I've got a reputation to uphold," he says, and pulls back, looking down at me.

"That's with the criminals, not your new colleagues." He smiles again. *Twice in one morning. I am honoured.*

He steps away and kisses my forehead before going out into the hall to get ready for work, while I clear the table and load the dishwasher.

"See you later, Gem," Dad calls after a few minutes.

"Have a good day," I say and wait for a moment, until I hear the front door close behind him, and I relax. It's not that my father puts me on edge. Far from it. It's just that he's been dreading the arrival of this new recruit ever since he was told about it. Now the day is finally here, I know he just wants it to be over, and for the man to settle in… as do I, because then we can all get back to normal.

I sit down at the table for a moment, wondering if 'normal' is really so wonderful. Dad seems to like it. He's relished routine for as long as I can remember, although he's probably been worse in the last five years, since Mum left us. He feels responsible for me now... me, and the rest of the village. Sometimes, though, I wish he'd lighten up a bit, and maybe find someone else to share his life with. He never listens when I suggest that to him, though. He seems to like things as they are, and I suppose 'normal' suits him better than me. I'm twenty years old and I'd have to say that 'normal' isn't really doing me any favours at all. I've got a job I love, and a roof over my head, food on the table and an element of security, but I know there's something missing...

Having someone to share it with.

That's like a gaping hole in my life. I've never had a boyfriend, or anyone special, unless we're counting the few kisses I shared with Dan Moyle in year ten. I'm not sure we can count them, though... partly because it was Dan, but mostly because there was never anything official about it. We'd been friends for years – probably since birth – mainly because our fathers have been lifelong friends too. Then, one day, at the beginning of year ten, he kissed me, right out of the blue, on the walk back home from the bus stop. He didn't say anything. He simply stopped walking, turned to me, and kissed me. Just like that. I liked it, and he must've done too, because he did it again... and I liked that even more.

Neither of us commented on the change in our relationship. We didn't see the need. We just went with it for a few weeks... until that awful day, just before Halloween. Dan had already dropped me off at my door, with a smile and a lovely kiss, and he'd walked along the harbour to the pub where he and his parents lived, letting himself in through the back entrance. His dad was out, but he found his mum, lying on the floor at the bottom of the stairs, surrounded by upturned cups and plates. He ran out onto the harbour, distraught and shouting for help. My father was passing, and took charge... realising straight away that Suzannah Moyle was dead. Dad got hold of Dan's father Ed, who'd gone to visit his mother, and told him to come home, without revealing why. Then Dad brought Dan back to our house. I was in the living room, eating custard creams and pretending to do my homework, when Dad came in, with Dan in tow, and I've never seen anyone look so altered. Dan had always been the life and soul of the party, but he was withdrawn, silent... shocked. Later on, when Ed got back, Dad took him into the kitchen and told him what had happened, while Dan sat in the living room with me. The door might have been closed, but I can remember the sound of Ed crying, even now.

It transpired that Suzannah Moyle had suffered a heart attack, which shocked the entire village, given she was only thirty-four. The fall down the stairs had nothing to do with her death. Dan's father went to pieces, and it fell to Dan to hold everything together. My dad did what he could, and I tried to support Dan myself. Things were never the same between us, though. We stayed friends, because that was set in stone. But the kissing stopped. That fledgling part of our relationship floundered on the rocks of his grief, and there was nothing we could do about it.

Months later, when Dan finally resurfaced, I was busy with my schoolwork, and he got into surfing... and started going out with Teagan Penrose. I didn't mind in the least. He was happy, and Teagan's fun-loving attitude to life brought him out of himself. I still had his friendship, which was what I valued the most. I needed it, too, when my own mother left, about a year after Dan's mum died. She literally disappeared into the night without a word, other than the note she left for my dad. I didn't get to read it because it was addressed to him, but when I asked him what she'd written and why she'd left us, he just replied that she'd said she had to 'find herself'. I can remember being astounded by that... and confused. But Dad was hurt, so I couldn't talk to him. I turned to Dan instead, because I had no-one else, and he listened to me rant about how selfish Mum was. He put his arms around me while I cried, because I felt so unloved and so abandoned. That was something he probably understood better than anyone. And even though we both knew there was nothing between us anymore, other than friendship, we were both okay with that.

His relationship with Teagan Penrose didn't last more than a couple of months, I don't think. I can't remember now. I know it wasn't very long, and after her, he had a string of other girlfriends... while I waited for 'Mr Right' to come along.

I'm still waiting.

My confidence that he'll walk through the door one day remains undimmed.

As I've got older, though, I've wondered whether I'll know him when I see him... and if I'll know what to do with him. It's not as though I have a huge amount of experience with men, after all.

In fact, I don't have any.

I startle back to reality, realising the time, and get to my feet, pushing the chair back under the table. I quickly wipe down the work surface and the table with a damp cloth, so the kitchen is clean. Then I get out a packet of mince from the freezer. I can easily make either spaghetti bolognese or a chilli for dinner tonight, and either of them will keep quite well if Dad runs late. Once that's done, I slip on my shoes, tie my light brown hair up into a ponytail, pull on a jacket over the top of my jeans and jumper, and grab my handbag from the end of the stairs. Finally, I check I've got my keys, and head out of the front door, pulling it closed behind me.

Dad and I live in one of a row of about ten terraced houses right on the harbour, each of which is painted in a different pastel tone. Ours is the pale yellow one and, like all the others, has three steps from the front door, down to the pavement. Once I've reached that, I cross the narrow road to the other side. Here, a low wall skirts around the edge of the harbour, and I run my hand along its rough surface as I walk to work. Gazing out to sea, I watch the spring sunshine as it glistens in jewelled sparkles on the water, the small boats bobbing up and down on the gentle swell. I might have lived here all my life, but I never grow tired of this view, and I don't think I ever will.

I reach the corner opposite Bell Road, which leads up, away from the harbour. The doctor's surgery is up there, along with the Seaview Hotel. There's also a new art gallery that opened a few weeks ago, in readiness for the influx of holidaymakers that we always get at Easter. This is a popular tourist resort and they'll keep coming right through the summer months and into the autumn. Some people around here don't like that, while others welcome visitors with open arms… it depends on your perspective, and what you do for a living.

There are lots of houses in Bell Road, and the streets that lead off of it, but opposite the art gallery, there are some really pretty little cottages that I've always admired. I remember, when I was little, I used to wish I could live in one of them. Actually, I still do.

This next part of the harbour – the longest part – is where all the shops are… or at least most of them, anyway. We've got a butcher's, and a baker's… but no candlestick makers. We also have a café, a fish and chip shop, and an ice cream parlour, as well as a gift shop, a pharmacy and an estate agent's. Around the other side of the harbour, on the opposite corner to Bell Road, is Church Lane. Needless to say, that's where the church is, along with the police station. There's also a small Italian restaurant and the local garage, and beyond Church Lane, on the far side of the harbour wall, is the main car park and the pub. It's called The Harbour Lights, and is still owned by Ed Moyle, Dan's father.

Right in the middle of the row of shops is my place of employment... Imelda's Flower Emporium. 'Emporium' might seem a little grand for a florist's shop, but at least it's one of the few places around here that doesn't feature either the word 'Harbour' or 'Sea' in its name. Instead, it's called after its owner, Imelda Duffy... my boss.

I think Imelda is fifty, or thereabouts. She's very cagey about her age, but she's owned the flower shop for the last ten years, since she moved here from France. She lived there for about fifteen years and before that, she had homes in Florence and Athens. She's full of stories of great love affairs, and is a very cultured, free-spirited person, who says exactly what she's thinking, when she's thinking it... and I love her dearly.

I've worked for her for two years now, since I left college, with no idea what I wanted to do. I just knew I wasn't cut out for university, or anything else that involved leaving Porthgarrion. Imelda was advertising for someone to work in the shop, and when she offered me the job, I can still remember questioning her sanity.

"I know nothing about flowers," I said, marvelling that she was willing to take a chance on me.

"Neither did I, and I bought a flower shop." She chuckled and offered me a cup of coffee.

That sums up Imelda, really, and since then, I've spent my days surrounded by blooms and buds, and Imelda's sage advice. Until two weeks ago, that is, when she tripped outside the shop.

It seemed she'd sprained her ankle, but she hadn't; she'd broken it. As a result, she's been laid up in her flat above the shop ever since, and I've been running the place, single-handed.

I haven't minded… in fact, I've quite enjoyed myself.

I've re-arranged the shelving and some of the displays, and reorganised the filing system, and I've made a point of taking my brief lunch break upstairs with Imelda every day. That way, she doesn't get too bored, and she can keep up with all the gossip, which is what keeps her going at the moment.

I reach the flower shop and use my key to open up, sucking in the scent of slightly overblown roses, as I let out a shiver. That's got nothing to do with the sea breeze. It's because we keep the temperature fairly cool in here, which is good for the flowers, but not so great for me. Still, experience tells me I'll get used to it in a few minutes, and I go through to the back of the shop. I turn on the lights, because it's always a bit dark back here, and then put my handbag on the hook behind the counter. Then, shrugging off my jacket and placing it on top of my bag, I return to the spiral staircase and look upwards.

"Good morning, Imelda."

"Good morning," she says in reply. "Come on up." I tread carefully to avoid the ferns that adorn the first four or five steps, and make my way into the living room at the front of her flat.

As I push open the door, Imelda turns and smiles at me from her position on the sofa. She's dressed in a long, flowing skirt and frilled blouse, with her dark blonde hair piled up on top of her head. Her feet are out in front of her on an overstuffed footstool, and her ankle is encased in a cumbersome fracture brace, which she assures me is more comfortable than it looks.

"Did you have a good weekend?" she asks, sitting up with a little difficulty.

"Not too bad." I straighten the magazines on the table beside her and pick up the book that's lying on the floor. It's a romance novel, with a rather raunchy looking cover, and I raise my eyebrows at her. She smiles in return and takes the book from me, putting it down on her lap.

"I'm not dead yet," she says, and I chuckle, going over to the window and pulling the curtains all the way back to let a little more light into the room. As I turn, I take in the decor, which is typical of Imelda. The furniture is mis-matched, and brightly coloured, and there are throws and cushions everywhere… and while it may not be my style exactly, I do like it in here. It's comfortable, and lived in… and very different to the rather sterile environment I'm used to at home, where everything has a place.

I offer to make us both a coffee, and Imelda smiles her acceptance as I make my way through to her kitchen, which is more organised than her living room… but only slightly. Normally, when she's fit and well, we make our drinks downstairs in the small kitchen that's at the back of the preparation area behind the shop. But at the moment, it's easier to make Imelda's drinks up here and carry mine downstairs, and once I've poured us both a cup from the brightly coloured cafetière, I take hers through and give her a smile.

"I'd better get on," I say as I back up towards the door. "We've got our delivery coming in later on."

She smiles up at me. "You don't really need me at all, do you?"

"Yes," I say, and she chuckles as I grab my coffee from the kitchen and head back down the spiral staircase.

I love working here, especially now I've rearranged things so they're not quite so haphazard. The counter is at the back of the shop, beyond which is an archway that leads to the preparation area. This is where we produce any large orders that need additional space, and where we put the deliveries when they come in, so we can sort through them and organise everything before we put it out on display. Out here, in the shop itself, there's one wall which features two large, cream painted dressers, both of which house various vases, ribbons and pots. Then on the floor and the raised plinth by the door, there are wooden crates, wicker baskets, and galvanised buckets, all filled to the brim with fresh flowers. Putting my coffee down on the counter, I pick up two buckets and carry them outside, putting them down on the pavement along the shop front. It might be hard work, but I'm relieved we'll be getting one of our twice weekly deliveries before lunchtime, as our stocks are looking a little depleted and sorry for themselves this morning.

After I've straightened the buckets, making sure they're neat and tidy, and that no-one can trip over them, I stand for a moment and look out over the harbour. I wave to Rachel, who owns the bakery two doors down. She's just putting up a poster in her window, and I smile to myself, because while I may be a little lonely, and even a little bored, I am truly blessed to live in such a perfect place.

Chapter Two

Tom

"You do like the house, don't you?" I can hear the worry in my mother's voice and I smile to myself as I glance around my new living area. I'm already getting quite attached to it here, even if there are still far too many boxes to unpack.

"I love it, Mum. Stop fretting."

"Well, I've never chosen a house for someone else before," she says, and I suppose I can see her point. When I received my transfer to Porthgarrion, I knew I'd have to find somewhere to live, but it wasn't practical for me to keep driving down here to look at houses. So, I set my mother and Aunty Andrea the task of finding me somewhere to live. Of course, I didn't expect them to find me a house in the village itself, and I don't think they did either. But now I'm here, I'm glad they did. As I say, I like the house, and it's good that I can live in the community I'm going to be policing… as of tomorrow morning, when I start work, that is.

"So you don't mind the fact that there isn't a main bathroom?" There's a residual doubt in her voice. "Andrea and I weren't at all sure about that."

"There's a downstairs toilet," I point out. "That's all guests are ever likely to need." Assuming I have any guests, of course. "And I like the fact that it's all so open-plan."

"Even though it's not how you're used to living? You don't mind the fact that you can see the mess in the kitchen when you're sitting on the sofa?"

I smile. "I haven't had a chance to make a mess in the kitchen yet, or clear the sofa so I can sit down on it… but hopefully it'll encourage me to be more tidy."

I'm not convinced it will, and judging from the silence on the end of the phone, I don't think Mum is either. Still, I do like having everything so open, and I particularly love the upstairs, where there's nothing except my bedroom and the ensuite bathroom. That means both rooms are quite large, and the bedroom has windows overlooking both the front and the back, so it's really light and airy.

"What's the village like?" Mum asks. "Andrea and I didn't get much of a chance to look around. We were in such a rush to see the house." She's not wrong there. She and Aunty Andrea were busy looking at properties nearer to Newquay, where Mum now lives, when the agent called and told her about this place. He'd been to see it, but hadn't had time to put it on the market yet. She liked the sound of it, though, and she and Andrea dashed over to take a look.

"I don't really know. I've only had a quick glance round it myself."

"I can't think why," she says, with a hint of humour in her voice now. "It's not like you've had anything else to do."

"No… just shopping, and staring at packing boxes… and trying to work out how I'm going to squeeze the contents of a three-bedroomed house, into a one-bedroomed one…" I let my voice fade.

"Are you okay?" she says.

"Yes, I'm fine."

"Not missing anything about your old place?"

"No. It was the right decision to move down here."

"And you're not missing anyone connected to your old place?"

"If you're referring to Kelly, then the answer is 'no'. We broke up years ago."

I think my mother has always been under the impression that, because Kelly and I bought a house together, we must have been in love – or at least destined for something more permanent. In reality, it was the opportunity to make money that captured our imaginations, when we first saw the run-down Victorian semi-detached house in Wimbledon. We'd been seeing each other for about a year at the time, but had never tried living together. In fact, we rarely even spent the night under the same roof, as I often worked shifts. We were both renting flats in different parts of town, enjoying a fairly active social life, when an estate agent friend of Kelly's pointed out the house to her, telling her about its 'potential'. For some reason, we saw ourselves as budding property developers, and having pooled our resources and scraped together enough money for the deposit, we got it for a steal. Then we set about the mammoth task of refurbishing it, kissing our social life goodbye, and working most evenings and pretty much every weekend to fix it up… while our relationship slowly fell apart.

I relished the challenge, learning how to plaster, mastering the basics of plumbing and becoming a dab hand with a drill and sander. Things were taking shape. At least, they were in my mind's eye… and then Kelly left me.

I've never been sure whether it was me or the house that she got fed up with, and by the time she left, I'd given up caring. Things hadn't been working out between us for quite a while, and when she finally slammed the door, yelling her undying hatred for me, my foremost emotion wasn't regret, it was relief.

Looking back – which I don't very often – I wonder how and why we ever got together. We had almost nothing in common and we argued quite a lot to prove it. But then, once in a while, I remember the sex, and I have to smile, because Kelly was really quite adventurous... and I liked that. At least, I liked it while it lasted. It was only afterwards that I realised great sex isn't enough of a basis for a relationship... and that Kelly had never been 'it' for me. She'd never been 'the one'.

I've often heard about that elusive 'one' person... the single individual you're meant to spend the rest of your life with. The one who captures your heart, claims you, owns you, because just the thought of being apart from them is more than you can contemplate. So far, however, I've never actually come across anyone I've been able to tolerate for long enough to even consider calling them 'the one'.

I live in hope, though. Deep down, I know there's someone out there for me, someone who I'm meant to be with... who I'm meant to care for and keep safe, and be happy with. Who knows? Maybe one day, I might bump into her... just when I least expect it.

Call me a romantic, if you like. It's quite an appropriate description, I think. Although I nearly had the romance knocked out of me by my break-up with Kelly. Not because she was a great love of mine, but because it was so drawn-out, and it became about the money... about the house. She knew I loved that place. She knew I had plans for it... but she demanded I buy her out. I suppose that was fair enough. Except she also knew I couldn't afford her demands. The alternative was to sell up and lose the house, and probably most of the money we'd invested, because it was only half-finished and not worth a great deal more than we'd paid for it.

We argued long and loud, our disputes becoming more and more vitriolic. I really couldn't see a way out of my predicament, and was getting desperate, when my mother decided to sell her house and move to Cornwall. She said she'd let me have the money I needed. I accepted, on the basis that it was a loan, although she told me I didn't need to hurry to pay her back, and it was with great relief that I finally got Kelly out of my hair.

With no social life to speak of, it took me less than a year to complete the refurbishments on the house. It was hard work, but it added a huge amount to the value of the property – as I discovered when I came to move.

"So, what did you make of the bits you saw?" my mother asks, breaking into my thoughts.

"Of what?"

"The village." She must think I'm so dense… but I've got a lot on my mind.

"It's quaint. There are some shops, right down on the harbour. And there's a hotel and an art gallery opposite the house."

"I remember seeing the hotel," she says. "But not the art gallery."

"It's quite unobtrusive."

"Am I right in thinking there was a pub somewhere on the harbour too?" she asks.

"Yes, it's close to the police station."

"That's handy," she says and I smile to myself. I'm not sure whether she means it'll be useful to have somewhere local to go after work, or whether she's referring to the fact that it won't be too far for me to drag the drunks back to the police station. Either way, she has a point.

"There's a little campsite as well… at the top of the hill, before you come into the village."

"That probably gets quite busy in the summer," she says, and I can't disagree with her. "You will be happy there, won't you?"

Her remark is rather unexpected. "Of course I will, Mum."

"It... it's just, I know you only moved to be close to me, and I feel responsible."

She sounds almost upset. "You're not responsible at all."

"Well, if I hadn't upped sticks and moved down here when your father left, and then broken my wrist last year, you wouldn't have felt the need to apply for the transfer, would you?"

"Probably not. But I don't regret it."

"Promise?" she says.

"Promise. Besides, it wasn't your fault Dad left, and I don't blame you for wanting to be closer to Aunty Andrea. As for breaking your wrist, that was an accident, so stop blaming yourself."

I'm not sugar coating my answer, or just saying any of that to make her feel better. It genuinely wasn't her fault that my father left her after more than thirty years of marriage. She said at the time that her life felt like it was falling apart, and wanting a fresh start – away from it all – seemed only natural.

She didn't just randomly choose to move to Newquay, though. She's not that scatty. Not quite. But after what Dad had done, she was bruised and battered... mentally, if not physically. Not only did he cheat on her, by having an affair with his secretary – of all things – but he ran his business into the ground at the same time. That last element shouldn't really have impacted on my mother. She had nothing to do with his company. There was some unpleasantness, though, from his creditors. Dad has used their home address to run his business, and promptly vacated when the going got tough... or, to be more precise, when the bailiffs came knocking. I dealt with most of that for her, even though I had no idea where my father had gone, and once they realised she had nothing to do with his business, or his debts, they left her alone. Still, the sour taste was too much for her, and when Aunty Andrea suggested a week away with her and Uncle David in Newquay, Mum jumped at the chance. She needed it too, and before I knew it, a week became a month. What none of us had expected was that a month would stretch too and, eventually, would become permanent. The first I knew of it was when Mum called and asked me to put her house on the market. It was her house, after all... not Dad's. She'd inherited it from her parents and – fortunately for her – she'd never given him any rights over it. To start off with, I was unsure about her 'move', and I told her so. I wasn't certain about her motives, and I thought the timing was a bit too soon after the break-up with my dad. I was worried she was over-reacting, and that she might regret it later on. However, when I came down to Newquay the following weekend, just to talk it all through with her, I realised she was right, and I was wrong. I'd never seen her looking so cheerful, or so relaxed, and I knew then that she'd made the right decision. Obviously, she didn't stay with Aunty Andrea for long, and once the sale of her house had gone through, she bought herself a little bungalow. It's about a five-minute walk away from her sister, and over the course of a long weekend, I helped her move in.

She settled in straight away, and I started travelling down from Wimbledon roughly once a month to see her. That was going just fine for us until about four months ago when I got a call from Aunty Andrea to say that Mum had taken a fall. It wasn't a bad one, but it was bad enough for her to break her wrist, and while Aunty Andrea and Uncle David, and the neighbours all rallied round to help, I felt like I was too far away to be of any use.

So I put in for a transfer. And I have every intention of making the best of it, despite my unspoken doubts. Because, regardless of everything I've said to my mother, I've got some doubts.

The decision to transfer from the Met to the Devon and Cornwall Constabulary may have been mine, but I'll admit, I'd expected that I'd be moved to somewhere like Truro, or St Austell. I'd even have accepted Plymouth. That's only just over an hour away from Mum's place… and is certainly a lot closer than Wimbledon.

When they said 'Porthgarrion', not only did I have to look it up on a map, I had to wonder what I'd let myself in for. I suppose, from the perspective of being close to my mother, it's pretty good, at just under half an hour's drive along the coast. But my doubts don't centre around the location. They centre around my profession. I've always worked in large police stations, with lots going on and plenty to keep myself busy. I've never even contemplated what it might be like to police a small village like this, where the locals all know each other, and I'm the outsider… although I know I'm about to find out.

"Are you going to come and see me soon?" Mum asks.

"Yes. How about next weekend?" I know I should probably be unpacking. I haven't done nearly as much as I'd hoped, but she seems keen to see me.

"You have remembered it's Easter, haven't you?"

"Yes. I'm working Friday and Monday, but I can come over on Saturday or Sunday, if that works for you."

"What about Saturday?"

"That's fine."

She sighs. "I suppose I'd better let you get to bed."

"Hmm… I have to be up early. It's my first day and I don't want to be late."

"It wouldn't set a very good impression," she says.

"Not really, no."

We say our goodbyes and I look around at the room I'd hoped to have finished unpacking by now.

I only moved down here yesterday, but the removals men were gone by mid-afternoon, and I've had the whole of today… and yet it feels as though I've achieved nothing. Okay, so I spent yesterday familiarising myself with the house, after which I drove out of the village to the supermarket to stock up. When I got back, it was all I could do to cook myself a pizza and eat it, before falling into bed. Today has been all about clothes… namely unpacking them and preparing my uniform, ready for tomorrow. At least that means my bedroom is quite tidy, by comparison with the rest of the house. Once I'd finished all of that, I went for a quick walk around the village, just to get my bearings, before coming back and making myself some dinner.

I'd hoped to get more done downstairs… but time seems to have gone nowhere.

Speaking of time, I check my phone to discover it's already gone eleven, which means I really should get to bed. I'm already nervous about starting work tomorrow and the very last thing I need is to be late.

It's the sun streaming through the window that wakes me, and I groan. I remember thinking to myself yesterday morning, at roughly this time, that I really ought to hang the curtains. Except I obviously forgot, because here I am again, being woken at dawn. It's my own fault. I should have been more organised. There's no point in me lying here ruing my mistakes, though. I've got to get up for work in an hour anyway, so I throw back the covers and pad through to my ensuite bathroom, flicking on the light and stepping straight into the shower. This is really more of a wet room than a bathroom, with just a single glass panel between the shower and the toilet, but no actual cubicle. The floor has terracotta tiles and is heated, and I noticed yesterday that it dries off really quickly once you've finished. The walls are white, as are the fixtures, and it's the only part of the house that has a modern feel to it.

I step out again, wrapping a towel around my waist, and brush my teeth, waiting a while for the mirror to de-mist. Then I shave, by which time, like the tiles beneath my feet, I'm just about dry.

In my bedroom, I put on my uniform and make the bed, heading downstairs, where I let out a sigh, because the boxes are still looking at me with an air of disapproval.

Still, there's not a lot I can do about that now… and I head into the large alcove that passes for a kitchen, putting on the kettle, before I realise I'm running early… very early. That being the case, I might as well make use of the hour that I've gained from having woken up at the crack of dawn, and do something productive, especially as there are a great many boxes piled up on the table. Most of them are labelled 'kitchen', and rather than standing here staring at them, I could actually unpack them.

It strikes me as odd how different my gleaming white plates and stainless steel saucepans look in this slightly rustic kitchen. It has pale cream cupboards, a beechwood work surface, and quarry-tiled floor, without a single straight line anywhere. The contrast couldn't be greater between this and the kitchen in my old house, which was dark grey, very angular and modern, and incredibly functional. As I look at the four cupboards, and then back at the six boxes I've still got to unpack, I wonder where I'm going to put everything, and whether I was completely mad when I thought I could downsize to this extent.

Beds haven't been a problem in themselves. Of the three bedrooms I had in Wimbledon, I only used one to sleep in. The larger of the other two was set up as a gym, in that it housed my rowing machine and my weights. The smaller one was an office-cum-guest room, with a sofa bed against one wall, and a small desk against the other. Although I wasn't too fussed about the sofa bed, or the desk, one of the key requirements in my new home was that it had to have somewhere I could put my gym equipment. And I got lucky here. Underneath the house is a garage, and the previous owner had converted an area at the back of it into a workshop. I knew straight away that was going to be perfect for me, and although I haven't had time to set anything up in there yet, I will. One day.

For now, I'm keeping myself in shape by moving boxes around, trying to see whether I can fit everything in. After three-quarters of an hour, I'm down to one 'kitchen' box. It contains wine glasses, and I decide I can buy myself a small free-standing cupboard which will fit neatly into the far corner of the dining area. I'll use it for the glasses, as well as the table mats and coasters, which are around somewhere…

I finish drinking my tea and quickly pour myself a bowl of cereal, now that I've got a bowl to pour it into. Then I sit down and eat at my cleared dining table, while searching online for a cupboard that will look right in here. I can't go for anything modern. The cottage is over two hundred years old, so 'modern' wouldn't work at all. But I manage to find something eventually, that's roughly the same shade of cream as the kitchen cupboards, and I order it. Unfortunately, it can't be delivered for a week or two, but the wine glasses are perfectly safe in their box for now…

I leave the house at a quarter past eight, trotting down the steps that lead up to my front door, and going down Bell Road and out onto the harbour. It's a bright sunny morning, and even if there is a slightly chilly wind, I don't really feel it as I stride along the footpath. Most of the shops are currently closed... except for the baker's which is just opening up. There's a lady standing by the door. She's got long, light blonde hair, tied up in a ponytail, and a slim figure, encased in jeans and a t-shirt, although they're mostly obscured by a navy blue apron, with the words 'Harbour Bakery' printed on the front. She looks up as I walk past, and says, "Good morning."

I repeat the greeting back at her, and she smiles as I pass on by.

I'll say something... at least the locals seem to be friendly, if nothing else.

When I reach the corner, I turn right into Church Lane. The police station is immediately on the right, opposite a neat row of five houses, the words 'Fairview Terrace' etched above the top window of the middle one. Taking a deep breath, I mount the three steps that lead to the main door, which I push open and enter inside.

Police stations have always reminded me of schools... at least in some ways. There's a hierarchy within them, that's for sure. And somehow they have a unique smell, which is hard to place. To me it's always reminiscent of boot polish and pencil shavings. An odd combination, I know, but that's what it reminds me of. They're also very different places when they're empty. It's as though the personality of the building takes over from the occupants. That's how this place feels now... even though I know it can't be completely empty, because I just walked in through the door, and that must mean someone is here.

I stand in the foyer, waiting. There's a door to my left and in front of me is a counter that separates me from the space behind it, which looks like something out of a 1950s television series. The sort of television series in which the main protagonist is a wily, chain-smoking police detective, who passes through the front of the station every day, en route to his office… somewhere in the bowels of the building. Except I'm not sure this place has any bowels. Either way, the front office features two desks, facing each other, both of which have files piled at one end, and on one of which is the oldest computer I've seen in my life. I may not be a technological wizard myself, but I think it might be older than I am, and I wonder to myself if there's a handle somewhere to wind it up. There's a small bank of filing cabinets off to one side, and in the centre of the right-hand wall is a door, which suddenly opens to reveal a tall man who's dressed in a sergeant's uniform. He's carrying a file, which he appears to be reading, and he looks up at me as he comes further into the room.

"You must be Hughes," he says, frowning.

That greeting doesn't feel quite as welcoming as the lady at the baker's, but I nod my head and hold out my hand across the counter.

"Yes, sir. Tom Hughes."

He looks down at my hand, and then back at my face, and I withdraw my hand, wondering why I offered it. It's not something I would have done at home… but then I have to remind myself that this is my home now, and that some things never change. Sergeants being one of them.

"Well, Constable Hughes," the sergeant says, with emphasis on my rank, "you'd better come in."

He moves forward and presses a button beneath the counter, which opens the door to my left, with a click, and I pass through to the inner sanctuary of the police station.

The sergeant puts his file down on the corner of one of the desks and folds his arms across his broad chest.

"I'm Sergeant Quick," he says, introducing himself. He's got dark brown eyes, to match his hair, which is just tinged with grey at the temples, and if I had to guess – which fortunately I don't – I'd say he's around forty years old. I'm probably two or three inches taller than him, but then I'm taller than most people, being six foot five. That was something a lot of my former colleagues used to rib me about, but Sergeant Quick just looks me up and down and moves over to the filing cabinets, walking ahead of me, but clearly expecting me to follow. "I'm sure you'll notice some differences between the way we do things here, and what you're used to," he says. "We don't have any of your modern gadgets down here. We have to rely on good old-fashioned police work." He turns to face me, leaning against the last of the cabinets. "That might not be something you're accustomed to, but you're going to have to get used to it, because I don't have time to carry you."

"I don't expect you to… sir." I add the salutation as an afterthought, and he knows it.

I can feel the hostility pouring off of him, even though I've done nothing to deserve it. Not to my knowledge, anyway.

I'm just about to ask if I've done something wrong when the door behind me opens and another police constable steps in from the foyer. He's a few years older than the sergeant, with salt and pepper hair and a friendly smile, which seems to be aimed at me.

"You must be the new man." He looks up at me. He's just under six feet tall, so the looking up bit is required.

"Yes. Tom Hughes."

His smile widens. "Welcome to Porthgarrion. I'm Geoff Carew."

"Nice to meet you, Geoff." I smile back at him, because this is more like the greeting I'd hoped for. "Is it just the three of us?"

"No," Sergeant Quick says, as though my question was naïve. Or stupid. Or both. "We've got a couple of Specials, and two PCSOs as well."

I nod my head, trying to feel bolstered by the fact that our staff comprises the three of us, plus two volunteers and two community officers, who have quite different powers than those of us on the regular force.

"Don't even think about looking down your nose at PCSOs and Specials," Quick says. "They might not have a prominent role to play in the big cities, but they're an essential part of policing around here."

"I'm sure they are, sir." I feel a little embarrassed that he saw through me so easily.

Geoff offers to make us both a cup of coffee and I'm relieved when Sergeant Quick accepts, giving me a quick glance. "We'll drink that, and then I'll take you out on patrol," he says, moving past me and picking up the file from the corner of the desk before he makes his way back into his office. He doesn't close the door, though, so I can hardly bombard Geoff with all the questions that have already formed in my head… and to which I'd dearly love to know the answers.

Geoff comes over to me and nods towards the small kitchen area in the corner. "Excuse me," he says, and I move aside to let him pass. As he does, he leans in and whispers, "His bark is worse than his bite," giving me a wicked smile, which I have to return. "You can take the desk with the computer on it." Geoff nods back in that direction. "I'm no good with technology, and I usually man the front desk."

"I'm not great with computers myself. In fact, I struggle to use my phone."

He chuckles and turns around while waiting for the kettle to boil. "I can see we're going to get along just fine," he says. "I've got no time for these youngsters who can't keep their eyes off of their screens for more than ten minutes."

"Then you won't have any complaints with me."

He nods his head and makes the coffee, handing me a cup, before he carries one through to Sergeant Quick. I make my way over to the desk and sit down, the chair swinging back slightly, and I take a moment to right myself.

"I probably should have mentioned that the chair has a mind of its own," Geoff says, coming back out and grinning at me.

"I'm sure I'll get used to it."

He leans forward. "You think you'll be here long enough?"

"I hope so. Why?" Does he know something I don't?

"No reason." He shrugs. "It's just that the last two men we've had come down here from the Met haven't exactly had what you might call staying power."

"Oh, I see. Is that why the sergeant is a little… negative?" I lower my voice, hoping Sergeant Quick won't hear.

"I couldn't possibly say," Geoff says, with a smile and a wink, letting me know I've hit the nail right on the head.

I've only just finished my coffee when Sergeant Quick appears in the doorway to his office.

"Are you ready then?" There's an impatient tone to his voice, as though he's been waiting for me.

"Yes, sir." I get to my feet and, without a word to Geoff, who's looking through the files on the other desk, I follow the sergeant out through the door and into the foyer.

It's a sunny morning and, as we exit the station, I pull out my sunglasses from my breast pocket, putting them on. I note, but ignore, the way the sergeant rolls his eyes at me before he turns and points up the hill, away from the harbour.

"Up there is the church, and the Italian restaurant that opened last year, and the garage, which is owned by Tim Burgess." I make a mental note and nod my head as we turn around again and start towards the harbour, sticking close to the building as a car passes, taking the corner far too quickly and clipping the kerb. "Idiot," Sergeant Quick mutters under his breath, but he lets the matter go. We turn to our right, where there's a public car park, which is half full at the moment. Beyond that is the pub, The Harbour Lights. We walk towards it and I notice a man outside, watering several tubs of flowers. He's about the same height as the sergeant, but with blond hair... the kind of blond that never changes, never shows any grey, and belies a person's age to perfection.

He glances up as we approach, and a smile forms on his lips. "Morning, Rory." He nods at the sergeant and I realise that must be my superior's first name.

"Ed," Sergeant Quick says, as the publican looks at me, raising his eyebrows. "This is our new recruit, Constable Hughes... from London."

He says the last word with an element of disdain and I want to correct him and say I'm not really from London... I'm from Wimbledon. Except that would be petty. And besides, correcting one's senior officers never ends well.

"Please... call me Tom." I offer my hand, which is accepted this time, in a firm handshake, that affords me some relief. Experience has taught me that some people shy away from befriending police officers, but I want to make friends here. It's my home now.

"Ed has a son called Dan," the sergeant says, once the introductions are complete. "He teaches surfing during the summer months."

"Here?" I look around at the enclosed harbour, which has three sides and a narrow opening out to the sea, and where there doesn't seem to be much 'surf' to speak of.

"Yes," Ed says, before the sergeant can. "There's a club about a mile or so up the coast, where they've got one of those artificial wave machines." He sounds like he barely understands what he's talking about. That's all right, though… I don't understand it either. "Dan works there during the summer, teaching holidaymakers."

"I see." I don't… not really. Surfing has never held any interest for me. But there aren't many opportunities for it in SW19.

Before we can get into any more detailed conversation, or I can ask what the landlord's son does for the rest of the year, Sergeant Quick takes a half step away. "We'd better be moving on," he says. "I'm just showing Constable Hughes around the harbour, so he can get his bearings."

Ed nods his head, and although I want to point out to the sergeant that I already got my bearings yesterday, I know better than to argue. So, instead, I tell Ed it was nice to meet him, and he tells me to drop in for a pint sometime… when I'm off duty, of course. I'm more of a wine man, but I don't bother telling him that. It was nice of him to make the offer.

I rejoin Sergeant Quick and we double back on ourselves, passing the end of Church Lane again, and walking along the fronts of the shops, starting with the estate agent's.

"Is there much call for an estate agent here?" I recall my own experiences in buying my house, which was handled by an agency in Newquay.

"They're also a letting agent, and they manage at least half the holiday homes in the village, so they keep themselves busy," the sergeant says, sounding affronted. "They don't open until ten," he adds, contradicting himself as he nods towards their obviously closed door, and we move on next to the pharmacy. That's open and I take a step towards it, surprised when Sergeant Quick doesn't follow.

"Are we not going inside?" I ask, turning back to him.

"You'll never remember everyone, if I introduce you to them in one go," he says. "And besides, this place is best avoided at the moment, unless absolutely necessary."

"Why?"

"Because the pharmacist, Shannon Truscott, has just gone through a very nasty divorce. She's a bit anti-men these days. So, unless you really need something from there, I'd steer clear." He doesn't bother with a smile, but I appreciate the warning. It's the most friendly thing he's said to me since I arrived at the station this morning.

We step aside, letting a lorry pass from behind us, watching as it pulls up outside the florist's shop, a few doors away, the driver jumping down from the cab.

"That'll be Imelda's latest delivery," the sergeant says, with a nod of his head, and I wonder to myself if anyone so much as sneezes around here without him knowing.

The next shop is the baker's where I saw that lady this morning, and as we pass, she's outside again, this time admiring a cake in the window.

"Is that your latest creation, Rachel?" Sergeant Quick asks, standing right beside her.

"It is." She nods her head, her voice a little wistful.

"It's beautiful," I say, and she looks around the sergeant at me.

"Why, thank you… stranger."

The sergeant rolls his eyes and makes the introductions again, telling me that this is Rachel Pedrick, third generation baker… and evidently creator of the most extraordinary cakes, if the one before me is anything to go by. I'm assuming it's for a wedding, judging by the flowers that decorate the top and sides of it. Obviously, I've never contemplated matrimony and all the periphery that goes with the big day – not having actually found 'the one' yet – but I can still appreciate the amount of work that must have gone into creating such a masterpiece.

Rachel averts her gaze back to the cake in question. "I think I need to turn it to the right, just slightly," she says, and disappears back into the shop, calling out her goodbyes over her shoulder.

"She seems very dedicated," I say, as we move on.

"She is. She inherited the baker's shop from her mother, but branched out into this fancy cake decorating about a year ago. I think she saw it as a tremendous risk, but she's making a go of it."

"It must be hard work."

He looks at me. "We're not afraid of hard work down here, you know?"

I let out a sigh. I'd thought we were getting along a little better... except it appears I was wrong. He seems to take offence at everything I say. Far too easily, if you ask me.

We come next to the café where the owner is just opening up, setting out a few tables along the pavement. He looks like he's about forty years old, with dark blond hair and a deep tan, and he nods towards the sergeant, who waves in return.

"That's Carter Edwards," he says as we move on without stopping. "He's been here for about five years. No-one knows anything about him... not even me. We just know he makes a mean cheese and ham toasted sandwich, and that his full English is too good to be bad."

"There are worse things in life," I reply, relieved that whatever it was that irked the sergeant, it seems to have passed. At least for now.

We by-pass the florist's, where the lorry driver is currently offloading huge boxes of flowers directly into the shop, and move on to the shop next door. This is double-fronted, one side being a butcher's, while the other is a fishmonger's. The first window has a full display of meat on offer, while the second has fish of just about every variety, nestling on a bed of ice. I can't help thinking, as we pass by, that I wish I'd noticed this place before I went to the supermarket. I'd much rather buy my meat and fish locally, and purchase just what I need, rather than having to get two of everything, which seems to be the way with supermarkets. It means a lot less waste… or the sometimes worse alternative of finding unidentified objects in my freezer several weeks down the line, and having to take pot-luck with dinner. As I glance inside the shop, I also notice that, at the back, they've got some refrigerated units, with a few basic items, like milk and cheese, and cream, on offer… and there's also a small rack of fruit and vegetables. So I guess this must be the local village store, for want of a better description.

"This is the Harbour Store," the sergeant says as we stroll past, and I'm relieved I didn't say anything now. The name above the door gives away the shop's function, and the sergeant would doubtless have thought me stupid for pointing out the obvious. "It's run by Bryn and Joan Evans… from Cardiff."

"They've moved here recently, have they?"

"No." He shakes his head. "They've been here for about twenty years now."

I find it interesting that, even though Mr and Mrs Evans have been here for such a long time, the sergeant still finds it necessary to tell me where they're from. They're outsiders. They're not 'from here'. It doesn't augur well…

Next, we come to a fish and chip shop, which is currently closed – not surprisingly, considering that it's barely nine-thirty in the morning – and we continue on to the gift shop.

"That's owned by Michael and Melissa Cole."

"Husband and wife?" I ask and he shakes his head.

"No. They're twins." He stops and looks up at the shop front. "When I was a boy, this used to be a toy shop… but their father couldn't make a go of it. The situation wasn't helped by the fact that he got dementia, so Michael and Melissa took over and turned it into a gift shop. They still sell some toys, and a few bits of hardware, to keep them going through the winter. It's not the same, but times change… I suppose."

He shakes his head, acknowledging the need for change, but only with great reluctance.

Finally, just before the turning into Bell Road, where I live, we come to the ice cream parlour… Harbour Ices. Again, it's closed, and according to the sign on the door, it won't open until eleven o'clock today.

"Ember Penrose runs this place." The sergeant stands still for a moment. "She makes the ice cream as well, although I have to say, she's got some strange ideas about flavours."

That's probably another of those changes he doesn't approve of. If it's not vanilla, he doesn't like it, I'll bet.

We've reached the end of the short parade of shops now, but the sergeant continues across Bell Road and stops on the opposite corner, pointing up the narrow street.

"The Seaview Hotel is up here," he says. "So is the art gallery, although that's quite new to the village… and you'll also find Doctor Carew's office."

"Carew?" I recall Geoff's surname.

"Yes. Our GP, Robson Carew, is Geoff's son."

"Right… I see."

He turns around, surveying the harbour.

"It's not the biggest patch in the world." His eyes twinkle as he takes in the view before him.

"I'd noticed," I say, and then regret it, as he turns to me and frowns.

"Don't be fooled." His voice has hardened now, and he walks back along the harbour, letting me fall into step beside him. "We still get our fair share of crime… and of idiots. Especially during the holidays season. You've arrived just in time for that, what with Easter coming up. Things won't quieten down again until late October, so don't think you can rest on your laurels and put your feet up, just because you've come from the big city."

"I wasn't…" I say, but he holds up his hand, and I stop talking.

"We've had a spate of bag snatchings over the last couple of weeks," he says, shaking his head. "It's happened three times now, and I'd like it resolved before we get inundated with holidaymakers, because that won't do our reputation any good at all… as a village, or a police force."

"No…" I can't think what else to say, so I don't bother.

His eyes narrow, and he glares at me. "Still, you probably won't be around long enough to worry about that, will you?"

"Yes," I reply, before he can find any more ways to put me down. "I've got no intention of going anywhere… sir." I add the afterthought – again – and he shakes his head.

"We'll see," he says. "We'll see…"

As he turns away, I can't help but feel his disappointment. I'm not sure whether that's because he's anticipating my failure, or because he's sensed I'm so determined to prove him wrong.

Chapter Three

Gemma

I've closed the shop for half an hour, so I can have lunch with Imelda. Normally, when she's on her feet, we take it in turns to have a break and something to eat. That's not an option at the moment, though, and she's insistent that I don't work right through. She's firm in her belief that, if someone wants to buy flowers from the shop, they won't mind waiting half an hour… and if they do, then it's tough, because a person has to eat. Those are her words, not mine, but I think I agree with the sentiment. Mostly.

Either way, I've made us some ham sandwiches in Imelda's tiny kitchen, along with a cup of tea, and we're sitting together in her living room. Her crutches are propped up beside her, and judging from her position, she must have got up at least once during the morning. I know she's not incapable… mainly because she reminds me of that quite often herself. But I enjoy coming up here and making our lunch… and sitting with her while we eat. It gives me a chance to talk.

She seems to have read a little more of that book I handed her earlier, and it's lying on the sofa beside her. Part of me wants to ask her about it, because I'm intrigued. The man on the cover has an incredibly muscular chest, like a bodybuilder, and his blue eyes are really piercing. I can't help wondering what it would be like to be the object of such a man's attentions, but I'm not sure I'm brave enough to ask. In any case, I've got other things to talk about. More important things. Or at least, more work-related things…

"I had a call this morning from the manager of the Seaview Hotel," I say, taking a bite from my sandwich.

She looks up, raising her eyebrows. "He's new, isn't he?"

"I don't know about new. I think he's been there for about six months."

"Which is new by Porthgarrion standards."

I smile at her. "His name's Stephen Goddard. He phoned because he wants to place a regular order for flowers… for the hotel."

Imelda sits up a little now, looking a lot more interested. "How regular?" she asks.

"Weekly, I think." I put my plate down on the low coffee table and pull the piece of notepaper from my jeans pocket, unfolding it and reading… "He wants us to do arrangements for the reception area… probably two or three. Then he wants flowers for the restaurant tables, which they can put into small vases themselves. And he wants us to provide ad hoc arrangements for whenever they have anyone using the honeymoon suite."

Imelda nods her head as I hand her the piece of paper and pick up my sandwich again.

"Well, this is very nice."

"What? The sandwich, or the potential order?"

She turns and smiles at me. "Both," she says.

"I told him you'd probably offer him a discount." I hope I haven't stepped out of line. "Is that okay?"

"Yes… yes, of course. I wouldn't expect to get a big order like this, without offering some kind of reduction." She puts down the piece of paper beside her and takes a bite from her sandwich. "I'll look through it this afternoon. It'll give me something to do… and you can send him the prices before you go home. If that's all right?"

"That's absolutely fine. I'll come up about five-thirty, shall I?"

"Perfect." She grins and sighs deeply, before twisting in her seat slightly, getting comfortable. "Did your father bring that new constable in for a visit yet?"

I shake my head. "No. I think I caught sight of him and Dad walking past earlier on, but the delivery driver was here, so I didn't get the chance to have a proper look at him… and anyway, Dad was blocking my view."

"What's your dad told you about him?" she asks. She knows him as well as anyone else, and understands that the arrival of a new recruit will have bothered my father, and played on his nerves… just like it has done.

"Not much. Except that he's come down here from London for personal reasons. That's all I know, really. Obviously, Dad thinks he's going to be trouble… because he'll have 'big city' ideas about policing and won't fit in with our ways of doing things."

Imelda rolls her eyes. "It's good to hear Rory's being positive."

I chuckle. "You're preaching to the converted, Imelda. He's always like this whenever there's someone new starting."

"Well, I think he finds it harder since your mum left… to trust people… you know?"

I can remember what he was like before, and there's no denying he used to laugh more. We both did.

"I suppose so. I just wish he'd try to be more positive sometimes. You know… hope for the best, rather than expecting the worst."

"I lived with a man who was a bit like that once," she says a little randomly, which isn't at all unusual for Imelda. "It was when I was in Athens."

"Was he Greek?" I ask, and she shakes her head.

"No, he was American, actually. He was a journalist who was living there, and we met in a rather lovely taverna, and just seemed to hit it off… or at least it felt that way. But most love affairs are like that, at the beginning… at least in my experience. In his case, it didn't last very long. He was just too downhearted for me, and in the end I couldn't be around him anymore. I don't know if it was because of all the things he'd seen in the world, or whether he was just a glass half empty kind of man, but he always seemed to look on the dark side of everything. It didn't matter how much I loved him, I couldn't live like that. He nearly drained the life out of me in the end…" She looks thoughtful, and perhaps a little sad, but before I can say anything, the phone rings in the shop, and I have to rush down the stairs to answer it.

Imelda's words ring loud in my ears throughout the afternoon, even as I'm re-arranging the new flowers, getting them to look their best in the window display, and I find my thoughts drifting to Dad. I didn't mean to make him sound so negative. He's not like that most of the time, and he'd never do anything to hurt me. He's put me first all my life… but especially since Mum left.

I suppose, though, if I'm being honest, I have been more aware of late that Dad's not happy. He's been on his own for a long time now, and although his job keeps him busy, there's more to life than work… I know that. Still, he's unlikely to discuss such things with me. We're close, but we're not *that* close.

At five-thirty, I go upstairs again, and Imelda shows me the prices she's done for Stephen Goddard, going through them in some detail. She's worked them out on her laptop, and done him a proper quotation on the flower shop's headed notepaper, which she prints out to the printer that's downstairs behind the counter.

"You can phone it through to him, if you want," she says.

"I think I'll take it up there. It's practically on my way home, and he might appreciate the personal service."

She smiles at me and nods her head. "That's a good idea. We may as well start as we mean to carry on. And, who knows, seeing your pretty face might be enough to sway the deal in our favour."

Her compliment makes me blush. I'm not used to being called 'pretty', or even being noticed, for that matter. I've lived here all my life, so I've just kind of blended in, to the point of becoming invisible. Still, I wish her goodnight before I go downstairs. I grab the quotation and fold it up, putting it into an envelope and then I pull on my jacket and take my bag from the hook and let myself out of the front door, locking it behind me.

The harbour is still busy. It's Easter next weekend and the schools have already broken up. That signals the start of the holiday season here, so it's no surprise there are tourists drifting along the dusky harbour side, buying ice creams and gifts, or making their way to the pub for an early evening drink.

I head in the opposite direction, turning left up the hill that forms Bell Road and by-passing those pretty little houses I've always liked. They're set over three floors, although the ground floor is taken up by a garage, and they have stone steps with a wrought iron railing, leading up to their front doors. I cross over the road, walking past the new art gallery, before I turn the corner and come upon the Seaview Hotel. Set well back from the road, with a D-shaped driveway, the hotel is painted in a soft cream colour and has a green awning at the front, with the hotel's name emblazoned in a golden script. I enter through the main door, into the large foyer. Its red carpet is luxurious underfoot, and there's a round table in the centre of the room. I can see that an arrangement of flowers would look perfect on there, because at the moment, it looks a bit lost, and rather pointless. The wide staircase is straight ahead, and the reception desk is off to my left, so I make my way over, clutching the envelope that contains the quotation firmly in my hands.

"Is it possible to see Mr Goddard?" I ask the man standing behind the desk.

"Yes. I'm Mr Goddard. How may I help?" I'm a bit taken aback, because he's a lot younger than I'd expected him to be. The man in front of me is probably in his early thirties, which seems quite young to be a hotel manager. He's also very handsome, with dark brown hair that's cut quite short, and hazel coloured eyes that are currently looking at me, a little quizzically.

"Yes... sorry. I'm Gemma Quick... from the florists?" I give my answer as a question, hoping he'll remember our conversation from earlier.

"Oh... yes?" His voice is no longer deferential and kind. Instead, he sounds a little more aloof, now he knows I'm not a guest, and he raises his eyebrows at me expectantly.

"I—I've brought the prices you wanted."

I hold out the envelope and he takes it from me, putting it down on the desk in front of him. "I'll look at it later on," he says. "And I'll be in touch."

"Oh... okay."

I feel completely dismissed now, but before either of us can say anything, the phone rings.

"Was there something else?" he asks and I shake my head, leaving him free to pick up the telephone and put on that obviously fake considerate voice of his as he announces the name of the hotel and asks if he can help whoever is calling.

I turn my back on him and make my way over to the door, wondering why I bothered coming. I could just as easily have phoned the prices through… or better still, e-mailed them, and been completely impersonal. Like him.

As for Imelda's suggestion that he'd be swayed by my supposedly 'pretty' face… well, that obviously had no bearing on the situation. He didn't even notice me.

I walk slowly back down Bell Road, taking my time and, to cheer myself up, I let my eyes wander over to the little houses on the other side of the street again. They really are small. I think they only have one bedroom, but size isn't everything, and although I've never actually been inside any of them, I just love the way they look. There are three of them, all lined up together, and all painted different shades of blue. The one in the middle is my favourite, because it's a cornflower blue, which I particularly like. The light is on in the front window, but as it's above my head height, I can't see inside. I wouldn't be so nosy as to try, either… even though I'm intrigued. It's not that I want to know who lives here, but I'm dying to see what the houses look like on the inside. I've always wondered whether they're as lovely as they are on the outside. I hope they are, because it would be very disappointing to find they're just plain and boring, with no character to them at all.

Turning left at the end of the road, I make my way along the harbour until I reach our house, and then let myself in. I'm still trying not to take Stephen Goddard's attitude too personally, and am surprised when the smell of onions being fried with garlic greets me as I step inside.

"Dad?" I say, hooking my bag over the end of the stairs.

"In the kitchen."

I hang up my jacket and kick off my shoes, going down the hallway and into the kitchen at the end, by-passing the living room and the formal dining room that we rarely use these days.

"You're cooking?" I state the obvious as I come into the room and see him standing by the stove, stirring something in a frying pan.

"Yes. I finished work earlier than I expected, so I thought I'd make a start on the dinner." He nods towards the pack of mince that I left on the draining board this morning. "Spaghetti, or chilli?" he asks, as though he read my mind. It wasn't hard, though. We are quite predictable in our diet. In this house, mince usually means one of two things.

"I don't mind," I say and he looks up at me.

"What's wrong?" he asks.

"Nothing… except I've just been dismissed."

He drops the spoon he's holding, and it clatters into the pan. "Imelda's fired you?"

I laugh as he struggles to fish out the spoon, frowning at me. "No… silly. That's not what I meant."

"Then what did you mean?"

He opens the pack of mince as he's talking and tips the contents into the pan, stirring as he looks at me.

"I meant that I've just been to the hotel, to drop off some prices, and the manager was a bit… dismissive. I can't think of any other way of putting it."

"Didn't he like your prices?" Dad asks.

"He didn't even look at them… which is annoying, considering he'd asked for them in the first place. Imelda had spent most of the afternoon working them out too, and I'd offered to drop them off on the way home."

"And he wasn't interested?"

"Not really."

"Sounds like he needs to be taught some manners." Dad huffs out a sigh and I go over to him.

"I'm sure he will be," I say, leaning my head against his shoulder. "But that doesn't mean you have to fight my battles for me. All right?"

He hesitates and then quietly mumbles, "All right. If you insist, but if he does it again, you let me know…"

"Yes, Dad." Before he can say anything else, I change the subject. "Do you want me to take over the cooking while you change?"

He glances down at his uniform. "I suppose so," he says. "The last thing I need is to get spaghetti sauce down my front."

"We're having spaghetti then, are we?"

"No, not necessarily. We can have chilli, if you'd rather."

"No, spaghetti is fine with me."

He nods his head and hands me the spoon before he leaves the room and goes upstairs. I'm left stirring the mince, pondering over the fact that this was one of the few things my mother taught me to cook… and wondering – not for the first time today – why she left us. My parents seemed happy to me. I don't remember any arguments, or even raised voices. All I remember is that one day she was here, and the next she was gone. It's strange… I can go for weeks and months without thinking about her, and then I have days like today, where her departure leaves me puzzled and doubting. I've never really understood why she left. 'Finding herself' was a pathetic excuse. I'm not even sure what it means, but I don't see why you need to abandon your family to do it. Maybe there was more to it than that… something she wasn't willing to admit to in her letter? I'll never know now, though. I can hardly ask Dad, and he's not likely to volunteer the information either. It's not something we discussed at the time. Dad just told me what her letter had said, and made it clear he didn't want to talk about it anymore. She'd hurt him… that much was obvious. She'd hurt me too, and although I was desperate for answers, I couldn't ask him why she'd left me behind. It would have sounded like I didn't want to be here with him… like I'd rather have gone with her, and that wasn't the case at all. I love my dad, and I love living here with him. It's just that sometimes, I wish I understood.

Over dinner, which we eat in the kitchen, as usual, I ask Dad about his new recruit and he shakes his head slowly from side to side.

"Was it that bad?" I twirl some spaghetti onto my fork and stare across the table at him.

"It was almost exactly as I expected it to be," he says, putting down his cutlery and taking a sip of wine. We don't always drink alcohol with dinner, but it seems to go with spaghetti. Besides, I felt the need to have a glass of wine, after the way Stephen Goddard made me feel… rejected, and cast off.

"So you don't think he'll last?"

Dad picks up his fork again, but rather than eating anything with it, he twists it around on his plate, like a child trying to find a good excuse for not having done their homework. "He didn't seem to understand that we don't run a twenty-four-hour service down here, or that the station closes at six… and that it's been working fairly well for us for quite some time." He's not wrong. It does work well for us. I'm not saying that nothing ever happens after six o'clock at night, but if it does, although there are official channels to be gone through, someone usually just comes and knocks on the door to let Dad know. It's quite informal, but that's how everyone likes it.

"I'm sure he'll get used to it," I say. "It must be very different for him."

He puts his fork down again, not bothering with the distraction of playing with it anymore. "He's just another typical London boy." For a second, his voice reminds me of Stephen Goddard's. I can hear the dismissive tone, and I hope he didn't adopt that when he was talking to the new man himself, because that would have made him feel very unwelcome. "Thinks he can just come out to the country and tell us how to do everything. He won't stay the course. You mark my words."

"That's… that's a bit negative, Dad."

"Maybe," he says, although I don't think he's heard what I've said. "But it's going to be a baptism of fire for him, and I'm not sure he's got what it takes."

"How do you mean?" I ask.

"He's arrived right at the beginning of the holiday season, hasn't he?" he says, like he's pointing out the obvious, and I'm being dense for not realising. "We're going to be rushed off our feet for the next few months, with strangers coming and going. New faces always make things more difficult."

"Yes, except everyone here is a new face to him. And anyway, don't you think he'll be used to strangers, and having lots of different people around, coming from London?" I may never have left Cornwall, but I can imagine there are a lot more people in London than we ever get here, even when we're at our busiest.

"He probably will be," Dad says, tilting his head to one side. "But he'll also be used to having a lot more facilities, and back-up. He won't be used to having to think on his feet, not like we do down here… so let's just see how long he lasts, shall we?" There's a slightly gloating tone to my father's voice which I don't really like, not that I comment on it. I don't get the chance, before he adds, "I'll give him until the August bank holiday before he's begging to go back to the Met."

I suck in a breath and let it out slowly, and although I've never met this man from London, I can't help feeling sorry for him.

Chapter Four

Tom

I let myself into the house, turning on the light, and drop the keys onto the box, which I conveniently left by the front door. Then I lean back against it and sigh as I gaze around the room.

I regret more than ever now that I didn't spend my weekend more wisely, unpacking and making some space to sit down. I could do with opening a bottle of wine and just crashing on the sofa for an hour… or three. But I can't, because – as I said to Mum yesterday – the sofa is still buried under boxes… so, while the very last thing I want to do after today is to unpack, I have little choice in the matter. If I don't, then I'm never going to be able to put my feet up.

Pushing myself off the door, I dodge through the boxes and climb upstairs into my bedroom, where I strip out of my uniform, leaving it on the bed for now. I won't shower yet. I have a feeling I'm going to get hot, and maybe even bothered, over the next few hours. So instead, I just put on some jeans and a t-shirt and head straight back downstairs again. I grab a knife from the kitchen, and once I'm back in the living area, I open the first box that comes to hand, smiling to myself. It's full of books, and although that makes it heavy to shift from the sofa onto the floor, at least I've got somewhere to put the contents. There are two very handy bookshelves that have been built-in either side of the granite fireplace, and I make light work of unpacking the first four boxes I come across. Doing so frees up the sofa, and I feel like I've actually achieved something with the last hour of my life.

To celebrate, I open that bottle of wine. It was one of several I picked up at the supermarket, and I rescue a glass from the box I left in the kitchen this morning, pouring a generous measure. Then I take the knife to the empty boxes, including the ones I unpacked before I went to work. Folding them flat, I go out to the kitchen area, the right-hand end of which leads onto a short hallway, past the cloakroom, to the back door, and I stand at the top of the steps that lead down to my small courtyard garden. It may be almost completely dark out here now, but I can still see that the area is roughly square, with high walls surrounding it on all sides, and is paved, with a raised flowerbed on one side. Judging from where I know the sun went down, it looks like it'll catch the light in the evenings, which is nice. I like it out here, and make a mental note to myself to spend more time in this rather secluded little space. I'll need to get myself some garden furniture if I'm going to do that though… and I might look at that later on, after I've eaten. In the meantime, I lean the boxes up against the wall, knowing they'll be safe there for now. I'll be adding to them later on, as I progress with my unpacking, and I'll take them to the tip on Saturday, when I go to visit my mother.

Newquay is only a very simple drive away, although I've got to say, after today, a part of me wishes I'd moved there instead of to Porthgarrion. Don't get me wrong, I really like my house, and the more I'm unpacking and am actually able to see of it, the more I'm liking it. I still want to live in the community that I'm going to be policing, but Sergeant Quick hasn't exactly been welcoming. Also, having now seen most of the village, I can't help thinking that Newquay would probably have more to offer in terms of a social life. However, on the down side, I would have been living right on my mother's doorstep, so I probably wouldn't have had a social life in the first place. She'd have wanted to know exactly what I was doing all the time… and who I was doing it with.

Still, it doesn't really matter now, does it? I'm here. So I'm going to have to make the most of it.

I go back into the kitchen and take a sip of my ice cold wine, looking around at all the work I've still got to do, and trying very hard not to feel too downhearted. Although it's not the work that's getting me down. It's today.

I never expected to feel quite so alienated from the people I'm working with. Yes, I expected there to be differences. Porthgarrion isn't London. It isn't even Wimbledon. There was bound to be a bit of a learning curve for me. I'd hoped for some help with that though… and instead, I've found resistance.

I'd also hoped that I might be made to feel welcome, rather than judged. After all, I'm fairly sure I got an excellent report from my previous station commander, and I'm not aware of anything negative on my record. But Sergeant Quick found fault with everything I did and said… even when I didn't actually say anything.

Okay, so I know I might have seemed a little negative about the Specials, but that's only because of previous experience with one or two of them at my old station. They could sometimes be a little self-important, and one of them in particular caused more trouble than was strictly necessary. I can appreciate that, down here, they probably have more of a role to play, though, and I'm not sure I needed to have that fact rammed down my throat. I also didn't appreciate the way he introduced me to the two

PCSOs – Justin and Kenneth – as 'the latest' man from London. That suggested I'm just one in a long line. It also made me wonder what might have happened to my predecessors, but given the way Justin and Kenneth looked me up and down, I'm not sure I want to know.

Of course, that brief scene only happened after we'd made it back to the station. First, we had to get round the rest of the village, and while we'd already seen the shops along the harbour front, that didn't mean we were finished. Not by a long shot.

Sergeant Quick decided we should make our way back as the village slowly came to life, with the locals and a few holidaymakers coming out to do their shopping. The holidaymakers might have ignored us, but the locals all seemed to know the sergeant, and either nodded or waved at him, exchanging pleasantries as we walked back along the harbour. They eyed me with suspicion. It was like they knew I didn't belong, and gave Sergeant Quick a look of sympathy, as though they felt sorry for his troubles… me being the main 'trouble' in his life, I presumed.

When we got back to the station, Geoff was busy dealing with a member of the public at the desk, so Sergeant Quick let us in through the side door. He used a four-digit code, which he gave me, telling me to remember it. His tone made me wonder whether he thought I'd have some difficulty with that. I didn't react. I just made a mental note of the digits, feeling grateful that I'd be able to come and go without having to announce myself. Then I stopped in my tracks as I came face-to-face with the two PCSOs who'd obviously arrived for work in our absence.

Justin is probably in his early twenties, while Kenneth is a little older, and they both looked at me with an air of suspicion, which I found less than comforting. They weren't as hostile as Sergeant Quick, but there was none of the country welcome I'd been hoping for, and as I sat down at my desk, I wondered what I'd let myself in for.

That feeling didn't improve when I looked at the reports that relate to the bag snatchings that have taken place over the last few weeks. I was comparing the notes and checking the map on the wall, trying to familiarise myself with the areas of the village where the crimes had taken place, when Sergeant Quick came out of his office. He stood beside me, looking over my shoulder.

"Solved it yet?" he asked, his voice laced with sarcasm.

Justin laughed, and Kenneth quickly joined in, before the two of them left to go out on patrol, shaking their heads at my expense. I wanted to answer back, but I didn't. I held my tongue and ignored them all. It felt like the wisest thing to do, in the circumstances.

I take another sip of wine and roll my shoulders, trying to release some of the tension, resolving that, although I'm going to visit my mother on Saturday, I'm going to spend Sunday unpacking my gym equipment – such as it is. I'll need to find a way of unwinding if I'm going to make a success of staying here, and working out has always done it for me in the past… that and sheer bloody-mindedness. I think I'm going to need a lot of that right now, because no matter how much they might try to treat me like an outsider, I'm determined to make this work. I've sold my house in Wimbledon and, having repaid my mother, even though I've got a reasonable nest-egg in the bank, I couldn't afford to move back there, even if I wanted to. Not only that, but I like the idea of living closer to Mum. And I'm stubborn… very stubborn. There's no way I'm going to let a country copper prove me wrong. I can cope with being out here in the sticks. I can even cope with a bit of judgemental bullying. In fact, I can cope with pretty much anything… so if they think they can get rid of me, they've got another thing coming.

My stomach grumbles and I check the clock on the microwave, quite surprised to see it's already gone seven thirty. It's no wonder I'm hungry. I only grabbed a quick sandwich from the baker's at lunchtime… and speaking of the baker's, the lady there, who I seem to remember was called Rachel, was about the only person I came across today, who was even remotely close to my age.

I smile to myself as I pull out a sauté pan and put it on the stove, adding a little olive oil, before going over to the fridge and pulling out the cod I bought for tonight's dinner. I suppose, if I'm going to find anyone to socialise with, I might have to spread my wings a little. Rachel was nice enough, but I'm not sure she was my type. I've never thought of myself as having a type before, but if I did, I don't think Rachel would be it. I didn't feel any kind of spark with her, and I've always felt something in the past… even though I've never actually come across 'the one'. There's always been a moment when I've looked at them, and they've looked at me… and I've known that something would happen between us. It might only be a few dates and the odd kiss, or it might be a full-on relationship, like it was with Kelly, but either way, I've always known right from that first meeting. And that tells me that, while Rachel was very pretty and easy to talk to, she's not for me.

While the oil heats, I season the fish and put a few new potatoes into a pan of boiling water, as I contemplate the prospect of starting a whole new relationship at my age. I'm not ancient or anything. I only turned thirty a couple of weeks ago. But I suppose I feel like I've done it all before, quite a few times, and I don't relish doing it all again. Okay, so I enjoy that feeling of excitement when you first start seeing someone. I love that sense of wonder and the thrill of not knowing exactly where things are going… or where you'll end up. What I hate is actually meeting someone new for the first time. There's always a certain awkwardness about that, which I find difficult to overcome. I'm usually most concerned that I won't be able to have a conversation with the women I meet, especially when I tell them what I do for a living. That's caused an awkward silence on more than one occasion. But talking, and especially being open and honest with the person I'm seeing is really important to me. Because while I like sex as much as the next man, and I'll admit that a physical attraction is often a deciding factor when looking at a new relationship and wondering what to do with it, I want there to be more to it than rolling around in bed together. My time with Kelly taught me that, if nothing else.

Obviously, once you get beyond that first meeting… once you've decided you like the other person enough to progress to something more, then things are usually very different. They're much more relaxed and, like I say, exciting. It's just that – for me – getting to that point can be difficult.

And down here, I think they might be impossible…

I finish preparing my dinner, indulging in one of my hobbies – namely cooking – and then I set the table. Once I've dished up my pan-fried cod with new potatoes and green beans, I pour myself another glass of wine and switch on the television. I could get used to this open-plan living. I can watch the movie that's just started while I'm eating. In fact, I can see the whole of the ground floor, just by turning around, which certainly makes a change from the way my old house was divided into individual rooms. I may have liked that way of living at the time, but, as I said to Mum, I think I prefer this. It's more informal… more laid back.

And I'm feeling quite laid back now.

That's probably the wine though… so I'm not going to read too much into it.

By the time I've finished dinner, I'm quite into the movie, which is a science-fiction thriller, set on a space station, and I carry on watching it while I load the dishwasher and wash up the sauté pan. Then I continue to unpack the last of my books, leaving myself with just five more boxes to do, one of which contains the wine glasses from earlier. I'd like to feel quite pleased with myself, but three of the four remaining boxes contain pictures. I have a lot of pictures, and they're going to need hanging. Except I can't. Not at ten o'clock at night. Not unless I want to upset the neighbours. As for the last box, that contains curtains. I remember how it felt to be woken by the dawn sunrise, and I rummage through, finding some that I know will fit the bedroom windows, and put them on the stairs, ready to take up with me. I don't care what time it is, I'm hanging them tonight.

Then, stacking the rest of the boxes neatly underneath the window, I gaze around the room and let out a sigh. At least I can sit on the sofa now... and I can use the dining table. The house feels a little more homely with my books on the shelves. It'll be even better once the pictures are hung, but that's a job which is going to have to wait for now.

The movie has finished and I'm tired, so I turn off the television and switch off the lights, locking the doors, before I grab the curtains and make my way up the stairs. I might be tired, but I sit down on the edge of the bed and browse a few websites on my phone until I find some garden furniture that I like. I add a small barbecue, and order everything for delivery on the same day as my new kitchen cupboard, as luck would have it. Then I hang the curtains. It takes a couple of attempts before I get them to fit the window properly, but when they're done, I head into the bathroom. I wasn't wrong... I am hot, and I strip off, leaving my clothes in a pile on the floor before stepping into the walk-in shower and turning on the water, letting it flow over my body while my head rocks back. I didn't think I minded the fact that there isn't a bath here… but now I'm not so sure. The idea of a long soak sounds quite appealing. Even so, I take my time in the shower, and once I feel truly refreshed, I get out, drying off, and make my way into the bedroom, letting out a groan when I see that it's twelve-fifteen in the morning…

Why did I try to do so much in one evening?
I must be mad.

Chapter Five

Gemma

It's been a funny old week.

Dad's moods haven't helped. He's been out of sorts ever since Tuesday, when one of the PCSOs, a man called Justin Dodd, called in sick. He had a bad bout of flu, evidently, but you'd have thought he was making the whole thing up, from the way Dad was behaving. It wasn't Justin's flu that really put him out though, it was the way the new man from London stepped into the breach, without even having to be asked.

The new man – who Dad refers to as 'Hughes', not bothering to give him a first name – evidently offered to take Justin's turn on patrol duty. He suggested to Dad that, if he stayed out on the harbour for longer – rather than the two hours at a time that Justin and Kenneth usually do – then the bag thief who's been making his presence felt over the last few weeks, might decide to move on to pastures new. It seemed like a good idea to me, and I couldn't really understand why Dad was so disgruntled about it. But when I was telling Imelda about it on Wednesday, she suggested that the real reason was because Dad hadn't thought of it first. Naturally, I was tempted to leap to Dad's defence, but

I couldn't, not given the way he's been slating PC Hughes all week, for nothing in particular, from what I can gather. It seems all the poor man has to do is blink in the wrong direction and Dad finds fault with him.

I haven't yet met this unfortunate outsider myself, but I'm sure I will in due course. In the meantime, I've got problems of my own. Well, not problems, I suppose… but worries.

It's Easter Saturday today. That means we're bound to be busy, even though it's still early, so it's hard to tell how the day will go. What I do know, though, is that it's been nearly a week now since I took that price to Stephen Goddard at the hotel, and I've heard nothing from him. I would have thought, if he wanted us to supply the flowers, he'd have asked us to start quite soon… and certainly before Easter itself. Besides, he definitely said he'd be in touch, and he hasn't. So, I'm wondering whether he's changed his mind… and whether that's my fault. Maybe he thought it was unprofessional of me to take the price in by hand. Or perhaps he'd have preferred something more anonymous, like an e-mail. I'm not sure why, but I hope I haven't caused a problem by doing what I did. Imelda seemed to think it would be fine, but it seems very odd that he hasn't even called.

To take my mind off things, I'm freshening up the long-stemmed white roses. Some of them have gone brown around the edges, so I take them out and re-arrange the rest, just as the bell above the door rings. I turn to face a very tall man, wearing dark blue jeans and a grey and white striped rugby shirt. He's a stranger, but that's not unusual at this time of year. From Easter to October, the population of the village swells by at least fifty per cent. The hotel and self-catering cottages that lie up the hill account for most of the influx, but we also have a campsite. While I can't imagine many people want to camp in March, the site also offers log cabins, which I believe are quite warm and cosy.

The man in front of me might be a stranger, but he's also gorgeous... absolutely gorgeous. He reminds me of the man on the cover of Imelda's book. That might be because he's really muscular... which is made obvious by the way his rugby shirt clings to him. Or it could be the way his dark hair falls over his forehead just slightly, or that square jaw... or perhaps his dark blue eyes, which are currently staring at me, looking bemused. Suddenly I realise why that is. I haven't spoken. I've just been gazing at him, with my mouth open, for far too long.

"C—Can I help?" I say, stuttering, and he smiles, and completes the picture of perfection, revealing neat white teeth.

"Yes." His voice is deliciously low and deep. "I'd like some flowers, please... for my mother."

"Oh... okay." I suppose I should feel relieved that he didn't say 'for my wife'. Except that would be reading far too much into a situation that hasn't even happened... and probably won't. I make my way over to the counter, putting down the two white roses. "Does your mother like any particular kind of flowers?" I ask, and he smiles again.

"Probably. But I don't have a clue which ones... so it's best if we just go for something pink. She likes pink, but then I imagine most people say 'pink' when they're not sure."

I can't help smiling myself now. "Yes, they do. It's a safe colour for flowers."

"Oh." He winces slightly, in a jokey way. "Do I want to be safe? That sounds a little boring."

I shrug my shoulders as I bend to select some pale pink roses from one of the buckets. "I'm not sure it's possible to be boring with flowers, but if we're talking colours, then I prefer yellow... yellow flowers are more cheerful." A blush creeps up my cheeks. Why did I tell him that? I hope he doesn't think I was dropping any kind of hint that he might like to buy me flowers one day. I mean, I wouldn't say 'no' if he did, but I'd hate for him to think I was being pushy.

"Aren't all flowers cheerful?" he asks, and I turn my head to see him staring at me, like he's genuinely interested in the subject.

"No." I stand up straight, moving on to the pink carnations nearer the front of the shop. "Lilies are quite sad. They're often used in funeral arrangements, so a lot of people don't like having them in every-day bouquets. They're meant to represent the restoration of innocence in the soul of the departed…" I let my voice fade and then I cough. What's wrong with me? I don't normally talk to customers this much, and never in such detail.

"Do you believe in all that?" he asks, stepping a little closer, as I pick up a few stems of sweet william, arranging them in my hand.

"Believe in all what?" I focus on the man again, although I rather wish I hadn't. Just looking at him makes my breath catch for a moment, and I hope he doesn't notice.

"Souls departed?" he says, smiling once more.

"No… but I believe that flowers have meanings."

"They do?" He tilts his head to one side, mystified.

"Yes… take these sweet williams." I hold one out for him to see and then remember what they mean and wish I hadn't used them as an example.

"Okay." He studies the head of small pink flowers. "What do they mean?"

"They… they represent masculinity and um… gallantry."

I can't help staring at his chest as I'm speaking, but he doesn't seem to notice and just says, "I see. And what about roses?" He turns towards the multicoloured display behind me.

"That depends on the colour."

"Oh… so each colour has a different meaning?"

"Yes."

58

"Right… so what about the pale pink ones you're holding?"

"They signify admiration."

"And yellow?" he asks, his smile widening, as he refers to my own favourite colour.

"Friendship, and new beginnings."

"I'll bear that in mind," he says, enigmatically, before he moves around me, bends, and picks up a couple of white roses – the ones I was just re-arranging – handing them to me to add to the bouquet. "What about those?"

"Innocence." I feel myself blush and to cover my added embarrassment, I turn away and ask, "Do you have a budget in mind? Or should I just keep going for now?"

"We should probably stop at about forty pounds, if that's okay?" he says from behind me, and I smile to myself. He's generous… I'll give him that. He's also funny, and very sexy. At least he is in my very inexperienced, very innocent eyes.

"Are you on holiday?" I ask, trying to steer the conversation away from flowers and their meanings, in case he was thinking of taking us back there.

"No," he says and I turn, picking up some eucalyptus to add a bit of grey/green background colour. "I've just moved here."

"Really?" I'm surprised by that, and do a poor job of hiding it.

"Yes. I've bought one of the houses in Bell Road."

"One of those lovely little cottages opposite the new art gallery?"

"Yes."

"It's not the cornflower blue one in the middle, is it?" I ask, and he nods his head. "Oh… I love that house."

He smiles at my exclamation, although I wish I'd learned to think before speaking.

"Good," he says. "So do I. I haven't finished unpacking yet, but when I do, I think I'll love it even more."

A part of me is dying to ask what the house is like inside, but that would be too inquisitive... and far too cheeky. And I feel like I've already made enough of a fool of myself for one day.

"What made you decide to move here?" I ask instead.

"Oh... my mother," he says, rolling his eyes.

"Does she live here then?" I'd be surprised if she did, because I feel sure I'd know her... and I don't know anyone with a son who looks like this man.

"No. She lives in Newquay, and has done for the last few years. Neither of us are natives of Cornwall, but my Aunt married a Cornish man, and moved here when she got married, and when Mum came to stay after my dad left her, she decided she liked it down here, and never came home again."

"Goodness..." Now I really am surprised. Not that his mother wanted to stay in Cornwall, but that he's told me so much when he doesn't know me.

"I thought something like that myself, when she asked me to put her house on the market," he says, as I reach for a few peonies that are still in bud, and add them to the bouquet, knowing how beautiful they'll look in a few days' time, when they blossom. "But she's happy here."

"So, what made you decide to follow her?" I ask, even though it's none of my business.

"She had a fall at the end of last year and broke her wrist. I decided it was high time I moved closer, just in case..." He lets his voice fade, and I nod my head, as he says, "Half an hour's drive away is more than close enough," and we both start laughing.

I'm trying to decide whether to go with some more white roses, or whether to add in a darker pink. I could even go for the burgundy colour and am just reaching out for one when the bell above the door rings again and I flip around to see Stephen Goddard coming into the shop.

He nods in my direction and smiles, while standing off to one side, presumably to allow me the space to finish seeing to my other customer. Except his presence makes me feel on edge. I can't explain why, but it does, and I find I'm even more indecisive about the roses than I was before.

"I'm not in any hurry," the handsome stranger says, turning to Mr Goddard, and waving him forward with his right hand. "Please, go ahead."

Mr Goddard nods in agreement and steps closer, making me feel more uncomfortable still. To solve that situation, I move back towards the counter, putting down the stranger's flowers and stepping around the other side. That way, there's a barrier between me and the hotel manager.

"How can I help, Mr Goddard?" I look up at him and he smiles.

"You can call me Steve," he says, although I'm not sure how I feel about that. "And then you can accept my apology." His voice has that soft, considerate tone that he used when I first entered his hotel the other day, before he realised I was just a supplier and not anyone important.

"What for?"

His smile widens. "Because you were kind enough to come and see me at the hotel on Monday, and I haven't even had the manners to get back to you like I said I would. My assistant manager left nearly two months ago, and I've been rushed off my feet ever since. I'm afraid it simply slipped my mind."

"Oh... don't worry about it." I'm not about to tell him I've been worrying about it myself. He doesn't need to know that.

"Well, it was very rude of me, so I thought I'd come down here in person and tell you I'd like to go ahead with the order."

"That's marvellous." I can't help smiling now, because I'm genuinely pleased and I know Imelda will be too. "When would you like us to start?"

"Ideally, yesterday. I know you have to order in the flowers, and it's my own fault that I've left it too late to get anything organised for this weekend, but we've got a honeymoon couple coming next Friday… so is it going to be possible for you to prepare a large bouquet for their room? And we may as well have the ones for the reception at the same time, if you can manage it, of course."

"I think that'll be all right. I'll be able to e-mail the order through to the suppliers on Monday."

"Are you open on Monday?" he asks. "Even though it's a bank holiday?"

"It's holiday season. From now until October, we're open every day except Sundays. Imelda insists on one day of rest per week." I don't know why I told him that… except he's making me nervous.

He nods his head. "Lucky you. We don't even get Sundays off." He sounds a little disgruntled. "Fortunately, I've found a new assistant manager now," he says. "It's just a shame she can't start for a few weeks, but when she does, I'll be glad to have some spare time." I'm not sure why I needed to know that, but I just smile at him, aware of the fact that he's giving Imelda a big contract.

"What about the flowers for the restaurant?" I ask, getting back to it.

"Can you do those sooner, do you think?" he says. "It's just that the place looks a bit sad, with nothing much on the tables."

"Of course. I'll bring down some boxes of roses later on today, if that's all right?"

"That's absolutely perfect. But I'm sure they'll be heavy. I'll send someone down to collect them. About four?"

I nod and he smiles at me, a very different man from the one who dismissed me on Monday evening, and made me feel so unimportant. I'm aware of the stranger, though. He's still waiting over by one of the dressers, and while I don't want Mr Goddard to feel like he's in the way, I'm not sure what more we can have to say to each other.

"Was there anything else?" I ask, getting to the point. "I think Imelda explained the payment terms in her quotation, didn't she?"

"Yes." He nods his head and then leans over the counter. "I was wondering," he says, lowering his voice, "whether you might like to come out for a drink with me, maybe tomorrow night, as you won't have been working? I'll be on duty at the hotel, but we have a very nice cocktail bar, and as long as I'm on the premises..." He lets his voice fade and I lower my eyes, wondering how to say 'no' without causing any offence to Imelda's newest client.

"I—I'm sorry. I'm afraid I'm not free tomorrow night, but thank you for asking."

He frowns. "Perhaps another time, then?"

I smile. "I'm quite busy at the moment, what with it being the holiday season," I say, trying my best to turn him down, without actually saying 'no'.

"Okay. Well, if you find yourself with a free half hour one evening, you know where to find me."

He's persistent, I'll give him that, although I don't say anything else, leaving my response as non-committal as possible, and he smiles before he turns around.

"Sorry for keeping you waiting," he says to the stranger.

"No problem." The man smiles and nods his head at him as Mr Goddard goes back out through the door.

Once we're alone again, I look over at the stranger and find he's staring at me. I'm not really sure what his expression means, but I much prefer his attention to that of Stephen Goddard...

and I just wish the hotel manager had chosen a different time to come and call.

Chapter Six

Tom

I have to revise my earlier opinion about there being no-one in Porthgarrion of my own age that I might want to spend time with… because I'm looking at her right now, and she's beautiful. What's more, I can definitely feel that spark, in a way that I've never felt it before. Okay, so she's younger than me, but not by much, I don't think… and what does that matter, when she's a walking goddess?

She's around five foot eight, in her neat flat shoes, which is the perfect height for me. Her jeans and pale pink blouse show off her slim figure, and she's got light brown hair, tied up in a ponytail, not to mention the most incredible amber coloured eyes, and full generous lips… which make me think about how long it's been since I kissed a beautiful woman. Not that I've ever kissed a woman as beautiful as she is, because I don't think such a person exists… other than here, in this florist's shop, in Porthgarrion.

She's been arranging my mother's flowers while we talk… well, flirt, I think. At least I'm flirting. I'm not sure whether she is. She's blushing quite a lot, and that makes her even more attractive in my eyes, because when her cheeks flush, she looks kind of innocent... as well as beautiful... and sexy. It's an interesting, unusual, and very enticing combination.

It was hard not to notice the way she stared directly at my chest when she started talking about masculinity and gallantry, as the meaning of one of the flowers she was holding. I can't remember which one it was now, because I was too mesmerised by her and her reactions, which is why I was so desperate to continue with our conversation. Frankly, I've never been that interested in flowers, or what they mean, but she clearly was, and because of that, I wanted to know about them too. That's part of getting to know a person, isn't it? Taking an interest... finding out about the things that matter to them. And because it mattered to her, I kept asking... until she changed the subject and enquired whether I was on holiday. I'm not sure why she did that. The rose we'd been discussing was a white one, which meant innocence, if I remember rightly. I'm not sure why she'd have found that an embarrassing thing to discuss, but she clearly did... and I went along with the change of subject, and told her about my house. I almost burst out laughing when she said how much she loved it, but I controlled the urge and just smiled instead and then told her about my mother, because that seemed like a safe topic.

We were getting along really well. There was none of that awkwardness that usually seems to come with first meetings – at least in my experience, anyway – and I felt really comfortable just talking to her... until that other man arrived.

The woman's reaction to him was very interesting. We'd been standing quite close together and talking, while she selected the flowers for my mother's bouquet, and she'd seemed quite at ease. But when the other man came in, and I suggested he could go ahead of me, because I wasn't ready to leave yet, the woman made a point of going around the counter and putting a very definite barrier between them.

The man seemed friendly enough, so I was struck by her response to him and, although it might have seemed like I was eavesdropping, I stayed close enough to hear what they were saying… just in case. I'm still a police officer, after all…

His name was Stephen Goddard, and I got the impression that he's the manager, or at least part of the management at the hotel.

He told the woman that she should call him Steve, but I noticed she didn't, and that after he'd made that suggestion, she avoided calling him anything at all. I found that quite intriguing. It suggested to me she didn't feel comfortable with the informality he seemed to be encouraging between them. She wanted to keep things professional… which was confirmed when he asked her out for a drink. The moment he issued his invitation, I stopped being a police officer, my whole body froze, and I waited with bated breath for her answer. When it came, I couldn't help thinking that her reason for declining him sounded a little lame, but I didn't overthink that. I was too busy working out how to hide my relief that she hadn't accepted… and wondering how I might go about asking her out myself. It wasn't going to be easy, considering she'd just told Stephen Goddard that she was too busy to see anyone, either tomorrow night or any time soon.

I'm still contemplating that when he turns and addresses me. I have to concentrate on listening and speaking, accepting his apology for holding me up – which he hadn't – and watching while he leaves the shop. Then I turn my attention back to the beautiful woman who I'm now absolutely determined to spend some more time with… somehow.

She's looking at me, with her head tilted to one side, her lips twitching upwards, and as far as I'm concerned, that's promising. She could barely raise a smile for Stephen Goddard... and hopefully that counts in my favour.

"Where were we?" she says, with a kind of false geniality to her voice as she picks up the flowers she'd been arranging for me from the countertop, coming back around this side.

"I've got no idea." I step a little closer to her. She looks up into my eyes and blinks a couple of times, two tiny dots of red appearing on her cheeks. "But I have a question."

I can't ask her to go out with me straight away, not right after Stephen Goddard did. That would be crass. But maybe I can work my way up to it...

"Yes?" she says, tipping her head the other way.

"Yes... I was just wondering what colour roses you were planning on giving Mr Goddard?"

She purses her lips, like she's trying hard not to smile, and then she looks around at the display before us.

"Probably the peach coloured ones," she says, pointing to them with her free hand. "We've got quite a lot of those at the moment and they're not a popular colour at this time of year. People like them more in the late summer and autumn."

I nod my head. "I see. And what do peach coloured roses mean?"

She loses the battle with her smile, her eyes sparkling, as she says, "They have quite a few meanings, but among them is the closure of a deal."

I laugh, and so does she, covering her mouth with the backs of her fingers.

"Are you really busy tomorrow night?" The words leave my mouth before I can stop them, and she looks up at me, her hand falling to her side again.

"N—No." She blushes properly this time.

"Then why did you say it?" I ask, smiling to let her know I'm teasing her, just a little.

"Because I didn't want to go out with him," she says, with astounding candour.

"Would you like to go out with me?" I let the words hang between us, but they don't stay there for long, because they're captured by her slight gasp, which becomes a slow smile, and I feel a warmth building inside me. It starts somewhere in the middle of my chest, spreading outwards to the very tips of my toes. I've never felt anything like it before and for a moment, I'm quite distracted. I'm not so distracted that I don't notice the woman nod her head, though. "Is that a 'yes'?" I say, just to be sure.

"Yes. I think I'd like that very much."

My smile is automatic, and for a long moment, we just stand and stare at each other. That ought to feel awkward, but it doesn't. It feels perfectly natural.

"Would you like to come to the pub and have a drink with me then?"

"Yes." She lowers her head, and although I'm tempted to reach out and cup her face, to raise it up, so I can look into her eyes, I don't. That would be too intimate… too soon.

"Where can I pick you up from?" I ask her instead and she raises her head, unaided, her eyes clouded with something that looks like doubt.

"You don't have to pick me up. I'll meet you at the pub."

I'm not sure about that, but she seems nervous about me collecting her and although I'm not sure why, I accept her suggestion.

"Eight o'clock?" I say and she nods.

"Perfect."

Yes… I think you probably are.

Once I've been to the tip to drop off the boxes that I don't need anymore, the drive to my mother's is straightforward. It's a lot more straightforward than it used to be when I lived in Wimbledon and had to set aside an entire weekend for my visits. As it is, I'm staying for lunch, and then I'm taking Mum to Aunty Andrea's for dinner tonight, before driving home to Porthgarrion.

I spend a lot of the thirty-minute journey glancing down at the beautiful hand-tied bouquet that the woman in the florist's finally arranged for me. I'm also thinking about her smile, and that I'm going to see her again tomorrow evening… and when I'm not doing that, I'm kicking myself because I forgot to ask her name.

Obviously, I can find that out tomorrow, when we meet at the pub, but I feel a bit of a fool for not bothering to ask such a simple question. My only excuse for my forgetfulness is that I was too preoccupied with admiring her… and then with thanking my lucky stars that she said 'yes' to going out with me.

I pull up outside my mother's small bungalow and walk around the car to grab the flowers, by which time Mum has opened the front door and is standing on the threshold, smiling at me. She always looks so diminutive, but then she is a foot shorter than me, and I think that's partly what makes me so protective of her. That and the fact that my father treated her so badly.

"Oh… it's so good to see you," she says, grinning.

"It's good to see you too, Mum." I walk over and hand her the flowers.

"They're beautiful." She bends to smell the blooms and then puts her free arm around me, giving me a hug.

"Are you all right?" I ask, as we go into the house and I close the door behind us.

"I'm absolutely fine." She walks through to the kitchen, and I follow. "I've finished physiotherapy now, and my wrist is almost back to normal. I just have the odd moment of weakness, but nothing major."

"That's good." I look down at her. "You've done something to your hair."

"Yes." She gives her dark head and instinctive pat. "I got a shorter cut, and your aunt persuaded me to have a change of colour."

"It's not a massive change, Mum." Actually, the colour looks about the same to me.

She smiles. "No, but at least you can't see the grey now." She puts the flowers on the table and bends to retrieve a vase from the cupboard beneath the sink. "How's the house?" she asks, as she stands up again.

"The house is good… or it will be, when I've finished the unpacking."

"And how's work? Are you settling in?"

I sit down at the kitchen table while she arranges her flowers. "I'm not sure 'settling in' is quite the right word. Maybe it's best to say I'm finding my feet."

She looks over at me. "Is it that bad?"

"It's not bad. It's just different."

"To what you're used to?" She tips her head to one side.

"To what I'd expected."

"Well, you are based in a small village. It was never going to be like London."

"I know. But everything seems so…" I struggle to find the right word.

"Old fashioned?" she says, and I smile.

"Yes… and insular. One of the PCSOs called in sick earlier in the week, and I stepped in and took over his patrols, without waiting to be asked... or told. You'd have thought I'd committed some kind of cardinal sin, instead of trying to be helpful. I don't think they like change very much."

"Then I wouldn't rock the boat, if I were you." She probably has a point, but I didn't think offering to help qualified as 'rocking the boat'.

"Shall I put the kettle on?" I ask, and she nods, fetching some cups from the cupboard.

"You're happy though, aren't you?" she says wistfully, clutching them to her chest and staring across the kitchen at me.

"Of course I am." I give her one of my best smiles, and she returns it, and although I'm tempted to tell her about the woman I met this morning, I resist. Partly because I've got no idea whether anything will come of it – no matter how much I want it to – and also because I forgot to ask the woman's name, and my mother is bound to think I'm a complete idiot for that. I know I do.

After lunch, we take a walk over to Aunty Andrea and Uncle David's house, which isn't very far away, and I'm surprised to find that one of my cousins is there too.

Sarah lives in Sussex, with her husband James, and I didn't realise they were visiting this weekend, although I suppose Easter is a good excuse to get away. I haven't seen them for ages and after we've all greeted each other, we sit down in Andrea's living room, where the reason for Sarah's visit becomes clear. She's come down to tell her parents that she and James are expecting their first child, and they break the news to us, too. Andrea and David have clearly known since yesterday, when Sarah and James arrived, and somehow my aunt has kept the news to herself for twenty-four hours. I'm not sure how though, because she's bubbling with excitement. Mum is thrilled too, and we both offer our congratulations, and after the hubbub has died down a little, it's James who turns to me and makes the inevitable statement…

"It'll be your turn soon…"

"It will if he ever settles down," Uncle David says, from his seat in the corner of the room.

They're joking, but their comments hit home, and I think my mother notices because she leaps to my defence.

"Give him a chance," she says, frowning. "He's just moved over two hundred and fifty miles. I doubt he's even met his neighbours yet, let alone any young ladies."

"Are there any young ladies in Porthgarrion?" Aunty Andrea asks, smirking at my mother's turn of phrase.

"A few," I say, giving nothing away and, sensing my discomfort, Sarah gives me a smile and tells us about how awful her morning sickness has been. That seems to capture everyone's attention, and at least diverts them away from me for a while.

We end up having a lovely afternoon and evening with them, and no-one mentions my relationships – or lack of them – again. When it's time to go, I make a point of giving Sarah a hug and thanking her. She smiles at me again.

"Just ignore everyone," she says. "Focus on being happy in yourself and the right woman will come along."

I'm on the verge of telling her that I think she already has, but I hold my tongue. I don't want to tempt fate.

Today has been good and bad.

The unpacking has taken up a lot of my day, as has hanging the pictures and tidying up. I'm also preoccupied, though… or at least impatient to see the woman from the flower shop again, and to discover her name. I want to spend some more time with her... just to look at her for a while, because even thinking about her makes me feel warm inside, so looking at her has to be better than that... right?

The house is much straighter than it was and I've now only got the box of wine glasses to unpack, which is going to have to wait for my new cupboard to arrive. I even found the time to sort out the area at the back of the garage, arranging my weights and my rowing machine in there. And I managed a thirty-minute workout, too. I wasn't sure I needed it, after moving everything around, but it felt good to just let off steam for a short while, before I jumped into the shower and freshened up, ready for tonight.

Now I'm getting changed into jeans and a smart shirt, I can't decide whether I'm nervous or excited. I think I'm a mixture of the two... and that's probably a good thing. It feels okay to be slightly nervous. After all, I'm meeting someone I'm very attracted to, and I don't want anything to go wrong. I think my excitement is understandable, too, though. Probably for exactly the same reasons.

Despite being busy, and nervous, and excited, I have reached one decision. It's something I've been thinking about all day, off and on, and it's that I'm not going to tell her what I do for a living. Not straight away. I'm going to see how things go between us, maybe have a few dates with her first – assuming we get that far – before I drop the bombshell that's often been the ruin of things in the past. She's different, and the last thing I want to do is have her running for the hills, just because she's wary of my job.

There's nothing to be wary about, but that's not always how other people see it, and I want her to get to know me as a man, rather than as a police officer, who also happens to be a man.

I'm ready a little early, but decide to make my way to the pub, anyway. I hate the idea that she might get there before me and feel uncomfortable having to wait… I'd much rather it was the other way around. So I walk along the harbour side, looking out at the silhouettes of the bobbing boats against the slightly pale skyline. The sun hasn't long since set, and I think to myself that while it may be quiet here – certainly compared to Wimbledon – I can't deny it's very beautiful.

The pub isn't too busy, considering it's the holiday season, and I go over to the bar and order a glass of Merlot, which the barmaid hands across to me, before I turn and find a table from which I can see the door. I notice that Ed, the landlord, doesn't seem to be present tonight, but I'm not complaining. He'd probably want to make conversation after we met at the beginning of the week, and I'm not really in the mood. I'm feeling more nervous than excited now, so I'm not sure how I feel about making small talk. Although I suppose I'll be doing that soon enough with the woman from the flower shop. Will that be small talk though? I hope not. And will she even turn up? I'm just wondering whether she only said 'yes' to meeting me to get me out of her hair, when the door opens and she comes in, looking around until our eyes lock. She smiles, and all that nervousness simply disappears.

I get to my feet, and take a moment to observe the pretty dress she's wearing beneath the jacket she's just shrugging off. Her hair is hanging loose around her shoulders, and she's put on a little make-up. I don't give myself time to think that through, or wonder if it might be for my benefit. Instead, I go over and offer my hand, which she accepts, letting me lead her back to the table, where I take her jacket and hold out a seat for her.

"Would you like a drink?" I ask as she sits down and looks up at me.

"Yes, please… a dry white wine."

I nod my head and smile, and then hang her coat up on the rack, beside mine, before making my way across to the bar, floating on air, because she's here. She's really here…

The barmaid pours the wine and hands it over, and once I've paid, I go back to the table and sit opposite the woman, placing her drink in front of her.

"I'm Tom," I say, staring right at her, and she smiles.

"I've been wondering what your name was. I can't believe we both forgot to ask."

"Neither can I. But now I'm at a disadvantage… because you know mine but I don't know yours."

"Gemma." Her voice is a quiet whisper.

"It's nice to meet you Gemma," I say, raising my glass to her.

She raises hers in return and says, "It's nice to meet you too." I don't want her to ask about what I do for a living, so I immediately ask her how long she's lived in the village, and she looks up at me and smiles. "All my life."

"You've never lived anywhere else?"

"No." She takes a small sip of wine. "I've rarely been anywhere else. There's a small junior school here, but for senior school and college, we had to go to Padstow on the bus…" Her voice fades and she looks down at her hands, which are resting on top of the table.

"You've been further afield than Padstow, surely?" She shakes her head. "What about holidays?" I can't hide my surprise.

She shrugs. "When I was growing up, my parents always had to work at their hardest during the holidays – like most of the people in the village – so we stayed here. When you live somewhere as lovely as this, you don't worry about going anywhere else."

"You talk about your parents in the past tense… are they…?" I leave my sentence hanging, unsure how to finish it, but she smiles and shakes her head.

"They're not dead," she says. "But my mum left about five years ago. She wanted to find herself, or at least, that's what she wrote in the note to my dad. I suppose I have a tendency to always talk about her now as though she isn't here anymore… because she isn't. Especially as finding herself seems to have amounted to forgetting all about us…" She stops talking abruptly.

"I'm sorry." I can see how much her mother leaving has hurt her, even though she must have been in her late teens or early twenties when it happened, and I reach across the table and place my hand over hers. She jumps slightly, but doesn't pull her hand away, and I let mine rest there, noticing that her fingers are cold, although her skin is soft.

"These things happen. You said your dad left your mum, didn't you?"

"Yes." I nod my head. "It was good to see her yesterday. She was looking a lot happier, and more relaxed."

"Do you think that's because you've moved here?" Gemma asks.

"I doubt it. I think it's because she's moving on."

"She's met someone else?"

"No. Not that I'm aware of. What I meant was, I think she's getting on with the next stage of her life."

She manages a smile. "I wish she could persuade my dad to do something like that," she says, with an air of despondency.

"Why? Is he still struggling?" I take an interest, because it clearly bothers her.

"I think so. I think he might be lonely, although I doubt he'd admit it."

"At least he's got you here in the village, close by," I say, and she frowns.

"I—I probably didn't make that very clear, did I?"

"Make what very clear?" I'm not sure what she's talking about.

"I still live at home… with my dad."

"Oh. I see."

I suppose it's not that surprising. Not in this day and age… and not in a village like this, where house prices are so high. If she wants to stay here, in the only place she's ever known, living with her father is probably the only option she has at the moment. I can't imagine she earns a huge amount, working in a florist's.

"How long have you worked in the flower shop?" I ask, changing the subject, because she seems embarrassed… again.

"A little over two years. I knew nothing about flowers when Imelda offered me the job, but she's an excellent teacher."

"I'd say you're probably an excellent student," I say, without a hint of false flattery. "You certainly seem to understand flowers, anyway."

"Oh… you're talking about their meanings?"

"Yes. I was impressed…" *And not just with your knowledge of flowers.*

"That's something I learned in my own time, after a man came into the shop on my first Valentine's day there. He bought a couple of bunches of tulips, and then told me they were for his wife of fifteen years. I thought it was odd and asked him why he wasn't buying roses, like most people do. He explained that roses – specifically red ones – represent love, but that tulips are about that one perfect love… the one you'll never let go. Until then, I'd never even realised there's an entire language surrounding flowers, but I went home that evening and looked it up on the Internet… and started learning all about it."

I smile at her, because she's clearly so enchanted by what she does, and it's impossible not to feel that, and be drawn in by it too. "So, all those men who've been buying red roses for Valentine's Day have been getting it wrong?"

"Well, not really. Red roses still stand for love… love, and… passion." She hesitates over that last word, and blushes again, and then says, "But if you want to *declare* your love, then it's really all about the tulips."

"I wonder how many women would appreciate that?" I ponder out loud and she tips her head to one side, like she doesn't understand, so I explain, "Most women would gush over a dozen red roses, but would they have the same reaction to a dozen tulips?"

She smiles and shakes her head. "Probably not, no."

"If only they knew…" I muse and we both take a sip of our wine.

The evening passes far too quickly, and before we know it, the bell above the bar is being rung, signalling that it's time for 'last orders'.

"Heavens," Gemma says, looking across the table at me as she finishes her second glass of wine. "I didn't realise that was the time."

"Neither did I."

It's the truth. We've done nothing but talk and gaze at each other for the last two and a half hours, and it's been incredible. She's fascinating and beguiling, and as for that spark… that's been more like a bolt of lightning every time she's smiled, or looked at me.

"Can I walk you home?" I say, as she bends to pick up her handbag from the floor.

"You don't have to. It's very safe around here."

"I know it is… but I'd still like to see you to your door. I'm not ready for the evening to end yet." That might sound corny, but it's true, and judging from the smile that forms on her lips, I think she might feel the same.

"That would be lovely," she says, and I stand, fetching our jackets and helping her on with hers before I pull on my own, and let her lead the way out through the door.

It's a lot cooler than it was earlier and I move around Gemma, so I'm the one taking the brunt of the wind, which is coming off the sea, as we walk along the well-lit harbour.

"Where do you live?" I ask, wondering how much longer I've got to enjoy her company.

"Just over there." She points towards the row of terraced houses opposite where we're currently walking, and I almost heave out a sigh of relief that we've got at least a few minutes left together.

"I've had a lovely time tonight," I say, taking her hand in mine.

She lets me and looks up, right into my eyes. "So have I."

There's something about her face… something pure and trusting, and as I hold her gaze, I know I have to tell her the truth. To do anything else would be wrong.

I stop walking, and because we're holding hands, she does too, and she looks up at me.

"Is something the matter?" she asks.

"Yes… at least… I'm not sure."

"What does that mean?"

"It means I've got a confession."

"A confession?" She moves away from me just slightly, although I keep hold of her hand, refusing to let her go, just in case she decides to run.

"Yes. I'd really like to see you again, but I can't ask you to do that, until I've told you the truth."

"This sounds… ominous." She fishes around for the right word, landing on one that probably feels appropriate… at least to her.

"I'm not sure whether ominous is how I'd put it," I reply, stepping closer to her, and feeling relieved that she doesn't move away again. "But telling people this has caused me problems in the past… and I really don't want it to this time… not with you."

Her brow furrows and I struggle not to smile because she looks so adorably confused. "What do you need to confess to?" she asks, in a hushed whisper. "Have you got a wife and seven children?"

"No, of course not."

"Okay… an ex-wife and seven children," she says.

"No. I've never been married, and I don't have any children. What I'm trying to tell you is that I've had a really lovely evening, but I have to admit, I've spent a lot of it trying to avoid telling you what I do for a living."

"Why?"

"Because I was scared you might not want to be with me when you found out."

I can't be any more honest than that, even though I still haven't told her the truth yet.

"What on earth do you do, then?" She's wide-eyed now, waiting.

"I'm a police officer."

There's a moment's pause and then she laughs, surprising me, as she puts her free hand over her mouth for a moment, before she says, "Why is being a police officer such a big problem?"

I laugh myself, out of sheer relief. "You'd be amazed by the number of people who've disappeared from my life upon hearing that."

"Seriously?"

"Yes. Seriously."

"Well, I'm not one of them," she says firmly, and I step even closer to her and lean down, brushing my lips across hers. She gasps in surprise and I take advantage of that moment, my tongue delving, exploring her. I don't want to hold back, so I release her hand and put my arms around her, pulling her close to me. She responds, her tongue dancing with mine, her hands gingerly progressing up my arms and resting on my biceps for a moment, before she raises them to my shoulders, and eventually around my neck. I hear a low groan echoing between us, and realise it's coming from me. It's answered by her soft sigh as her breasts heave into my chest and I change the angle of my head, deepening the kiss. Her breathing becomes more laboured… more ragged, and so does mine, and although I know what I want to do next, I restrain myself. I pull back while I still can, looking down at her upturned face, her eyes closed, her lips slightly swollen and I know, without a doubt, that I've found her.

She's the one.

Chapter Seven

Gemma

I wake, and it's as though I'm floating above my bed, my body as light as a feather, a smile permanently etched onto my lips, which still feel a little numbed from Tom's kisses.

God… he felt incredible. He was forceful and intense… and yet gentle and understanding. In fact, he was everything I've always imagined a man might be.

I raise my fingers to my lips, which feel surprisingly normal, and not swollen at all, even though they should be. Then I let out a slight giggle, stretching my arms above my head, as I remember our evening, and how interesting he was to talk to… and how interested he was in what I had to say, too. I liked that. It made me feel valued. Important. *Wanted?* I'm not sure, although his kisses seemed to suggest want… or need. Maybe?

God, I wish I understood romance a little better.

Then I might know what to make of it all. He seemed romantic, and caring… and considerate.

After all, he made a point of seeing me to the garden gate, and then kissing me again, right before he asked me if I'd like to have dinner with him… tonight.

I said 'yes'. Why wouldn't I? I want to see him again, which was just what he'd said to me… right before he confessed to being a police officer. I wasn't entirely sure why he made such a big deal about that. But then I suppose I've grown up around a policeman, so it's hardly going to shock me, as professions go. It puzzled me when he said that other people have backed away from him on finding out what he does for a living. I've never come across that with Dad… although we live in a small village, and maybe things work differently in big towns. I was about to point that out to him, when he kissed me, and literally took my breath away, and by the time he broke the kiss, I had other things on my mind. Things like how good his lips had felt on mine, and how nice it was to be held… and how much more I wanted, even though I'd never have admitted that out loud. I wouldn't have known where to start.

But that doesn't make it any less true.

Dad left very early this morning, passing me in the hall on his way out, as I went into the kitchen to have breakfast. His only comment was, "You got back late last night." I didn't get the chance to say that I didn't think eleven o'clock was so very late, or to tell him anything about Tom, before he'd disappeared out of the door and closed it behind him.

I felt his disapproval, though, and it did rather take the edge off my date with Tom. By the time I get to work, though, I've resolved to ignore my dad and listen to my heart… and at the moment, my heart is telling me that Tom is just right for me.

In fact, he's perfect.

He's so perfect, I'm finding it hard to concentrate on anything, and I've just had to double-check the order for the hotel. I was about to put it through to the wholesalers, when I realised I'd forgotten the bouquet he asked us to provide for the honeymoon suite. I'm sure we could have made up something from what we've got in stock, but that's not how it's supposed to work.

I go back through Mr Goddard's order, and cross-reference it with the one I'm about to place, to make sure I've got it right this time, and then send the e-mail, just as the shop door opens, the bell ringing out loud. I can't help smiling as Tom walks in, wearing the uniform of a police constable, and looking utterly divine in it. The fairly tight black top shows off his muscular physique and the combat-style trousers that merely look practical on my dad, seem very much more enticing on Tom.

"What are you doing here?" I ask as he steps forward, walking right up to the counter.

"I thought I'd come and see you."

He hesitates for a second, looking over his shoulder, then he steps around the counter and places his hands on my cheeks, gazing deeply into my eyes as he leans down and kisses me. His lips crush against mine, his tongue demanding entry and I grant it willingly, as he pushes me back against the counter. Within seconds, his feet are either side of mine, his body holding me in place, and I'm struggling to breathe, just as something digs into my ribs and I have to pull back.

"What on earth is that hard thing sticking into me?" I say and he smirks, letting his hands fall to his sides.

"Sorry?"

"That…" I tap on the front of his stab vest and realise what it is straight away. "Oh… it's your torch."

"Yes." He smiles properly now. "Sorry about that. I'm afraid police uniform isn't exactly conducive to kissing."

"No… not kissing like that, anyway."

He leans forward and kisses me again, but much more gently.

"Is that better?" he says.

"No. I liked how you kissed me before. But I don't suppose you're allowed to take your uniform off…" I stop talking and clamp my mouth shut, feeling the blush creep up my cheeks. "I—I meant for kissing… not for…" God, how I wish the shop floor would open up and swallow me.

Tom smiles, his eyes twinkling. "I know what you meant," he says, bringing his right hand up again and caressing my cheek with his fingertips. "And no, we're not supposed to take our uniform off… for kissing, or for anything else. At least, not when we're on duty. We can take it off at other times." His voice seems a little deeper than usual, and I feel a pool of heat which gathers in the pit of my stomach and seems to settle there. It's not an uncomfortable feeling. It's actually quite nice and I smile up at him.

"So, you won't be wearing it tonight then?"

"No. I won't." He gazes at me, his eyes darkening slightly, and I realise what I've just said. Before I can embarrass myself further, he smiles. "I'll be wearing something more casual, so I can kiss you… as often as you like."

Despite my embarrassment, I can't help smiling at the thought of being kissed again, and judging from the way Tom's staring at my lips, I don't think he's averse to the idea, either. But for now, I think it's best if we stick to more practical, manageable subjects… ones that don't involve his uniform.

"You didn't explain what you're doing here," I say.

"Yes, I did. I came to see you."

I shake my head. "No… I mean, what are you doing in the village?"

"I'm working. I was out on patrol this morning and I thought…"

"You mean… you work here?" I interrupt. "In Porthgarrion?"

"Yes. Sorry. I probably didn't explain that very well, did I? Still, look on the bright side, I've got the perfect excuse to call in every so often… and even if the uniform makes kissing a little tricky, it's still nice to see you."

I smile at his words, even though my mind's in turmoil. He works here… with my dad. That must make him 'Hughes', the man my dad can't seem to say a single good word about. The man who Dad thinks will be gone by the August Bank Holiday. God… I hope not. Because he's also the man whose kisses do lovely things to my body. The man who made a point of coming in here today, just to see me… and the man who's taking me to dinner tonight, without his uniform on, so he can kiss me as often as I like.

"Are you okay?" he asks, moving a little closer again, and I realise I've been staring at him for ages.

"Yes… I'm fine."

I can't possibly tell him who my dad is, though, can I? From the few things Dad's told me, I know he hasn't made Tom's first few days here very easy, or welcoming, and revealing who I am could make Tom's professional life even more difficult. Besides, telling Tom would mean telling Dad, and that feels like a bad ending waiting to happen. Dad's negativity would spell disaster for Tom and me… and for our future. Heavens… do we even have a future yet? Or am I moving too far, too fast, here?

Of course I am. We've had a few drinks and shared a couple of divine kisses… and I like him a lot. That doesn't mean I need to worry about the future. We barely know each other… so the fact that my dad is his boss doesn't need to be a problem. Tom doesn't even need to know. Not yet. And nor does Dad.

"I've booked a table at that Italian restaurant in Church Lane," he says, and I look up at him.

"Oh… okay."

"So, I'll pick you up at ten to seven?"

"No," I say, perhaps a little too quickly. "I'll meet you there."

He frowns. "I know where you live and it's hardly out of my way."

"I know. But… but I might have to work late, so it's best if I just meet you there."

He hesitates for a moment and then nods his head. "Okay. As long as you're sure."

"I'm absolutely positive."

The last thing I need is Tom knocking on the door and my dad answering it. I feel guilty for lying to him about working late, but it's best this way… and I'll tell him the truth, eventually. Once I know it matters. Once I know I matter, I suppose.

"Do you want me to wait outside for you?" he says and I focus on him again.

"Outside where?"

"The restaurant… tonight." He shakes his head, his brow furrowing, which is hardly surprising. I'm being spectacularly vacant, after all.

"Oh… yes. That would be lovely, if you don't mind."

"Of course I don't mind. I'll see you there, just before seven."

He leans down and kisses me again, and then turns away, giving me a wink as he leaves the shop.

I feel confused… almost agitated.

I really don't feel comfortable lying to Tom. But what else can I do? Telling him the truth feels like the worst idea. After all, he might not want to be with me anymore… not if his feelings for my dad are remotely similar to my dad's feelings for him. That doesn't even bear thinking about, though, because I've never felt this happy before in my life… and I'm not ready to give it up.

I'm not ready to give him up either… and I don't think I ever will be.

*

I gaze down at my tuna sandwich and wonder if my stomach is ever going to stop churning.

"What's the matter?" Imelda says and I glance up to find that she's staring at me, with a puzzled expression on her face.

"Nothing… except I think I might have made a huge mistake." I bite my bottom lip, the rolling of my stomach rising to epic proportions.

"In what way?"

"Because I've lied." I pause under her frowning scrutiny. "No… that's not strictly true. I haven't lied. I just haven't been completely honest."

"They're usually one and the same thing," she says. "But it might help me understand better if you gave me some context."

"It's about Tom," I say, my voice little more than a whisper.

"And who exactly is Tom?" she asks, sitting up and taking more of an interest now.

"He's the new police constable. The one from London."

"Oh. I see." She nods her head. "And what have you been lying to him about?"

"Like I said, I haven't been lying. I—I just haven't told him the truth."

"Which, as I say, is the same as lying. You know that yourself, Gemma. If you didn't, you wouldn't be so uncomfortable with the situation."

I wish I'd never started this conversation, but there's no point in not telling her now, is there? I've come this far, so I may as well go all the way… and besides, I could do with her advice, to help me make sense of it all.

"He came into the shop on Saturday," I say, starting at the beginning… or at least the beginning for me and Tom. "Only he wasn't in uniform, so I didn't know who he was."

"Okay."

"He bought some flowers for his mother, who lives in Newquay… and he asked me out for a drink."

Imelda smiles. "Well, that's nice. Did you go?"

"Yes. Last night. We had a lovely time… and afterwards, he told me he's a police officer."

"Why afterwards?" she says, looking confused. "Why not before… or during?"

"He said that sometimes people can react badly to hearing what he does for a living, and he didn't want to scare me off." I remember him saying that, and how his words left a warm glow deep inside me.

"So, he didn't want to lie to you, or deceive you?" she says, her brow furrowing.

"No. But obviously, I wasn't at all fazed about him being in the police force… because of Dad."

"Obviously." She nods her head.

"And I was going to tell him that, but then he… he kissed me."

"Oh…" She smiles. "Was it a nice kiss?"

"It was a lovely kiss." Her smile widens and I have to smile back, even though I'm still in such a muddle. "But this morning, he came into the shop, in his uniform, and after he'd kissed me again, I asked what he was doing here… and he explained he works here." I look directly into her eyes. "That was when I realised he's PC Hughes… the man my dad thinks is just passing through, and has no staying power whatsoever."

"Right…" she says slowly, like she doesn't understand what the problem is.

"I couldn't bring myself to tell him that my father is his boss." The words tumble out of my mouth and I let out a long sigh at the end of them.

"Ah… so that's the lie. Or at least, that's the lack of truth?"

"Yes. I know you're going to say I should have told him, but how could I? There's every chance he's not even serious about me, but if he is, it would probably make things very difficult for him at work. It might mean he wouldn't want to see me anymore… and as for how my dad would react…" I let my voice fade, before it cracks up completely.

"Do you think he might be serious about you?" Imelda asks.

"How on earth would I know?" I struggle against the tears that have unexpectedly formed behind my eyes.

"Do you want him to be?" she says, and I wish she didn't know me so well.

"Yes."

"Then you owe it to him to be honest." She looks at me long and hard. "I don't just mean that you need to tell the truth. I mean, you can't hide things… or keep secrets. That's not fair."

"But what about Dad? He's not going to like it."

"This isn't about your dad. This is about you and your young man… and being honest with each other."

A feeling of shame creeps over me, because I know she's right. I can't wait and see. I have to tell Tom the truth, before it's too late. "I'll tell him. I'll do it tonight."

"Good." She smiles and picks up her sandwich, taking a bite. "It's for the best, you know."

I smile at her, relieved that I've made my decision… and that I know I'm going to stick to it.

I just hope I don't regret it.

Dad beats me home tonight, but then I had a customer come in right at closing time, wanting a funeral arrangement. In those circumstances, I didn't really feel as though I could say 'no'. Of course, I didn't expect that the man would take nearly twenty minutes to decide what he wanted, or that he'd have to look up the details of where the funeral was, and that he'd want to talk for so long... but I didn't have the heart to rush him. Which means I'm now in a rush myself, and as I let myself in, I kick off my shoes and make for the stairs.

"Where are you off to?" Dad asks, coming out of the living room, heading for the kitchen.

"I'm going out tonight..." I put my foot on the first stair.

"Again?" he says, the tone of his voice making me stop in my tracks and turn to look at his stern face.

"Yes... again. And I'm running late."

"Are you seeing the same man you were with last night?" He frowns, and I can't help but feel a little insulted that he evidently finds it so hard to believe that someone would want to go out with me more than once.

"Yes. He's taking me out for dinner... to the Italian restaurant in Church Lane."

"This sounds serious." He tilts his head, his frown fading. "Maybe I should meet this young man."

"No." I realise too late that my reply is too hasty, and too loud, and Dad's frown reappears in an instant. "It's not serious at all," I say, before he can respond. I know that's a lie. For me, it's very serious, and as I said to Imelda earlier on, I'd like it to be serious for Tom too.

"Oh, I see," he says, and I almost hear his sigh of relief. "Well, you'd better get changed."

I manage a smile and run up the stairs, dashing into my bedroom and closing the door, as I try not to think about the fact that I've just lied to my father... on several levels. Not only did I not tell him I'm going to be having dinner tonight with PC Hughes, who he really doesn't seem to like very much... but I also told him I'm not serious about Tom, when I am. Although I suppose that second element isn't really a lie. After all, if Tom isn't serious about me, then it won't matter how I feel, because nothing will come of it, anyway.

Feeling a bit depressed at that thought, I quickly undress, and put on a hint of make-up, before combing out my hair, and putting on my dark red sweater dress, which I like, because it's simple, but looks good… or at least, I think it does.

Checking my watch, I notice I've only got fifteen minutes until I'm due to meet Tom, so I pull on my black boots and run back down the stairs, where Dad's waiting for me. I wonder if he's been standing there all this time, but he can't have been. Surely?

"You look nice," he says.

"Thank you."

"You won't be late home, will you?"

I shrug on my jacket and grab my handbag. "No. I've got work tomorrow."

He nods his head. "Okay… well, have a nice time."

"Thanks, Dad."

I go over to him and kiss him on the cheek, returning the smile he gives me, before I let myself out of the house and pull my jacket tight around me. It's chilly tonight, and I hop down the steps onto the pavement, and start the walk around the harbour.

I'm just approaching Bell Road when a man appears out of the shadows and I let out a yelp of surprise, stopping dead.

"Sorry." I hear Tom's familiar voice as he steps into the light. "I didn't mean to frighten you."

"What are you doing here? I thought we were meeting at the restaurant."

"We were. But I decided that, as we both have to walk in the same direction, we might as well walk together."

That's such a sweet thing to say, and I smile up at him. He leans down and kisses me, letting his lips rest on mine as he pulls me in close to him and holds me for a moment, before he releases me again, a slight smile etched on his face.

"I'm glad I don't have my uniform on," he says, winking, and I giggle as he takes my hand in his and we walk together.

"I was nearly late," I say, as we pass Imelda's shop.

"Well, you said you might be." I recall my white lie from earlier, which turned out to be completely accurate.

"I had a man come into the shop, wanting a funeral arrangement. He seemed really sad, and I ended up talking to him until quarter past six. I had to rush home and change really quickly to get back out in time."

He looks down at me. "That was kind of you... staying and talking to him, I mean."

I shrug, feeling embarrassed by his compliment. "He wasn't from the village. He said he'd been recommended to us by a friend... so I could hardly disappoint, could I?"

Tom's still gazing at me, and I look up into his eyes. "You think that's all it was, do you? You think you gave up your time, just because it made the shop look good?"

"Well... no. I felt sorry for him."

"Exactly." He stops walking, bringing me to a halt, and with his free hand, he cups my cheek and leans down, kissing me a little harder, his tongue finding mine in a slow, romantic dance. "You're very sweet," he says, eventually breaking the kiss, before he turns and starts walking again.

I'm not sure what that means, but I need to know.

"How do you mean 'sweet'?" I ask. "Do you mean I'm sweet for talking to that man, or that I taste sweet?"

He turns and smiles, his eyes twinkling in the street lamps. "Both."

I'm not sure that helps with understanding his meaning, but I smile up at him anyway as we turn the corner into Church Lane. We pass by the police station, and go up the hill a little towards Sapore di Mare, the new Italian restaurant, which has been open for just over a year now. The owners are a middle-aged married couple and they're no more Italian than I am, but the illusion seems to work, and the restaurant is popular with holidaymakers.

Tom holds the door open for me, and we pass inside, where a waiter takes our coats and hangs them up on a rack by the door, before showing us to a table near the back of the restaurant, handing us menus as we take our seats. The lighting in here is quite dim, although there are candles on the tables, and I smile across at Tom, who takes my hand in his.

"It's good to see you again," he says.

"It's good to see you too."

I know I've got to tell him about Dad, but I don't have to tell him yet. We can at least order our food first… and maybe have a drink.

"I've had such an awful day," he says, laying his menu on the table in front of him, without even looking at it. "I swear, apart from that brief interlude when I came to see you earlier on, it's only been the thought of seeing you tonight that's kept me going."

"What's been wrong with your day?" Dad didn't mention that anything significant happened today, but I suppose I wasn't at home long enough to give him the chance.

Tom sighs, shaking his head. "I probably shouldn't say."

"Why not?" For a second, I wonder if maybe he's heard that his boss is my father, and whether this is his way of letting me know… but he looks into my eyes and somehow I know that's not the case.

"Because I imagine you know almost everyone in this village, and me talking out of turn about my boss might make you feel uncomfortable."

If only you knew… "If you need to talk, then talk," I say out loud, and he sighs again.

"Sergeant Quick seems to have taken an instant disliking to me," he murmurs, a shadow crossing his face. "I don't want to sound paranoid, but it feels like he's going out of his way to make my life miserable. He spent most of the afternoon finding fault in everything I did… and when that wasn't enough, he belittled me in front of everyone else at the station."

"In what way?" I ask, feeling ashamed of my father already.

"I had to ask him a question about the computer system." He shrugs his shoulders. "I'd already explained that I'm a technological dinosaur, so I don't know why he was surprised I needed help. What I don't understand is why he had to answer me in such a condescending way, in front of everyone else." He stops talking. "I'm sorry. I don't mean to sound like a whining baby. That's not my style. It's just hard fitting in, and I've had a bellyful of Sergeant Quick's attitude today. Ignore me."

That's such a horrible thing for Dad to have done, and I put down my menu, placing my other hand on top of Tom's.

"Of course I won't ignore you. And I'm sorry." He looks up.

"What are you apologising for?" His confusion is obvious, and not at all surprising. He doesn't know that I'm saying sorry on behalf of my father, does he? He puts his hand on top of mine, so we've made a tower, and looks down at the construction, smiling. "Let's forget about work, shall we?" he says, raising his eyes to mine again. "Let's order some food, and some wine, and talk about anything but police sergeants."

"Okay… if that's what you want."

"It is."

He takes away his top hand, and I do the same, dismantling the tower, and we open our menus. The words swim before my eyes though, and I struggle to focus, because for all my good intentions, I know now that I can't tell him who I am… or who my father is. Given the state of their professional relationship, it would drive a wedge between the three of us, and I don't want that to happen. I love my father… obviously, and I know that, despite his recent behaviour towards Tom, he's not normally so cruel. I really like Tom too, and I don't want whatever is going on between us to end. But I think it might, if he finds out who my father is.

That means I'm going to have to stay quiet for now, and hope they iron out their professional differences. Maybe then I can tell them what's going on, and we can all laugh about it. I only hope they work things out soon though, because I'm really not comfortable keeping my secret… from either of them.

Dinner has been lovely. We spent a lot of the evening discussing food, and I discovered Tom likes to cook… not just to eat, like most of us, but for the enjoyment of it. It was lovely to watch him enthuse over something he's clearly so passionate about.

At the end of the evening, once he's paid the bill – which he insisted on – he helps me into my jacket, and we go back outside into the chilly night air. Once we're at the end of Church Lane, he puts his arm around me, rather than holding my hand, and we slowly start our walk back around the harbour.

"Can I see you tomorrow?" he asks, and I look up at him.

"Yes, if you want to."

"Of course I want to. I was wondering if you'd like to come to my place? I'd like to cook something for you."

I smile, recalling our conversation. "You would?"

"Yes." He stops walking outside the pharmacy and turns me to face him. "And I'd like to spend some time alone with you… just the two of us."

He leans down and kisses me, his lips crushing mine, and as I sigh into him, a thought crosses my mind. He wants to be alone with me… so does that mean he's going to have expectations?

God knows…

The good Lord might also be the only one who knows whether I want to fulfil them… because I don't have a clue.

Chapter Eight

Tom

Gemma's kisses are like nothing I've ever felt, and I've never had to fight so hard to control my reactions to anyone before. Because I've got to be honest, after we finished dinner tonight, I was really tempted to ask her to come back to my place… to spend the night.

I let myself into my house, closing the door behind me, and smile as I recall the one thing that stopped me. It didn't have anything to do with the fact that I only met Gemma a couple of days ago, or even that my house still isn't as tidy as I'd like it to be. I refrained from inviting her because she seems so easily embarrassed… even though she's quite good at causing that embarrassment herself. Like she did this morning, when I kissed her at the shop. My torch must have been prodding into her side, and she made that comment about something hard sticking into her. It was a challenge not to smile then. I was very aroused at the time, and for just a split second, I wondered if she'd noticed. I'd been trying my best to keep my distance… but even as her meaning became clear, she made matters worse – at least for herself – by asking if I'm allowed to take my uniform off. That was so funny, and yet I couldn't laugh, because her comment was made with such innocence. I felt completely beguiled by her then… just like I did this evening, when she asked whether I'd called her sweet because of how she tasted. I knew she was talking about our kisses, but the thought of tasting her more intimately almost made me groan out loud. It was hard to resist the urge to tell her I've thought of very little else since Sunday night, other than being alone with her… but tomorrow night, I'm going to do just that, because when I asked if I could cook for her, she said yes.

I'm tired now, and I don't need anything, so I don't bother turning on the lights and, after I've taken off my jacket, I head upstairs and get undressed, falling into bed, and gazing up at the ceiling.

I'm not going to read too much into tomorrow night. I'm just going to take it as it comes. It is only our third date, after all, and just because I want her like I want to breathe, and I'm struggling to think about anything else but her during every waking moment, doesn't mean she feels the same way. She didn't run for the hills when I said I wanted to be alone with her, but I'm not going to overthink that either. We could be on different wavelengths. So, we'll just wait and see what happens. If that turns out to be an evening spent talking and kissing, and finding out more about each other, then I won't be complaining. If it turns into an evening spent naked, either in my bed, or on the sofa, or anywhere else in my house, then I'll be the happiest man in the world.

I wake this morning with a smile on my face, because I know I'm going to see Gemma tonight, and that we're going to be alone. I'm still not expecting anything to happen, but just the thought of being alone with her is enough to get me hopping out of bed with renewed vigour in my step.

That's a minor miracle after the day I had yesterday. I wasn't kidding when I told Gemma it had been awful. It had. I've never been so humiliated as I was yesterday afternoon, when I had to ask Sergeant Quick for his help with the computer system, and he showed me up in front of everyone… even the two Specials, who were at the station at the time. One of them – Naomi, I think her name is – gave me a sympathetic look, once Quick had gone back into his office, but I wasn't in the mood for sympathy.

I'm also not in the mood for another day like that though, especially when I've got such a magical evening to look forward to, so after I've showered and got dressed, I have breakfast and make my way to work, determined to avoid Sergeant Quick as much as possible. It seems to be the best way, if you ask me.

When I arrive, I almost groan out loud, because despite my plan, only Geoff and Sergeant Quick are in the office and I nod a greeting at them before going over to the kitchen and putting the kettle on to boil. At least making the coffee will keep me occupied and out of the sergeant's way.

"I think you need to let her make her own choices," Geoff says, and I realise I've entered half-way through a conversation.

I'm not sure what they're talking about, and I don't intend getting involved either. The sergeant will only tell me it's none of my business and, in reality, it isn't.

"I'm not saying she can't make her own choices." Quick sounds fed up. "I'm just saying I'd like to meet him… that's all."

"Hmm… so you can vet him, and tell her she's making the wrong choices," Geoff says as I come out from the kitchen area to ask if they want a cup of coffee. Geoff turns towards me, before I've even opened my mouth, a light smile on his lips. "What do you think, Tom?" he says, and I notice Sergeant Quick scowling at him.

"I'm not sure I think anything." I'm trying to be diplomatic. Or at least non-committal. "I don't know what you're talking about."

Geoff looks up at Quick, grinning. "Then let me explain… the sergeant here seems to think he's entitled to meet his daughter's new boyfriend…"

"I don't think I'm entitled," Quick interrupts. "I just think it would be nice to know who she's spending her time with, and I don't see why she won't let me."

Maybe because she thinks you'll scare the poor bloke off, I muse to myself, but I don't comment out loud.

"What do you say, Tom?" Geoff asks.

"I think it probably depends on their relationship," I say, with great reluctance.

"Mine with my daughter?" Sergeant Quick jumps down my throat.

"No. Your daughter's with her boyfriend, assuming he qualifies for that title in her eyes." He waits, like he expects me to explain. So I do. "If she's serious about him, then I'd say at some stage you should probably expect to meet him. But not at the very beginning of their relationship, because they'll be wanting to spend some time by themselves first."

Quick stares at me. "That's a very mature attitude." He sounds surprised, and probably, because of that, has paid me a compliment for once.

"I'm not exactly a child," I say, and he almost manages a smile.

"Did she say it was serious?" Geoff asks, getting back to the point of their conversation. "Or are you just overreacting?"

I'm glad it was him who said that, and not me.

Quick turns to him and frowns. "Actually, she told me it wasn't serious…" he says, like he's thinking out loud.

"In which case, I think you should leave well alone," Geoff says. "She's young. Let her have some fun."

Quick shakes his head. "You seem to forget… it was only a month or so ago that she was still a teenager."

Geoff leans forward. "And you seem to forget that when you were her age, you were already married, and about to become a father."

Quick frowns. "I know… and look where that got me."

Geoff falls silent, and I wonder about that remark, as the two of them stare at each other.

"Can I get either of you a coffee?" I ask, breaking the silence, and their conversation, I hope, because I'm not really interested in Sergeant Quick's domestic problems.

"No, thanks." Quick glances at me, and goes into his office, closing the door behind him.

"I'll have one, please," Geoff says, with a smile, and I return to the sanctuary of the kitchen.

My day goes so much better than yesterday, perhaps because Sergeant Quick seems preoccupied with his personal issues, and doesn't have time to pick holes in me, and what I'm doing. I wonder to myself whether he'd allow me – or anyone else – to be so distracted, but I don't say a word. I just relish a quiet day, and when it's over I make my way home, take a quick shower and change into jeans and a shirt, and then set about getting the dinner ready.

I've gone for something quite simple, which I've made before… namely, haddock parcels, and I popped out at lunchtime and bought some haddock fillets and vegetables, dashing home and putting everything into the fridge. So, all I've got to do is season the fish and prepare the vegetables, and then wrap it all up in individual greaseproof paper parcels and put them in the oven. Once that's done, I've still got enough time to give the living room a quick tidy and lay the table, before Gemma knocks on the door at seven o'clock precisely.

I let her in, unable to stop myself from smiling as I take her coat and hook it up, turning to briefly feast my eyes on her skin-tight jeans and fitted white blouse, right before I pull her into my arms and kiss her. I can't help myself and she responds, her tongue clashing with mine in an instant, and I feel the heat rising between us. She's breathing heavily, her arms around my neck and her fingers twisting into my hair. I let my hands wander from her waist, my right one roaming up and down her back, while the left one finds its way up her side, coming to rest on the curve of her breast and she moans loudly, tilting her hips. She must feel the same way I do… she must want more.

I break the kiss, struggling for control, and look down at her upturned face, all too aware of the tension between us, which is entirely sexual. The light in her eyes tells me she can feel it too, and while I'm tempted to suggest we adjourn to my bed, I don't… but only because we've got the whole evening, and there's no need to rush.

"Hello," I say instead, realising that we've kissed, and touched, and come close to doing a lot more than that, but we haven't actually spoken yet.

"Hello." She smiles and bites her bottom lip, and I reach up and release it with my thumb, holding her still before leaning down again and nibbling gently on it myself. She sighs and clutches at my arms, her hands gripping my biceps as she hitches in a breath, right before I release her.

"Would you like some wine?" I offer and she nods her head and lets me take her hand, leading her into the kitchen.

"I love your house." She sounds a little dreamy, and I turn to see her looking around, her eyes alight. "It's just how I imagined it would be."

I remember now that she told me she's always liked these houses, and I smile down at her as I let go of her hand and fetch the wine, and the two glasses that I pulled from the box earlier on, when I was laying the table.

"I've got a new cupboard coming soon," I say as I open the wine. "It's going in that corner." I nod towards the side wall. "And I've also ordered some garden furniture."

"Do these houses have gardens, then?" She sounds surprised.

"Not as such. I've got a courtyard… although you wouldn't want to sit out there now, because it's freezing. But I have high hopes for the summer."

"I'm sure it'll be lovely," she says, watching me pour the wine and taking the glass I offer her. We clink them together, our eyes fixed on each other as we both take a sip… the moment only interrupted by the buzzer on the oven announcing that our dinner is ready.

I'm sure the meal tastes fine. In fact, I know it does, because I've made it before… and Gemma keeps telling me how wonderful it is. Except I can't taste a thing. I'm too captivated by her to even think straight, let alone allow my senses to function properly… and I hate having three feet of oak table between us when I want her in my arms.

We finish eating, and I'm relieved I can clear away the dishes and join her on the sofa, bringing our wine with me. I sit beside her and turn, that unspoken tension building to a crescendo as I pull her into my arms and kiss her. I gently push her back until she's lying down and I lower myself on top of her, taking my weight on my elbows. Gemma moves one leg aside and I shift into the space she's created, knowing she'll be able to feel my arousal, because there's no hiding it now. She pauses, seeming to hold her breath, and then sighs and changes the angle of her head, bringing her hands up onto my shoulders, just as I pull back and trail gentle kisses along her jawline and down her exposed neck. Her body shudders as I raise myself up, noticing her closed eyes, slightly swollen lips and flushed cheeks, and I balance on one arm, undoing the first button of her blouse to reveal the top of a white lace bra. She startles then, and her eyes shoot open, as I move down to the next button.

"W—What are you doing?" she asks.

"I'm undressing you."

Her eyes widen. "I—I've never…"

I still, my hand poised. "You've never what?"

"I've never done anything like this before."

I move my hand away from her blouse and let it rest beside her head, uncertainty prickling over my skin.

"Can I ask you something, Gemma?" Doubt is clawing at my voice now, making it crack slightly. She nods her head, and I take a breath before I say, "How old are you?"

"I'm twenty."

I kneel up, gazing at her afresh, and notice what I should have seen before… that her embarrassment and her innocence have a foundation in her youth.

"Twenty?" I repeat, on a whisper, pushing my fingers back through my hair.

"Yes. Why? How old are you?" she asks.

"I'm thirty. Ten years older than you." I don't know why I feel the need to point out the age gap, but I do, although I regret the words the moment they've left my lips. Gemma's eyes glisten over with tears and she pulls up her legs and twists around, standing and dodging past the coffee table as she makes for the door.

"Hey…" I clamber to my feet and follow her, grabbing her wrist as she reaches for the door handle, her coat forgotten in her panic to leave. "Where are you going?"

"Home."

She won't look at me, but stares at the door instead.

"Why?" I step between her and her way out, placing my hands on her hips and moving her slightly.

"Because you don't want me anymore."

I can't believe I heard that right, but the look on her face tells me I did. "Whatever gave you that impression?"

"Your reaction." I feel like the biggest loser in the world now, because she saw right through me, and I know I'm going to have to be honest with her.

"Okay. I'm sorry about that. It was just a shock, that's all. I'd thought you were a little older, and hearing you say 'twenty'… well, it came as a surprise. I'm sorry if that's the wrong thing to say, but that's exactly how it was."

"How old did you think I was then?" She tilts her head to one side, frowning up at me.

"Truth?" I ask and she nods.

"Of course I want the truth."

"About twenty-four or twenty-five, I suppose."

She blushes and shakes her head. "Do I really look that old?"

"You don't look old at all. You look beautiful… and I apologise for getting it wrong." She relaxes slightly and I step away from the door, closer to her, putting my arms around her now. "And if you honestly think I don't want you, then I'm clearly doing something very wrong."

She blinks a few times and lowers her head. I copy her, only now noticing that her blouse is still gaping open, giving me a perfect view of the tops of her breasts, encased in fine white lace. I close my eyes. It feels wrong to look without her knowledge, or

107

her permission, and I lean back instead, opening my eyes now and staring at her as she raises her face to mine.

"Do you want to do that up?" I say, nodding towards her blouse.

She glances down and while I expect her to blush, and quickly refasten her buttons; she doesn't. Instead, she looks up at me again and whispers, "I don't know."

"You don't know?"

"No. I feel like I don't know anything at the moment… I'm so confused."

I smile, because she's so sweet. "That makes two of us."

"I'm sorry."

"What for?"

"Because I don't mean to confuse you," she says, sighing deeply. "And I certainly don't mean to tease you, but the thing is, I don't know what I want… and you're not from around here, so…"

"What has that got to do with anything?" I interrupt, surprised by her remark.

"Can't you see? We could… we could get together… we could sleep together, and then sometime later on, you could decide you don't like living here anymore… or that you don't like working here anymore… and you could leave."

I can't help smiling again, simply because she's thinking ahead. A long way ahead… and that feels good, because I am, too.

"I'm not planning on leaving," I say and she looks into my eyes, like she's searching for the truth, which is all she's ever going to get from me. "I like it here, Gemma. It's taking me a while to get used to the slower pace of life, but I'm working on it. I'll admit my job might not always be perfect, but I do still like it… and I really, really like you."

"I really, really like you too," she whispers, and I feel my heart do a kind of somersault in my chest, and wonder if 'like' was the right word for me to use just then. It might be early days for us, but 'like' already feels inadequate. I've never used the word 'love' out loud before, in this context, but 'like' doesn't feel enough. Before I can utter another syllable though, to tell her I think I'm falling for her, or maybe that I've already fallen, she adds, "But even if you're not going to leave, and even if you do really, really like me... that doesn't help me understand what I want."

"What *don't* you want?" I ask. "It might be easier to start there and work backwards."

"I don't want you to leave," she says, and I pull her closer to me.

"I think we've already established, I'm not going anywhere." *Especially not now you've said you really, really like me.*

She nods her head, smiling, and whispers, "I don't want you to stop doing all the things you do to me."

"But you're not ready for anything else yet." I say and she rests against me, her shoulders dropping, like she's feeling deflated by the whole thing, which isn't how this is supposed to work at all.

"I don't know." She sounds confused still, and frustrated. "I'm sorry if we're going round in circles, Tom, but when you're kissing me, I feel very ready... like I want you to keep going, and never stop. Except that can't be right, because if I was really that ready, why did I stop you?"

"Whoa... can you slow down for a second?" I lean back and bring my hands up, cupping her face, holding her and fixing her with my eyes. "I wasn't asking a question just then. I was making a statement. You're not ready."

"I'm not?" Her brow furrows.

"No. You've obviously got doubts…"

She tries to shake her head, even though I'm holding it. "I don't have any doubts about you," she says.

"That's good to know," I reply, smiling, and then I move a little closer to her. "This is my fault, Gemma."

"No, it's not."

"Yes, it is. I moved too fast."

"You weren't to know how… how inexperienced I am," she mumbles.

"No. But it's only our third date… and I should've waited a little longer. I—I let my need for you get in the way of common sense."

"Need?" she queries.

"Yes. Need."

"You need me?"

"God… yes."

She sighs. "Don't you think common sense is overrated sometimes?" she says softly and I laugh.

"Yes, I do. But, I should still have been a more responsible boyfriend… and I'm sorry."

"Did you just say boyfriend?" She ignores my apology, her eyes widening.

"Yes. Isn't that what I am?" I suddenly feel like I'm standing on quicksand, completely unstable and unsure of myself.

"Yes. If you want to be."

"Of course I want to be."

She smiles and I feel the ground strengthen beneath me. "Does that make me your girlfriend?" she asks.

"Yes, it does."

I'm not giving her options, or alternatives, but judging by the way her smile is broadening, and the sparkle in her eyes, I don't think she needs any.

"S—So what do we do now?" she says, a little nervously.

"We wait."

She frowns. "Wait? Nothing else? We just wait?"

"This isn't the kind of waiting you'd do at a bus stop, so you don't have to worry about getting bored." She chuckles. "We can carry on doing what we were doing before, as long as you're happy with that, and we can try new things, when you become more comfortable."

"So we're not really waiting at all… we're…" She struggles for the right word.

"Getting to know each other," I suggest, and she smiles.

"I like the sound of that."

I lean down to her, brushing my lips across hers. "Hmm… so do I."

I deepen the kiss, her tongue caressing mine, as her breathing changes and she crushes her breasts against my chest. I groan at the contact, aware that the buttons of her blouse are still undone, and with that thought, I grind my hips into hers, letting her feel my arousal. She moans and sighs and puts her hands on either side of my neck, pulling me closer, until we're both breathing so hard, I can hear my own heartbeat… and maybe hers too.

I pull back eventually and gaze down at her.

"I think I'm going to enjoy waiting for you," I whisper, and lead her back to the sofa.

Chapter Nine

Gemma

What a night…

What a rollercoaster of a night.

I stretch my arms above my head, and look out of the window at the blue morning sky, and I can't help smiling, because that really was a night.

Okay, so it wasn't all good. Dinner was amazing, and as for Tom's kisses… they just get better all the time. When he undid the buttons of my blouse, though, I was so confused, I didn't know what to do. I was torn between wanting him and an overriding feeling that it was all happening too fast. I felt bad for stopping him, but what else could I do, when it didn't feel right? Of course, I never expected him to react so badly to discovering my age, although with hindsight, I think that was more of a misunderstanding than anything. But in that moment, as I looked into his eyes, I felt scared that he didn't want me anymore… and in my fear, I ran. Or I tried to. He stopped me though, and then he explained… and after that we talked. God, did we talk. It was a very intimate, personal conversation… but then, I suppose we had been about to do some very intimate, personal things, and the need to communicate about that was important. At least, that's what Tom said to me as he walked me home, after he'd spent another hour or two kissing me.

"I know this is all new to you," he said, as we turned the corner at the end of his road and the wind caught in my hair. "But you must talk to me whenever you need to… if you're unsure about anything."

I turned to face him. "Like what?"

He smiled and shrugged his shoulders. "Like anything we're doing… or anything you want to try doing. I won't know if I'm getting it wrong, unless you tell me. We have to be honest with each other."

Of course, at that point, a wave of guilt washed over me, as I remembered that I still hadn't told him the truth about who I am… or who my father is, to be more precise. That was only compounded when I thought about our conversation, and how he'd promised to wait for me. He'd called me his girlfriend, showing his commitment to me, and yet I couldn't even be honest with him. I still can't, because I can't lose him. Not now… not when I know I'm falling for him…

"Did you have a nice time last night?"

Dad looks across the kitchen table at me, spreading marmalade onto his toast.

"Yes, thank you."

He nods, and then a smile settles on his face. "You don't need to worry," he says. "I'm not going to hassle you about whoever it is you're seeing. You've told me it's not serious and I believe you. You're young, Gemma… you should be out enjoying yourself."

I feel even more guilty now than I did upstairs. Up there, I was just beating myself up over lying to Tom about Dad. Down here, not only am I lying to Dad about seeing Tom, but I'm also pretending my feelings for him aren't serious, when the reality is so different.

I can't admit to that, though.

"I'm seeing him again tonight," I say instead.

He raises his eyebrows. "Four nights in a row?" He puts down his knife, taking a bite from his toast. "Going anywhere nice?"

He's fishing, I know that much, but at least he's not talking about wanting to 'meet' Tom anymore.

"I think we're going to the hotel for cocktails."

"Ooh… very fancy." He puts on a slightly mocking voice, but he's smiling and I know he means well.

I quickly finish my breakfast and get on with preparing the stew I've got planned for dinner tonight. It's going in the slow cooker, so it'll be ready for when Dad and I get in from work, and I can change afterwards and meet Tom at the hotel, as we've arranged. Personally, I think I'd rather spend the evening at Tom's house again, but he suggested the hotel, when he kissed me goodnight, and I wasn't about to say 'no' to seeing him.

Not when he means the world to me… already.

My day has been quite good.

The weather has been fantastic, so we've been busy. That always makes the time go quickly and while I was disappointed that Tom wasn't able to come in, I caught a glimpse of him through the window. He waved to me and gave me the most gorgeous smile… and my heart skipped a beat. I knew why he wasn't able to come in too. It was because there was another bag snatching on the harbour. That's the fourth one now, and it was outside the pharmacy this time. There was a lot of activity from both the public and our small police force. Dad popped in to tell me what was going on, and asked if I'd noticed anyone hanging around – which I hadn't. Of course, when I went upstairs at lunchtime, Imelda wanted to know all the details… and I was relieved about that, because it meant we didn't have time to talk about Tom, and the fact that I still haven't told him the truth about who I am. I know she'd be disappointed in me, and I'm not sure I can face that.

By closing time, all the excitement has died down, and it's fairly quiet again, other than a few holidaymakers strolling along the harbour.

I'm able to leave on time tonight, so I don't have to rush home, as I'm not meeting Tom until eight. But, given all the activity earlier, I'm not surprised to discover that Dad isn't home yet, and I help myself to a portion of stew, because I don't really have time to wait for him.

Dinner is really tasty, and once I've finished it and put my plate into the dishwasher, I make my way upstairs and quickly shower, before drying my hair, applying a little make-up and putting on some black underwear and lace-topped hold-ups. Then I stand in front of my pine wardrobe, in my bedroom at the back of the house, and stare at my clothes, wondering what on earth I should wear.

I'm not exactly overflowing with cocktail dresses, but I do have a really nice black dress, which I bought when I was leaving college and a few of us had a night out in Padstow. It's not too short, but it is very fitted, and off the shoulder, so I won't be able to wear a bra, being as I don't own a strapless one. I hesitate for a moment, with my hand on the hanger, wondering if I should go for something else. The problem is, what? I've got summer dresses galore, but it's March, and they're not really appropriate, and while this dress is sleeveless, I can team it with my black leather jacket and I know it looks good.

Oh, to hell with it.

I pull out the hanger, and before I can give too much thought to what Tom might think, I remove my bra again, and put on the dress, doing up the zip at the side and then turning to check how I look in the mirror. My face is a little flushed and my hair is a mess again, but there's something different about my appearance. I'm not sure what it is, and I don't have time to wonder now… because if I'm not careful, I'm going to be late.

Dad must have come home while I was in the shower, because when I come down the stairs, hanging onto the bannister at the bottom so I can put on my shoes, he comes out of the kitchen, still in his uniform, and stares down at me.

"Goodness," he says.

"What?" I look up at him and he raises his eyebrows.

"You look…"

I glance down at myself, straightening my dress and feeling nervous now. "How do I look?"

"Beautiful," he says, as though the thought has only just occurred to him, and I disguise my relief. "Are you sure you're not serious about this man you're seeing?" He frowns at me and I tense again, although I hide that too as I lean up and kiss his cheek.

"I'm positive, Dad. Stop worrying."

He nods his head, seeming to accept my statement, and I grab my leather jacket from the coat rack, shrugging it on, before I pick up my bag and make for the front door, pulling it open.

"Not too late," he says, with a warning note to his voice.

"No, Dad."

I close the door behind me and carefully climb down the steps, taking care in my heels. I'm not used to wearing them, and while I know that my flat black boots or trainers simply wouldn't have worked with this dress, I wonder now about the wisdom of trying to walk in such high heels.

Still, I don't have far to go, although I wish that Tom had chosen tonight to meet me on the corner. He could have held my hand, or propped me up and saved me the trouble of feeling like I'm going to fall over, especially on these cobbles, which are treacherous at the best of times.

I make it to the hotel without breaking anything, but there's no sign of Tom, even though we arranged to meet outside. For a second, I feel slightly fearful. I don't particularly want to stand out here by myself, but I don't want to go in on my own either.

"Gemma?"

I turn at the sound of my name and sigh out my relief as I see Tom running up the driveway. He looks lovely, in dark trousers and jacket and a white shirt, although he seems a little flustered.

"I'm so sorry I'm late," he says, coming up and kissing me.

"You're not. Not really."

"Shall we go in? It's cold out here."

I nod my head and he opens the door, letting me pass through before him. When I turn back, he's standing, staring at me.

"Wow… it was dark outside. I didn't realise you looked so… I mean… wow."

I smile at his inability to string a sentence together and he comes and stands right in front of me, leaning down to kiss me again, but delaying a little longer this time.

"You look stunning," he says, rediscovering the power of speech.

"Thank you."

I try hard not to blush as he takes my hand and leads me into the bar, which is through an archway on the right of the reception area. Inside, I stop for a moment and gaze at the enormous room, decorated in dark wood, with lots of down-lighters and mirrors. I'm not surprised that Mr Goddard didn't ask for any flowers in here. They really wouldn't work… and while I'm thinking of Mr Goddard, I wonder if he's here, and what I'll say to him if we should meet.

"It's busier than I'd expected," Tom says, interrupting my thoughts and guiding us further into the room, towards a vacant table on the far side.

"Yes, it is." I glance around at the other guests, realising that, even if Mr Goddard is working tonight, he's unlikely to see me with all these other people here. I'm quite relieved about that. It could be awkward, considering I told him I was too busy to go out… and yet here I am.

It seems I'm a lot better at lying than I thought I was, and I find that thought quite depressing.

Tom's holding out my chair for me and I snap out of my momentary melancholy and shrug off my jacket, handing it to him, before sitting down. He leans over, his mouth beside my ear, and whispers, "Are you *trying* to drive me insane?"

I shake my head as he puts my jacket over the back of his chair and sits opposite me.

"No. Why would I be?"

"Looking as good as that, when I've promised to wait for you," he says, smiling, so I know he's joking, which is a tremendous relief.

"Oh, I see what you mean. It wasn't intentional. This is the only dress I own that felt appropriate for somewhere like this…" I glance around.

"I'm not complaining." He reaches out, taking my hand in his, as a waitress comes and stands beside us, expectantly.

"What can I get you?" she says and Tom looks across the table at me.

"I've never had a cocktail before," I whisper, hoping the waitress won't hear me, even though I'm fairly sure she will.

He smiles. "In that case, I've got two questions… do you like gin? And do you trust me?"

"I quite like gin, and I trust you absolutely," I say and his smile becomes a broad grin as he turns to the waitress.

"Two very dry martinis, please," he says, and she gives him a sympathetic look, presumably because he has the misfortune to be sitting with someone who doesn't know how to order a cocktail. Then she leaves, and Tom turns to me again, the smile still lighting up his face. "I'm so sorry I was late," he says, leaning in a little closer.

"You've already apologised once." I sit forward myself now. "And, as I said outside, you weren't late at all."

He delves into his jacket pocket with his free hand and pulls out his phone. "I only realised, when I was panicking about getting here, that I don't have your number. If I had, I could have called to let you know I was late home from work, and that getting here on time might be an issue…" He holds out his phone to me. "So, do you want to put your number onto my contacts lists, to save me from having a heart attack sometime in the near future?"

"You'll need to unlock it first," I say, but he shakes his head.

"No, I won't. My phone is ancient. It doesn't need unlocking."

I take it from him and glance down, seeing that he's telling the truth. It's a smartphone, but it really is quite old, and I smile up at him.

"I make no apologies." He holds up his hand. "I'm absolutely useless with technology, and I like my phone. It's small enough to fit into my pocket, and it does everything I need it to do… which is why I haven't changed it since dinosaurs roamed the earth."

I shake my head and smile at him, just as the waitress comes back and puts down two cocktail glasses containing clear liquid and olives on sticks.

"Thank you," Tom and I both say together, and she moves away again, before he and I lift our glasses and clink them together.

"Sip it," he warns and I raise the glass to my lips, taking a small sip of the slightly sour tasting drink, and just about managing not to choke at the strength of the alcohol.

"Do you like it?" Tom asks, putting down his glass.

I copy him and nod my head, because despite the strong flavours, it is really nice.

"Yes, I do. I'm not sure I could drink a lot of them though."

He chuckles. "You're not meant to," he says and nods towards his phone. "You still need to put your number on there."

"Yes, I do." I tap on the screen, finding his contacts list and I press on the icon, my smile fading when I see the names come up. The first few are all female and I read down the list… Alice, Amanda, Andrea, Becky…

I look up at him again, although he's slightly blurred now, thanks to the tears in my eyes, and he frowns.

"What's wrong?" he says.

I put his phone down again, pushing it across the table towards him. "Who are all those women?" I murmur through the lump in my throat.

He pulls his phone a little closer, and then focuses on the screen for a second or two, before he looks back at me again. "I'm sorry," he says. "I told you, I'm not good with technology, and I've never worked out how to remove anyone's number from the list."

I blink back my tears, or at least try to, and I swallow hard, before I ask, "Are… Are they all girlfriends?"

"Some of them are *ex*-girlfriends," he says, tilting his head to one side, like he doesn't understand what my problem is, which is confirmed when he grips my hand a little tighter and asks, "What's the matter, Gemma?"

I'm not sure how the man who helped me understand my feelings last night can be so insensitive today, but it seems it's possible. "What do you think?" I ask, my anger doing a good job of disguising my insecurity.

"I don't know," he says. "But I'm guessing you're having a problem with the fact that I've got a past."

"Well done." Anger can't disguise my sarcasm, and his frown deepens as he releases my hand.

"Gemma... I'm thirty years old. That means I've been doing this for ten years longer than you. Did you honestly think there wouldn't have been anyone else before you?"

When he says it like that, it sounds reasonable – even logical – and it's hard not to say, "No, I suppose not," although I still think he's being insensitive about the whole thing. But perhaps that's just my inexperience showing through... again.

He pushes his phone back across to me. "You still haven't put your number on there yet," he says and I pick it up.

"One on a long list?" I muse to myself, but he must have heard me.

"It's not a long list." He sounds defensive, maybe even a little hurt. "And if you want to, you can delete them... assuming you know how."

"I do."

"Okay... go ahead then."

The atmosphere between us is tense, but not in a good way, and I feel responsible for that... at least in part. At the same time, though, I hate the idea of him having this list of ex-girlfriends on his phone when he's supposed to be my boyfriend. That's what he called himself, after all.

"You're sure you want me to?" I ask.

"Of course." He takes my free hand in his again, which feels more comforting than I would have thought possible. "I'm not in touch with any of them. They're not important to me, and in most cases, they probably don't even use those numbers anymore. I'm just a bit of a loser with phones... and most other forms of technology. If you want to delete them, feel free."

Using my thumb, I click on the contacts icon again, and stare at the screen.

"You say that only some of them are ex-girlfriends?" I ask, looking back up at him.

"Yes."

"Okay... so what about Alice?"

He smiles. "She's my cousin. I'll be in trouble if you delete her, so please don't."

I nod my head and manage a smile. Just. "Amanda?"

"Yep... she can go. I went out with her about ten years ago, but I imagine she's probably forgotten my name by now. It wasn't the most memorable of relationships."

I click on Amanda's name and scroll down to the bottom of the screen, pressing 'delete contact', and confirming it when the window pops up.

"Andrea?" I say, going back to the main list, and Tom laughs.

"That's my aunt... Alice's mum, and the whole reason my mother moved to Cornwall in the first place... which I suppose is why I'm here too. I wouldn't dare remove her from my phone."

I manage a more genuine smile this time. "Becky?" I say, looking down at the list again.

"She was my father's secretary." Tom's voice has changed. It's harsher, and I look up to see a dark expression on his face. "I used to have her number in case I couldn't get hold of my dad, but he ran off with her about three years ago, and I haven't heard from him since. I don't even know if they're still together... and, frankly, I don't really care."

"Does that mean you want me to delete Becky's details?" I ask, feeling a little shocked.

"Yes, please." He smiles at me now. "I know that's the second time I've mentioned my father leaving my mother, and that I haven't given you the full story yet, but I'll fill you in on all my dad's sorry misdemeanours some other time... when we're not erasing my past."

He nods towards the phone again, letting me know I should continue, even though I'm not sure I want to anymore. I think I'd rather just leave... and maybe go back to his place, so we can sit and talk.

"Catherine?" I say, unable to hold in my sigh, because this feels really intrusive now.

"Definitely delete."

He doesn't say anything more, so I remove her, scrolling down past a few male names, and what appears to be his bank, until I reach the next female one. "What about Helen?"

"Oh God," he says with some considerable feeling. "Get rid of her. She was nothing but trouble."

I delete Helen's details and move on to Kelly.

There's a moment's hesitation after I've said her name, and I look up at Tom to see he's staring at me.

"Delete," he says simply, but with an unusual coolness to his voice.

"Why did you hesitate?" I ask him. His reaction was different, and I want to know why. "Is she important?"

"No. I told you... none of them are."

"Okay... I'll change the tense of my question. Was she important?"

"No, not really. We owned a house together... the house I sold before I moved here."

"So you only broke up with her recently?" I wonder if that's what the problem is.

"No. We broke up years ago. But things didn't end well between us. It got ugly in the end and all we did was fight over the house. I suppose I just got used to a feeling of dread whenever I saw her name come up on my phone."

"Did you love her?" I ask. "Before it got ugly, I mean."

"No." He doesn't hesitate this time. "I've never been in love." He stops talking rather abruptly.

"And yet, you lived with her?"

"Yes. It was a mistake, but by the time we worked that out, it was too late. Kelly was the one who left, but the relationship was going nowhere, and it was just a question of which one of us jumped ship first. I don't look back on that time with any kind of fondness, but being with Kelly and going through that break-up did me quite a few favours."

"Like what?"

"It taught me a lot about myself."

I don't know what that means, and I'm too scared to ask, so instead we both gaze at each other for a moment. I've got no idea what he's thinking, but I know I'm wishing we'd never started this.

"We're not finished yet," he says, tilting his head towards his phone.

"No." I look back down at it, and find the next name. "Monica," I say, a little half-heartedly.

"Please, please, delete her. She was a nightmare."

I do as he asks and then scroll down to Sarah.

"No," he says, after I've read out her name. "Sarah's another cousin. She's Alice's sister."

I skim over her name and then find, "Tanya?"

Tom smiles and shakes his head and just says, "Delete."

"Why are you smiling?" I ask as I remove her name from the list.

"Because she was a good laugh. Completely crazy, but a good laugh. I went out with her about a year before I met Kelly,

I think… and I don't have any bad memories of her at all. Unlike a lot of them."

"Why did you break up?" I ask.

"Her family emigrated to somewhere. It was all to do with her father's job, although I can't remember where they went now. She was twenty-one and had just finished uni, and had the choice of staying here, or going with them. She chose to go."

"Were you upset about that?"

"No." He shakes his head. "I didn't love her. I told you, I didn't love any of them. And I don't think she loved me either. If she had done, I imagine she'd have stayed here. Like I said, we'd had fun together… but that was it."

I look down at the phone again and scroll to the bottom of the list.

"That seems to be all of them," I say.

"Yes, I imagine it is." He leans forward. "And now, will you please put your number on my phone?"

"Are you sure you still want me to?"

"Why wouldn't I?" He frowns, evidently surprised by my question.

"Because I've just spent the last thirty minutes deleting and dissecting your past."

"So? I've already explained, none of them meant anything…" He leaves his sentence hanging and I try very hard not to read anything into that. It's hard, though, and as I tap my number into his phone, I have to wonder whether, in years to come, he'll do this again with someone else, and look back on our time together so dismissively.

Chapter Ten

Tom

The atmosphere between us, which is normally fizzing with sexual tension, currently feels edgy… almost brittle, and it's getting to me. I need to talk to Gemma. I need to know we're still okay… because it doesn't feel like it at the moment.

The problem is, that's not a conversation I'm willing to have here, in public, so I take back my phone and put it in my pocket and then get to my feet, pulling her up with me.

"What are you doing?" she says, wide-eyed.

"I'm taking you home."

"Home? But I…" Tears appear in her eyes, but just at that moment, the waitress comes over.

"Is everything okay?" she says, eyeing our half finished drinks, as Gemma turns her head, hiding her tears.

"Yes. Sorry… something's come up. We've got to leave." I pull out my wallet and hand the waitress a twenty-pound note.

"I'll get your change," she says.

"Don't worry… keep it."

"Oh… thank you."

I ignore her now and reach behind me for Gemma's jacket, helping her to put it on, even though she's keeping her head down and won't look at me.

"Please don't cry," I whisper in her ear and she looks up at last, her tears brimming and about to fall. Before she can say anything, or even try to, I take her hand and lead her back through the bar, into the reception area and then out of the front door, into the cool night air.

I can't believe how badly tonight has gone, but then I suppose I should have known when that woman turned up at the station, just as I was about to leave for the night. I should have realised then that I was destined to have a disastrous evening.

Geoff had already gone home and there was just me and Sergeant Quick in the building when the woman came in, fussing about something, and demanding to see the officer in charge. That was Sergeant Quick, of course, but he was on the telephone, so I tried to deal with her myself… which was my first mistake.

My second was to invite her to come into the office and sit down, which I only did because she seemed so flustered. What I didn't realise was that, once she got comfortable, it was going to be almost impossible to get rid of her again.

The reason for her visit, which took me ten minutes to discover, was that she'd seen a man 'acting suspiciously' by the pub earlier in the day. Ordinarily, I wouldn't have thought very much of that, but a bag had been snatched this morning, just outside the pharmacy, so anything suspicious was always going to be noteworthy. The problem was that, when questioned, this woman couldn't be sure what time she'd seen the man, or give an accurate description of him, other than that he was wearing a grey hoodie and was 'suspicious'. So, all in all, her statement was worse than useless.

Fortunately, I managed to remove her from the station by the time Sergeant Quick materialised from his office. He seemed quite surprised to find me on the premises still, and he locked up and bade me goodnight before I rushed home to get ready for my date with Gemma.

It was only while I was getting dressed that I realised I didn't have any means of contacting her to warn her I might be late… which was why I suggested she put her number onto my phone… and the whole evening fell apart.

How was I supposed to remember the contents of my contacts list, or that it still contained the details of every other girlfriend I've had in the last decade? I have to say, I was surprised there were only six of them. It felt like there were more than that at the time, but in hindsight, I suppose Kelly took up quite a few years… between the relationship itself and the fallout from it.

What I hadn't expected, though, was Gemma's reaction. She seemed genuinely hurt, and surprised, that she's not my first. At least, that's how it felt. But at my age, that's just ridiculous…

As we reach the end of the hotel driveway, I hear Gemma sniffle, and I stop, turning towards her, even though my house is only just across the street.

"Please don't cry," I whisper again, looking down at her. "Just wait until we get inside, and we can talk."

"Inside? But you said you were taking me home," she whimpers.

"I am… my home."

She sucks in a breath and bites her bottom lip. "I—I thought you meant my home," she says, still struggling with her emotions.

"No. I meant mine. We need to talk, Gemma."

She nods, and I put my arm around her, guiding her across the road and supporting her too. She doesn't seem to be very stable in her high heels. They look incredible on her, making her legs seem even longer and more shapely than usual… helped by the sexy black dress she's wearing. But I'm not sure high heels are very practical when coupled with cobbled streets.

We climb up the steps to my front door, and I let us in, flicking on the light and closing the door, before I turn to her.

"Tell me we're okay," I say, unable to wait a second longer.

"Sorry?" She looks up at me, confused.

"Tell me we're okay. Everything feels different between us tonight, and I need to know we're still okay with each other."

"Y—Yes," she says, with a degree of hesitation, which is unnerving, to put it mildly. "It was just a surprise, having your past put before me, in one go, in black and white like that."

I take off my jacket, and hers too, hooking them both up and trying very hard not to let my hands, or my eyes, dwell on her bare shoulders, as I lead her across to the sofa. I sit her down beside me and then take her hands in mine, twisting in my seat, so I'm facing her, because I need her to see the truth in my face.

"You understand, don't you, that I was always going to have a past? At my age, it was never going to be any different. I've slept with six women, Gemma. But none of them meant anything… and I certainly don't care about them now. You believe that, don't you?"

"Yes," she says. "But do you understand that being aware of your past is one thing… wanting to know all about the people in it is something else altogether. I may be young and… well, ignorant, I suppose, but even I'd worked out that there would have been other… other women in your life…"

"You're not ignorant," I interrupt. "You're innocent."

I feel the age gap between us more than ever… more even than last night, when I wanted her so much, and found out how innocent she really is.

"It makes no difference what I am," she says, her voice cutting through me, because I can hear the hurt in it. "The point is that, even though I can understand their presence in your life... in your past... I wasn't prepared to have them laid out in front of me like that, so unexpectedly. It... it wasn't very sensitive of you, Tom."

I gaze at her divine face, the doubt and insecurity written all over her perfect features, and I can't deny the truth of what she's saying. Suddenly I'm overwhelmed with disappointment... in myself, not her. Even if I had forgotten those names were on my phone, I should have handled the situation better. I should have thought about how it would look and feel from Gemma's perspective, and I probably should have taken her age and inexperience into consideration too... because, like everything else we're doing, this is new to her.

"I apologise." I move a little closer. "Please believe me... I'd genuinely forgotten their names were even on there. All I wanted was to have your number, so I could call you if I was running late. I didn't think about anything else, and if I've been insensitive... if I've hurt you, then I'm truly sorry." She leans her head towards me, and I copy her until our foreheads are resting together. "Am I forgiven?" I whisper, and she nods.

"Yes, you are."

"While we're sharing secrets, can I ask... do you have any?"

Her eyes widen slightly. "What do you mean?"

"I mean, is there anyone from your past that I should know about?"

She frowns. "No. How could there be?" She lowers her head, but I place my finger beneath her chin and raise it again, so she has to look at me. "I—I thought you understood..."

"I do. But that doesn't mean you can't have had a boyfriend or two."

She sucks in a breath, and I instinctively know that something's coming. "There was someone."

"Oh, yes?"

"I went out with Dan Moyle for a while, when we were at school. In year ten."

I smile at her, relieved that my phone didn't go that far back. If we were including all the girls I've ever dated – as opposed to slept with – right back from when it all started, with Sophie Westwood, in year nine, then I'd be in a lot more trouble than I already am.

"Dan Moyle?" I say, nodding my head. "Isn't he the surfing guy?"

"Yes." Her brow furrows. "You can't have met him, though. He's not here at the moment. He's away, taking part in a surfing competition, somewhere or other."

"I haven't met him. I've met his father. Sergeant Quick introduced me to him on my first day here, and he mentioned his son teaches people to surf, or something." She blushes and tries to look away again, but I don't let her. "Did you like him?" I ask, feeling a little confused by her reaction.

"No. I mean, yes… of course I liked him. I've known him all my life. But I didn't like him in the way you mean. He was good to me though, when my mum left and… and we're still friends." She looks up at me. Her blush is still there, but there's more to this than embarrassment. It's like she's scared.

"And you're worried I might not like that?" She doesn't answer, but the doubt in her eyes is enough of a give-away, and I move closer to her. "It's okay, Gemma. I don't have a problem with the two of you being friends."

"Really? I don't think I'd like it, if you were still friends with any of the women who were listed on your phone."

I smile. "Yes, but there's a big difference between the two things. You've known Dan all your life, and your friendship is important – to both of you, I would think." I move my hand and caress her cheek. "The women on my phone were just people who passed through my life. They don't mean anything to me."

"Nothing?"

"Absolutely nothing."

"Okay," she says, letting out a sigh.

"With that in mind, do you think we could put tonight behind us?" I suggest, because I really just want to get back to where we were before this all started.

"Yes," she says. "I think I'd like that."

"May I kiss you?"

"You don't need to ask," she whispers, leaning into me a little.

"After tonight, I think I probably do."

"No, you don't." My skin tingles and I edge nearer, but it's Gemma who closes the gap between us, and our lips meet in sudden, breathless need. I don't need to push her down onto the sofa tonight, because Gemma changes our position herself, and I feel her kick off her shoes before she lies down on her back without breaking our kiss, pulling me with her. There's something wild and unrestrained about this… and I'm as turned on as I've ever been in my life. My mouth devours hers, and my hands wander over her body, feeling her through the material of her dress. I wish to God I hadn't promised to wait. Somehow – although God knows how – I have to stick to my promise, and even though she's rocking her hips into mine, and I want her so much I ache, I hold back.

"Touch me," she whispers, on a stuttered breath, finally breaking our kiss and I lean up and gaze down into her eyes.

"Sorry?" I can't have heard that right, can I?

"T—Touch me."

I place my right hand on her cheek as I kiss her again, shifting my body slightly to one side and moving my hand downwards, caressing her neck and then her bare shoulder. She sighs into my mouth, and I continue to explore, feeling her rounded breast through the soft fabric of her dress, aware even then of her nipple hardening against my palm. She moans now, and I let my hand wander lower, across her flat stomach, further down to the hem of her dress, which I raise, feeling the tops of her stockings, and then the delicate, bare flesh of her thighs. Her legs tremble as I move higher, my fingers coming into contact with her fine lace knickers, which I carefully push aside, discovering her soft, smooth folds, which part easily to my touch. A guttural groan escapes her lips and as I stroke her, finding that sweet spot, she bucks her hips up into me, our kiss becoming ferocious in its intensity. She tries to part her legs, but the confines of the sofa are proving to be a barrier, and sensing her frustration, I stop, and I raise her skirt up higher, lifting her leg up on to the back of the couch, so she's fully exposed. Then I break our kiss and look down at her slightly glazed eyes, gazing back at me.

"Don't stop," she murmurs, and I smile.

"I won't." Just looking at her, I know she's still not ready for everything. Not yet. And I'm okay with that, because she wants this... and so do I.

I go back to where I was, my fingers easily finding their destiny, as I keep my eyes locked on hers, watching her breathing become more and more ragged until she's grinding her hips in a circular motion, reaching down and holding my wrist, keeping me where she wants me and looking up into my eyes the whole time.

"Don't stop," she breathes, barely in control... and then, without warning, her whole body starts to spasm and shake. She rocks her head back and screams out my name in a long, low cry as pleasure courses through her. It goes on and on, claiming her, until eventually she calms, although even then she continues to twitch and convulse in my arms.

As her breathing slowly returns to normal, I bring my hand up, and without losing eye contact with her, I put my fingers in my mouth, licking them, tasting her sweetness. She watches, fascinated, mesmerised, her lips parted, and after a few minutes, I move my hand away and lean in to kiss her. She pulls back, shaking her head, and I stop.

"What's wrong?" I ask.

"You… you're going to taste of me," she says, blushing.

"I know. And you taste so very sweet." I lean down again and this time she lets me kiss her, tentatively to start with, although within seconds, the fire is back, and our tongues collide in a breathless frenzy.

"This feels really unfair," she whispers, when I eventually pull back and I frown down at her.

"Why?"

"Because there doesn't seem to be anything in it for you." I smile now, but she shakes her head. "I might not have done any of this before, but even I know you're meant to get something out of it."

I brush a stray hair from her face and kiss her lips, just softly. "I am getting something out of it. Watching you come just now is the most erotic thing I've ever seen in my life."

Her brow furrows, and she pushes her head back into the cushion. "You're making that up," she says.

"No, I'm not." I lean up on one elbow, looking down at her. "Don't you get it yet?"

"Get what?"

"That I'm about as open as they come, Gemma. It's impossible for me to lie to you. I tried it when we first met, because I didn't want to risk spoiling things between us by telling you about my job. But when it came down to it, I couldn't lie. I still can't." I lean in and kiss her again, even though she's still looking a little doubtful, so I decide to take my courage in my hands and hope I don't regret it. "I guess in the spirit of being completely honest, I'd better own up…"

"To what?" She tilts her head to one side, looking worried.

"To the fact that I'm falling in love with you."

I can't tell her that I think I've already fallen, in case she runs a mile, or tells me I'm moving too fast. And I'm too scared of her rejection to give her a chance to respond. I'm scared she'll tell me she doesn't feel the same way. So instead of letting her have her say, I kiss her. In doing so, I capture the gasp that escapes her lips. Whether a gasp is good or bad, I don't know, but her kiss is like heaven, full of fire and promise, and that wild abandonment I saw in her just now when she came apart right before my eyes… and I try my hardest to reassure myself that a reaction that feels as good as this can't possibly be bad.

Chapter Eleven

Gemma

Tomorrow, it will be two weeks since Tom came into Imelda's shop to buy that bouquet for his mother, and asked me if I'd like to go out with him. I can't believe that just such a short time ago, I didn't even know him, and yet now, he fills my life so completely. When I'm not with him, I think about him all the time, to the point of distraction… to the point of breathlessness. And when I am with him, he fills me with pleasure beyond words.

That night at the hotel, and afterwards… it changed everything between us. I honestly thought I'd lost him then, especially when he said we were going home. We'd barely touched our drinks, and I thought that was it. It didn't matter about all the lovely things he'd said to me the previous night, when he'd said he'd wait for me. It was over. But it seems he thought the same thing too. It seems he was feeling just as insecure as I was, because the moment he got us inside his house, he begged me to tell him we were okay. That shocked me. I'd never seen him like that before… so nervous and uncertain. And while I was still confused about what had happened that evening, and a little cross about his insensitivity, I wasn't about to let go of what we had. I just needed him to understand, and once I explained how I felt, he did... and his apology was sweetness itself.

I craved him in that moment, and it seemed natural to ask him to touch me. I wanted to feel the connection between us. More than a kiss... more than his words. I'd called myself innocent and ignorant... and I was. I still am. When I felt his fingers on me, my body came alive, as though every nerve ending, from the top of my head, to the tips of my toes, was on fire. I remember begging him not to stop. I think I even said it twice, although I can't be sure. He did as I asked. He kept going, until a wave of overwhelming, tingling, quivering pleasure washed over me. It wasn't just one wave, though. It went on... and on. I screamed his name, unable to say anything more coherent than that one syllable, and I clung onto him, until eventually the waves subsided, the tide turned, and I gazed up into his eyes. I know I should probably feel embarrassed about how wild I became in those moments, but I'm not. I'm not embarrassed or inhibited about anything we do together, because Tom makes it all seem like the most natural thing in the world... and so it is.

It felt like the most natural thing in the world when he told me that night that he was falling in love with me, and I longed to tell him the truth about my feelings too... that I'm not falling in love with him, but that I'm all the way there. He didn't give me the chance, though. He kissed me again instead. I could still taste myself on his lips, and I got carried away in another of those moments that we seem to share more and more of these days. Our kiss went on for ages. It veered from deeply intense and passionate, to soft and playful, with barely a break, until he noticed the time... which was almost ten-thirty.

"I should probably get you home," he said, and with a last, slow kiss, he got to his feet and helped me to stand up too, before he straightened my dress, which was very creased and dishevelled. "Oh dear," he murmured, then added, "Sorry." His smile told me he wasn't sorry at all, but neither was I, and he leant down and kissed me again, before I found my shoes, clinging on to him while I put them on. "You're not very steady on those, are you?"

"No, but they're the only shoes I've got that go with my dress."

"I'd like to suggest relieving you of the dress, so the shoes won't be necessary anymore, but…" He let his voice fade, a wicked smile spreading across his lips. I had to smile back, even as I was shaking my head and trying my best to look disapproving. Of course, he made that even harder still by pulling me into his arms and kissing me ferociously.

Our walk home was slow, made necessary by my heels, and because I don't think either of us was in a rush to be parted from the other. When we got to my house, though, my intention of declaring my feelings for him, which I'd been dying to reveal ever since he'd asked permission to kiss me, vanished in a fit of nerves. I noticed that the living room light was still on, and the fear that my father might look out and see us became absolutely overwhelming. All thoughts of love disappeared in my panic, and I kissed Tom briefly before making my excuses to get inside.

I didn't think he'd noticed my haste, but by the next afternoon I was starting to wonder. We hadn't made any arrangements to meet up, and he hadn't been into the shop at all during the day. Had I offended him? Had he noticed something was wrong? Or, worse still, had my dad let something slip?

It was just after three o'clock when I heard the beeping of my phone in my handbag, and as there was no-one in the shop, I took advantage of my solitude and pulled it out, smiling as I looked down at the screen. The number wasn't familiar, but the message made it very clear who was sending it.

— Hello, beautiful. Sorry I haven't had time to come and see you. I won't bore you with how busy I've been, but I just realised we forgot to make any arrangements for tonight. Hopefully you're not busy, because I'm not sure I can survive an evening without you. If you're free, I thought I might drive you into Padstow for dinner. Let me know? Please. Tom xx

My smile broadened, and I felt like I was floating as I quickly added his number into my contacts list before typing out my reply.

— Hello. You don't have to apologise. I'm not busy tonight and I'd love to see you. Dinner in Padstow sounds lovely, although I'm not sure I wouldn't rather spend the evening at your house. Either way, as long as I'm with you, I'm happy. Gemma xx

I pressed 'send', still smiling to myself, and hoping my words might help him understand at least some of how I was feeling about him.

His reply was almost instantaneous, and I held my breath as I read…

— I'm so relieved. I'd love to spend the evening at my house too, but I'm supposed to be waiting for you… and I'm not sure I could survive a whole evening. We can go back there after dinner though, for a little while, if you like? Because there's nothing I want more than to make you happy. T xxx

I giggled, putting a hand over my mouth, and felt a warm glow fill my body. He wanted to make me happy. He'd said so in writing. I had the evidence in front of me, and as much as I wanted to just keep reading it, I had to reply…

— I'm sorry to make you wait. Hopefully, it'll be worth it. Dinner in Padstow and a 'little while' at your

place sounds perfect. And you already make me happy... all the time. G xxx

I wondered if I should have made my comment about the wait being worth it, but I'd already pressed 'send', so it was too late to do anything about it, and when his answer came back, I knew I'd been worrying over nothing.

— Don't worry. I know it'll be worth the wait. Shall I pick you up from your place? T xxx

Panic set in, yet again, and I wondered how to get out of his suggestion when I remembered the day's delivery.

— It's probably best if you pick me up from work. We've got a delivery coming in, and I might be a bit late. As long as we're not going anywhere too smart, I won't need to change. Is that okay? G xxx

I felt guilty for not telling him the truth, although I wasn't actually lying. There was a delivery due in, and it wasn't coming until quite late in the day. Okay, so that wasn't the real reason for me asking him to collect me from work, but I could hardly tell him the truth, could I?

My phone beeped, and I looked down at it, feeling a little less cheerful than I had a few minutes earlier.

— That's fine. I thought we'd go to a pub over there. Not being a local boy, I've found one on the Internet. It's just a quaint little place on the harbour, so you won't need to change. I will... but only because kissing you when I'm wearing my uniform seems to be a little difficult. And I want to kiss you. T xxx

— I want you to kiss me too. G xxx

I smiled again, thinking about his lips on mine as my phone beeped.

— I will. Later. I'll pick you up outside the shop at six-thirty. T xxx

The bell above the door rang out, breaking the spell of my dream, and because I didn't really need to reply to Tom, I put my phone away and got on with doing my job.

That night was, if anything, more spectacular than its predecessor. I think that was because it wasn't borne out of so much difficulty, and when we got back from the harbour-side pub in Padstow, we enjoyed an untamed, passionate hour or so discovering new realms of ecstasy.

Since then, we've spent every spare moment together, and he's taken me to even greater heights every time. I still haven't found quite the right moment to tell him I'm in love with him, but I will… soon.

For now, though, it's Friday night and Tom's invited me to his place for dinner. I'm excited. I want to see him. But I also can't help wondering whether he's changed his mind about waiting. His text message said he couldn't survive a whole evening of it, so does his I invitation mean he's grown accustomed to the situation and can handle it better? Or does it mean he doesn't want to wait anymore? I wish I knew. I wish I understood men and romance better. Then I might know what to expect. Tom said I should talk to him, but I don't always know how. I mean, how do I tell him that I'm not sure waiting is all it's cracked up to be? Yes, we have fun, and I love everything he does to me… or with me… whichever it is, but I keep asking myself what he'd think if I somehow found a way to ask for more.

After my shower, I put on some underwear and a simple navy blue wrap dress, with a pale grey cardigan over the top, and a pair of flat shoes, smiling as I remember Tom's comments about my heels and how he wanted to relieve me of my dress. I tingle at the thought and check myself in the mirror. My clothes are quite casual, but I look okay, and it's not like we're going anywhere, so I turn off the light and run downstairs, grabbing my bag.

"Considering you're not very serious about this young man of yours, you're seeing an awful lot of him." I stop at the sound of Dad's voice and turn to face him. "It's been a fortnight now, hasn't it?" he says.

"Nearly."

"And you're sure it's not serious?"

"I'm positive, Dad. I'm not even sure he's my type."

"Well, I suppose there's only one way to find out what your type is." He rolls his eyes with an indulgent smile. "But make sure you're being careful."

"I will. We're just having fun, that's all."

I go over and kiss him on the cheek, and he smiles down at me. I smile back, even though I feel guilty for lying to him, especially when I remember the scolding Imelda gave me earlier in the week. I'd only popped upstairs to see if she felt like a drink, and she finally cornered me into a confession that I haven't told Tom the truth about who I am yet.

"His relationship with Dad is really difficult," I explained.

"So you still haven't told your father the truth either?"

"No."

She sighed then, her disapproval obvious. "I can understand your predicament, Gemma, but as I said before, honesty is really important in relationships."

"I know."

How could I not know, when Tom's always made such a big deal about his own truthfulness?

"Why don't you tell your dad first?" Imelda said. "I'm sure, once he knows the situation, he'll behave differently towards Tom."

"Yes. He'll probably transfer him," I murmured, shaking my head. "This is all Dad's fault, really. If he wasn't making Tom's life such a misery at work, I'd be able to come clean."

She stared at me for quite a while then, before she said, "I'm not sure there's any logic to your argument, but even if there is, you're missing the point."

"I am?"

"Yes. Can't you see? It doesn't matter whose fault it is. You need to stop this charade and tell the truth... to both of them. Otherwise, when they find out, they're going to be very hurt and upset with you. Do you really want to do that to them?"

"No. Of course not."

I couldn't think what else to say to her, so I made us a fresh pot of tea and went back to work.

"Will you be late home?" Dad asks, breaking into my thoughts, and I notice he didn't give me his usual instruction about getting home at a reasonable hour, but asked the question instead.

"No, I don't think so. I've got work tomorrow."

"Okay. Well... I might go down to the pub later on, so if I'm not here when you get back, that's where I'll be."

"Oh... okay. Have a nice time."

He rarely goes out these days, but as I leave the house and close the door behind me, I wonder whether my absence from home is helping him. Perhaps spending more time alone is making him realise that he should be enjoying life a bit more, too.

I hope so, because it's high time he got back out there.

It's quite a mild evening, which is why I'm not wearing a jacket, and I make short work of the walk to Tom's house, climbing up the steps to his door and knocking on it, at exactly seven o'clock, as we arranged.

He opens the door within moments and gazes down at me. He looks utterly divine, in dark blue jeans and a white t-shirt that clings to his body, like it's moulded to him, which is exactly what I'd like to be at the moment.

"Hello," he says, taking my hand and pulling me inside and straight into his arms, as though he's been able to read my thoughts, his lips greeting mine as he kisses me deeply. I can feel my body responding to him, tingling and heating as his hands roam up and down my back, occasionally lingering on my behind, until he eventually breaks the kiss, leaving me breathless and wanting more.

"I like your way of saying hello," I say, gazing up into his eyes.

"I know. So do I. But the thing is… I've got a problem."

I frown. "You have?"

"Yes." He smiles. "As much as I'd like to keep saying hello to you all evening, I need your help with preparing the dinner."

He's teasing me. He's got that tone to his voice, and that tingling heat spirals up into shuddering, almost desperate need.

"Can't you cope by yourself then?" I struggle for some control of my body, and tease him back… which, with hindsight, seems like a silly idea when things are already so fiery between us.

"Yes." He surprises me with his reply. "But the problem isn't anything to do with the dinner itself."

"It's not?"

"No. It's that I've missed you so much since yesterday, I'm not sure I can wait until after dinner to touch you. So, I figured that, being as my kitchen is quite small, if the two of us were preparing food together, in such close confines, we'd almost certainly end up touching."

I can't help giggling and he pulls me closer to him, rocking me from one side to the other and grinning down at me.

"So? What do you say?" he asks.

"I think it sounds like you need rescuing." I'm surprised by the depth of my voice, and his eyes widen, right before he leans down and kisses me again. This time, I'm the one who breaks the kiss, because I'm in danger of asking for more, and as he stands up straight again, I catch my breath and murmur, "Shall we go and cook something?"

He nods and takes my hand, by-passing the living area on the way to the kitchen. Tom has a lot of books, neatly arranged on shelves in the alcoves, but my eyes are drawn to his dark grey sofa, where we've spent so much of our time lately.

"To be honest, there's nothing to cook," he says, turning to face me and walking backwards.

"There isn't?"

"No. I thought we'd have a salad tonight… a goat's cheese, walnut and pear salad."

"That sounds really nice."

"It does, doesn't it? It's not a recipe I've made before, but I decided that something simple and light might be a wise choice."

I want to ask him if there's a reason for that, but I'm too shy… and too uncertain about what I'll do when he answers.

Instead, I release my hand from his and, as he continues into the kitchen, I take off my cardigan, hanging it over the back of one of the dining chairs, and leaving my handbag on the table, before I join him.

"Where do you want me?" I say, and his eyes sparkle as he shakes his head.

"Is that a serious question?"

"Yes."

He sucks in a breath, and then reaches over to the knife block beside him, pulling out a large chef's knife, which he turns around and passes to me, handle first.

I take it and he stares at me for a moment, before opening the fridge and removing several ingredients, including two packs of goat's cheese, a bag of pears, two lemons and several types of lettuce. Putting them down on the work surface, he grabs a chopping board from beside the microwave and puts it next to all the ingredients, placing the pears on top.

"Can you cut those into slices?" he asks, turning to me. "And then put them in a bowl, with some water and lemon juice, to stop them from turning brown?"

"Of course."

I step forward as he moves to one side, and putting the knife down for a moment, I open the bag of pears, just as he comes and stands right behind me, his body almost touching mine.

"You're going to need a bowl," he says.

"Yes." He reaches up and opens the cabinet above our heads, taking down a mixing bowl and putting it next to the chopping board.

"That should be big enough."

I nod my head, and try to focus on the pear I'm holding in my left hand, even though Tom hasn't moved away. He's closed the cupboard door, but he's still standing right behind me, his presence making it hard to concentrate on anything. It's a situation he makes worse when he puts his hands on my waist, pulling me back onto him, so I can feel his arousal, hard against me. I sigh, because I can't help myself, and he leans in again.

"In answer to your question…" he says, his voice a soft, low hum.

"Wh… which question?" I stutter.

"Your question about where I want you," he says, grinding his hips into me, until my head rocks back and I moan involuntarily. "The answer is that I want you everywhere…" He kisses my exposed neck. "I want you on every surface in this house. Repeatedly."

"Oh, yes, please." I blurt out the words, and he spins me around, staring down into my eyes.

"Do you like the sound of that?" he says.

"Yes."

"In theory, or in practice?"

"Both."

He doesn't blink, or even seem to breathe, but takes the pear I'm still holding and puts it down. Then, with my hand in his, he leads me to the bottom of the stairs. He puts his foot on the first tread, but before he starts to climb, he turns and looks into my eyes.

"You're sure you want to do this?" he says.

I nod my head. "I'm sure."

We climb together, him one step ahead of me, until we get to the top, where there's no hallway and evidently no door, and as Tom flicks on the lights, I see that we've simply walked directly into his bedroom. There's a huge wooden framed bed against the wall, with a blue and grey tartan throw over the end, and bedside tables on either side. The curtains, which Tom goes and closes, are a similar grey to the one in the throw, although they're plain, and to our right is a chest of drawers and a wardrobe, in the same wood as the bed. In the opposite corner, I notice a door that's open, and although it's dark in there, I can make out tiles on the wall, so I presume that must be a bathroom.

I'm holding back slightly, staying at the top of the stairs. That's not because I feel nervous. I don't. I want Tom so much I can scarcely breathe. My hesitation is because I know that what we're about to do is an enormous step, and that once it's done, there's no going back.

Tom turns and looks at me and then retraces his steps, coming to stand directly in front of me. He reaches out to cup my face with his hands, his eyes a more startling shade of blue than ever, boring into mine.

"Just because we've come up here, we don't have to do anything you're not ready for. You can change your mind, Gemma. It's allowed."

He smiles and I smile back. "I know. But I don't want to change my mind. I want you."

He sighs, although a throaty sound escapes his lips at the same time, and he leans down and kisses me. There's something almost savage in his touch, and in the way his breathing hikes up a notch, as he devours my lips… and yet, he's gentle too, caressing my cheeks with his fingertips and turning us around to walk me slowly backwards towards his bed.

When my legs hit it, he pulls back, staring into my eyes, his own on fire as he tugs on the tie at the front of my dress, which undoes easily so he can unwrap me, pulling the flimsy garment from my shoulders and letting it fall to the floor at my feet. He doesn't look away for a second, but holds my gaze as he reaches behind me and unclasps my bra, releasing my breasts, the lacy covering falling from his hand when he finally lets his eyes drop.

"Oh… God…" he whispers, and his fingers graze over my exposed skin, before he bends his head, licking, sucking and biting on my pebbled nipples until I can hardly breathe. The thrill of anticipation is almost overwhelming and I'm about to reach around behind his head to pull him closer to me, when he suddenly releases me and drops to his knees. I hadn't expected that, but he looks up at me, his thumbs in the top of my knickers, as he pulls them down with slow precision, letting out a long sigh when I'm finally exposed to him.

"I had no idea," he says, his voice sounding a little strangled.

"About what?" I suddenly feel uncertain. This is the first time I've been completely naked in front of him. I feel vulnerable… embarrassed… and I pull my arms across my chest in a vain attempt to cover myself. Tom stands, looking down at me, and taking my hands, he pulls my arms back down to my sides again.

"I had no idea you'd be this beautiful," he says, still holding my hands. "I know this is all very new to you, but please don't hide yourself from me." He kisses my lips, just briefly. "Never hide yourself from me." He repeats his words, this time with a pleading note to his voice, and I nod my head.

"I won't."

"You should be seen… all the time," he says, releasing my hands and pushing my hair out of the way so he can plant soft kisses on my neck and shoulders. "By me… and only me."

It's as though all my senses are on fire. I want to feel everything there is to feel, and taste everything there is to taste… and see everything there is to see.

As though he's read my mind, he steps back and, with slow and deliberate movements, he starts to undress.

Chapter Twelve

Tom

I pull my t-shirt over my head, taking my time. I want to cherish every second of this, because I can't believe it's actually happening.

Waiting for Gemma has felt like perfect torture over the last few days... being with her and yet not completely 'being' with her; loving her and yet being too scared to tell her. I was worried she might think I was moving things too fast... pressuring her to do more than she's ready for. I've loved every second of what we've been doing, and pleasuring her has been magical... and I invited her here tonight for more of the same. It was always going to be hard to resist her, but I was prepared to do it. I *wanted* to do it... and I certainly didn't expect her to tell me that the wait was over. And to mean it.

That much was obvious from her reactions and from the look in her eyes. Even when I offered her the chance to change her mind, she didn't take it. She wants this as much as I do. I can tell just from the way she lets her eyes roam over my chest, and I smile at her attention and then unfasten my jeans, pulling them down, along with my trunks, before I stand up, naked, before her.

She tilts her head and steps a little closer, holding out her hand, tentatively, and running her fingertips down my chest and over my abs.

"I always knew you had muscles," she says, "but I never knew…" Her eyes widen and her tongue grazes lazily across her lips as she lets her eyes follow the path of her fingers, the fire and hunger building within them, as her hand slides lower, and then suddenly stops, her head shooting up to mine. Her expression has changed completely now, her need replaced with what looks to me like fear.

"What's wrong?" I ask her, stepping closer, but she moves away and looks down again.

"That… that can't possibly be right."

"What can't?"

"That." She points to my erection.

"What do you mean, it can't be right?" It looks perfectly okay to me… just the same as it always has.

"It can't possibly fit… in me," she says, shaking her head, and as realisation dawns, I reach out and grab her hand, pulling her back to me.

"It'll fit." I try to sound as reassuring as I can, reminding myself that, even though she wants this, it's all new to her… she doesn't really understand what 'this' is yet.

"It will?" She blinks a few times, although at least that fear has gone from her face now.

"Yes."

"Will it hurt?" she says, in a quiet whisper.

"Probably." I have to be honest with her, even though she tenses in my arms, and I hold her a little tighter. "I'll do everything I can not to hurt you though," I say and she relaxes just a little. "You must be full of questions, but try to forget about them and just answer me one thing…"

She looks up and nods her head. "What's that?"

"Do you trust me?"

"Of course I trust you," she says, without hesitation, and I smile and then lower her down to the mattress, her perfect body laid before me. She doesn't seem so shy now and gazes up at me, waiting. I wonder if she's expecting me to touch her, like she implored me to that night… and like I've done every night since, discovering new ways to pleasure her with my fingers, until she's either begging me for more, or to stop… or sometimes both. The thing is, tonight is different, and I want her experiences and her memories to be special… unique.

With my hands on her knees, I push her legs apart, holding them in place for a moment, before I kneel between them and lean in, running my tongue down her swollen folds. She shudders and gasps.

"Did you just lick me?" she says and I look up to find she's raised her head from the mattress and is staring at me.

"Yes. Did you like it?"

"Yes." She returns my smile with one of her own, and I bend my head forward and lick her again. "Oh, God…" Her voice is rasping. "That feels so good."

I don't reply this time, because the need to taste her honeyed sweetness is overwhelming, and instead I flick my tongue across her, delving and searching, sucking and biting, until she's arching her back off the bed and writhing in unbound pleasure.

"Please don't stop… please don't stop." She grinds out the words, her hips rising in desperation for more, as she parts her legs still further and brings her hand down on the back of my head. "Please, Tom…" she squeals and her body shudders and shakes, and then she stiffens and lets out a scream, before she thrashes wildly through waves of intense pleasure.

She's gasping for breath, but before she has the chance to calm, I reach over and grab a condom from the bedside table, pulling it over myself, even as I crawl up her still shuddering body, finding her entrance with ease. This might be Gemma's first time, but in a way, it's mine, too. It's my first time with a virgin, and I'm led to believe there are two ways of doing this: slow, or fast. Slow sounds ideal for me, but tortuous for Gemma... prolonging the agony. Fast seems like the better option... like ripping off a sticking plaster, getting the pain over and done with as quickly as possible, before moving on to the pleasure.

She tenses, uncertainty fuelling her fears, and I lean down onto my elbows, cupping her face and kissing her gently, letting her taste herself.

"Relax," I say on the softest of whispers, and she blinks, gazing up at me as I flex my hips, and in one swift move, push all the way into her. She yelps at the penetration, her cry piercing my heart, and I still, deep inside. I try to ignore her tight grip and the urge to move... to take her. Instead I wait, and wait... until she breathes out a long sigh and brings her hands up around my neck.

"It fits," she says, sounding almost drunk.

"We fit together perfectly." I kiss her again and then raise myself up, moving slowly and tenderly, taking my time. She grinds her hips, matching my rhythm and we stare at each other, our bodies joined, to the exclusion of everything else. Nothing exists but the sensation of being buried inside her. I can't see anything except her body beneath mine, her eyes glistening with heat, her face flushed with pleasure. I can't hear anything except her soft sighs, mingling with my own. They intensify yet more when she lifts her legs, wrapping them around me, binding us together in what can only be an instinctive move on her part. It's nearly enough to be my undoing, though, and because I want to make this as special for her as it is for me, I change the angle slightly, loving her just a little harder.

That's all it takes for her to tremble, to shake and then to cry out at the top of her voice, "I love you," just as I let out a loud howl and lose myself deep inside her.

I think it's minutes later, although it could be hours, my nerves are sparking still and I'm trying very hard to regain control, not only of my body but also of my mind. I can't wait, though. I have to know... I have to ask her.

"Did you just say you love me?" I breathe hard, gazing down at her.

She's flushed, breathless, twitching, the pleasure still fizzing through her body, but she looks me in the eye and nods her head.

"Yes."

"Thank God for that." I let out a long breath.

"What does that mean?" She frowns.

I lower myself down again, my lips an inch or two from hers. "It means I think I've been in love with you since I first walked into the flower shop. I just didn't know how to tell you. So I said I was falling for you instead, in case I scared you off."

She stares up at me, wide-eyed. "You've been in love with me all this time?"

"Yes. We're right together," I say, and she nods her head.

"I know."

"And I'm so in love with you."

She moves her hands, placing them around my neck, and pulls herself up, kissing me.

I want her again... already. And while I know I need to change the condom, I flex my hips into her anyway and she moans softly. "Never stop," she whispers, staring into my eyes.

"Loving you? Or making love to you?"

"Both," she murmurs, lowering herself back onto the mattress and gazing up at me.

"I won't. I promise."

Her smile is like sunshine after a storm, and it fills my heart with light and hope. "I love you so much, Tom," she says, and I lean down and kiss her... hard.

I'm not sure how long we've been lying here, cradled in each other's arms. I just know it feels right. It feels perfect, actually, because Gemma loves me, and I love her, and while I may never have made that kind of commitment to anyone before, saying that to Gemma felt wondrous and magical. And because of that, I don't want to move from here. Ever.

I'm about to explain all of that to Gemma when her stomach grumbles and she looks up at me, smiling, before we both start to laugh.

"I'm sorry," she says. "That was very rude."

"No, it wasn't. If anything, I'm the rude one. I invited you here for dinner, and I haven't fed you."

"Maybe not. But I'm not complaining."

I lean down and kiss her. "Why don't I go and quickly throw together that salad we started making earlier, and I'll bring it back up here? We can eat in bed."

"You can just throw it together, can you?" she says, teasing.

"Yes."

"And you don't want me to come down and help you?"

I smile and shake my head. "If you come downstairs with me, I guarantee we won't get dinner at all tonight."

"Why not?" I can't tell whether she's teasing now, or asking a genuine question, borne out of innocence, and I brush my lips against hers, eliciting a soft moan.

"Because, as I told you earlier, I want you on every surface in my house, so if I'm going to concentrate on dinner, rather than working out whether to start with the dining table, or the living room floor, or that bare patch of wall by the front door, where I haven't put any pictures up, I think it's best if you stay here."

She hesitates for a moment, breathing hard, and then says, "D—Did you just say something about a wall?"

I smile. "Yes. But before I get too carried away with the idea of taking you up against it, I'm going downstairs… alone."

I push myself up, planting a quick kiss on her lips, and then kneel, crawling off of the bed. Turning to look at her, it's hard not to groan out loud at the sight of her naked body sprawled across the mattress. But I manage to tear my eyes away and head for the top of the stairs.

"Aren't you going to put any clothes on?" Gemma asks, and I look back to see she's sitting up now, gazing at me.

"No. I don't plan on being away from you for long enough to bother."

She giggles and flops down onto the bed again, and although I'm tempted to go back to her, I feel like I should feed her. So I trot down the stairs and into the kitchen, where I gather up the salad ingredients and set about quickly chopping them into the bowl I'd already put out earlier, before serving it up into smaller dishes.

I can't stop smiling… but I suppose that's not surprising, really.

I'm in love.

By the time I go back upstairs, Gemma seems to have re-made the bed. Or at least, she's straightened out the bedding, and is sitting up, leaning back against the pillows. I go over and put the tray I'm carrying on the end of the mattress, before giving her a quick kiss, and handing her a bowl of salad. I leave her glass of wine on the bedside table and carry my own around to the other side of the bed, getting in beside her.

"Do you often have dinner in bed?" she asks, spearing a slice of pear with her fork.

"No. It's a first for me."

She twists slightly, so she's facing me, lowering her bowl a little. "Have there been any other firsts tonight?"

"For me?" I ask, because I'm fairly sure she's fishing, but I need to be certain.

"Yes. I think we both know that everything we've done tonight has been a first for me."

I smile and lean over, kissing her. "I know… and you have no idea how special that is."

Two dots of pink appear on her cheeks. "Don't change the subject."

"I wasn't." Putting my bowl down, I capture her face between my hands. "I've never made love to someone I'm actually in love with," I say, gazing into her eyes. "Nor have I ever made any kind of verbal or physical commitment to anyone before. I've never said 'I love you' to anyone in my life, either… not until tonight. And I do love you… so much."

She places her bowl next to mine, between us, and rests her hand on my chest. "I love you too," she says, and I bend my head to kiss her. "Have you really never said 'I love you' to anyone else?" she asks as she sits back up a little.

"No."

"And yet you've… you've slept with six other women."

I notice she remembered the number from the other night, when everything nearly went so wrong between us… even though it ended up so right in the end.

"Yes. You don't have to love someone to sleep with them."

"Don't you?" She looks genuinely surprised by that and I can't help smiling.

"No. I can tell you – after tonight – that being in love makes it a hell of a lot better, but it's not a requirement."

"I can't imagine doing what we did tonight and not being in love with you," she says, as though she's trying to make sense of things in her own head.

"I know… and that's one of the many, many, many reasons I love you so much." She tilts her head to one side and, by way of explanation, I add, "Because you've given me all of yourself, and held nothing back."

She sighs and leans in to me as I hand her back her bowl of salad, before picking up my own, and she nestles against me as we eat in a very contented silence.

Once we've both finished, I take Gemma's bowl and put it alongside mine on the bedside table and then I move us down the bed a little and explore every inch of her with my tongue, before proving to myself yet again how different it is to make love to someone, when you're so deeply in love with them.

"What time is it?" Gemma asks.

She's cradled in my arms, still a little breathless, her eyes sparkling and her lips swollen from my kisses.

"I don't know." I roll over and check the clock.

"It's just gone eleven."

"Oh my God…" She sits up, almost elbowing me in the face, and throws back the duvet, which is twisted around our bodies.

"Where are you going?" I lean up on my elbows, watching her as she clambers away from me.

"I have to go home."

"You do?" I can't disguise the disappointment in my voice, and she turns back to me, kneeling on the edge of the bed and biting her bottom lip. "Can't you stay the night?"

She shakes her head. "I've got an early start tomorrow… and my dad is expecting me."

That's not a remark I've heard for a very long time and I'm suddenly reminded of how young Gemma is, although I refuse to be bothered by the age gap between us. It's just something we're going to have to accommodate.

"I don't want you to go," I say, kneeling up myself now and reaching out for her, pulling her back down onto the bed and pinning her beneath my body. She gasps, but doesn't object. "I'd rather you could stay here with me, but I don't want to make things difficult for you, so I'll get dressed too and walk you home."

"You really don't have to. It's only around the corner and…"

"Are you serious?" I interrupt her. "I wouldn't have let you walk home by yourself even if we hadn't just spent the last few hours making love… but as it is…" I don't need to finish my sentence. She knows what I mean and she smiles her agreement before we both get up, gathering our clothes from the floor and pulling them back on. It's only when I'm completely dressed and I turn to look at Gemma that I laugh, because I can't help myself.

"I think you'd better go into the bathroom and see what you can do with your hair."

"Why?" She looks at me quizzically.

"Go and see for yourself."

She shakes her head and disappears into the bathroom, turning on the light and then letting out a yelp.

"What happened to me?" she cries and I go in, standing behind her as she looks in the mirror above the washbasin.

"Three and a half hours of sex," I say, smiling, and she looks up at my reflection.

"Your hair looks all right."

"I know, but mine's a lot shorter than yours."

I do my best to run my fingers through her hair, although it's fairly tangled, and she giggles at my half-hearted attempts.

"I've got a brush in my bag, downstairs," she says, turning to face me, and I put my hands on her hips, my feet either side of her as I step closer, our bodies fused, my arousal pressed against her hip.

"You're sure you have to go?" I ask, bending to kiss her. "If you stayed, you wouldn't have to do anything with your hair… and I can't think of anything I want to do more than wake up beside you in the morning."

She shudders in my arms, breathing hard already.

"I wish I could, but…"

"I know." I save her the trouble of explaining and kiss her instead. Then I lead her down the stairs, where she delves inside her handbag for a small hairbrush.

"Does that look better?" she asks, turning to me, after five minutes' de-tangling.

"I'm not sure. I think I liked you better all dishevelled."

She smiles, shaking her head, and puts her brush away, while I hold out her cardigan, helping her to put it back on.

"Are you going to be warm enough?" I ask, as we make our way over to the front door and I grab a jacket.

"I've got you," she says, looking up at me, her hands resting on my chest. "So yes…"

"You'll always have me." I wonder if that's too much, too soon… but then she leans up and kisses me, and I know it's nothing of the sort. It's the truth… and we both know it.

I wake this morning, with a smile on my face, and turn to my left, wishing I could see Gemma lying there beside me. I can't, but I don't think it'll be long before that changes. She seemed quite keen to stay last night, but all the while she's living at home with her dad, I suppose it's not that simple for her. She'd have to explain, for one thing, and that's never going to be easy.

I turn over, wondering whether I should suggest that she introduce me to her dad sometime soon. If he met me, and he knew how serious I am about her, he might be more amenable to her staying the night from time to time… or more often than that, perhaps.

I throw back the covers and get up, because even though it's Saturday, I'm still on duty, and I head into the shower, wishing more than ever that Gemma could be here and that we could have showered together. As I stand beneath the water, letting it wash over me, I wonder whether I might suggest that she comes with me next weekend to see my mother. I don't have any plans to visit Mum, but I'm sure she won't mind, and it might be a way to introduce the concept of 'meeting the parents', without putting too much pressure on Gemma to be the first one to do it.

Coming out of the shower, I check the time, and with a few minutes to spare, I grab my phone from the bedside table and type out a message, smiling as I do so.

— ***Hello, beautiful. I hope you slept well. I missed your kisses when I woke up this morning, but I'll call by later on and collect them, if that's okay with you. Love you. T xxx***

I get dressed, but stop, with my sock halfway on my foot, as my phone beeps and I pick it up, reading…

— ***Good morning. Can't wait to see you later. I slept very well, thank you… better than ever. Love you too. G xxx***

I smile to myself, typing back:

— ***That'll be the sex ;) xxx***

I don't expect Gemma to reply, but she does.

— ***No, it was dreaming of you. xxx***

I could reply that I dreamt of her too. It wouldn't be a lie. Still, I can tell her all about that later. Instead, I just send her a long line of kisses and continue getting dressed before I go downstairs. I pour myself a bowl of cereal and make a cup of coffee, hoping that my day won't be too busy and that I'll be able to fulfil my promise of calling into the florist's later on. I really need to kiss her… more than anything.

It feels like it must be my lucky day, because my morning so far has been really quiet, and by ten-thirty, I'm out on patrol and passing the baker's on the way to Gemma's shop. Rachel gives me a wave, and I wave back, not breaking my stride, because nothing's going to hold me up today.

I let myself into the shop, the bell ringing out above my head, and I sigh out my disappointment when I see that there's someone already here… and I'm going to have to wait. Fortunately, the woman concerned seems to be completing her purchases, taking down a glass vase from the display on the dresser and adding it to the bouquet that Gemma is just wrapping for her. Gemma looks up at me and smiles, but focuses on what she's doing. She turns, pulling out some tissue paper from beneath the counter and uses it to wrap the vase, before ringing everything through the till and offering the woman the chip and pin machine.

Only when she turns around does the woman notice my presence, and she blushes and nods her head before leaving the shop. People react in lots of different ways to seeing police officers. Blushing is one of them, and I've given up reading anything into it.

Besides which, I've got more important things on my mind, and I stride over to Gemma and lean down, gently kissing her lips.

"Is that your idea of a kiss?" she says, as I stand upright again.

"When I'm in uniform, and likely to injure you, yes it is." She chuckles and I run my finger down her cheek. "I really missed you this morning."

She blushes, in a much more provocative way than the woman who just left. "I—I missed you too."

"Good." I kiss her again, before pulling back, just in case I get carried away. I glance around the shop and look back at Gemma again, a thought occurring to me. "I wish I could buy you some flowers… but it's a bit tricky, with you working here."

She shakes her head. "I don't need flowers. I just need you."

I grab her by the waist and pull her into my arms, regardless of all my kit. "You've got me, Gemma. I'm yours."

She blinks quickly a few times. "I'm yours too."

I smile. "And how are you feeling today?"

"I'm fine." She looks a bit puzzled.

"You're not sore, or anything?"

"Sore?"

My smile widens and I realise I'm going to have to explain what I mean, and that she might quite like my explanation, given one of the things we talked about last night. "I've never slept with a virgin before," I say, keeping my voice to a quiet whisper while I hold her tight. "But I'm led to believe it's quite normal for the virgin concerned to feel sore afterwards."

"You've never…?" She stares at me, wide eyed.

"No. Never."

"So that was another first?"

"Yes. It was. And that being the case, I need you to answer my question."

"Why? I mean… why do you want to know?"

"Because I don't like the thought of hurting you, and because I'd like to make love to you again, as soon as possible… only I can't if you're sore. So, if you are we'll wait."

She grins. "In that case, I'm glad I'm not sore."

I laugh and pull her even closer to me. "How about tonight? Seven o'clock. My place." She nods her head with enchanting enthusiasm. "Maybe we'll even try to have dinner first this time?"

"Really?" She sounds skeptical, and I laugh again.

"Okay… we'll see what happens, shall we?"

"I prefer that plan." She leans up on her tiptoes, kissing me.

I deepen the kiss this time, only pulling back when it becomes necessary, and I step back from her, taking in her swollen lips and twinkling eyes.

"I can't wait until tonight." I walk backwards towards the door. "We can compare dreams."

"Compare dreams?" She looks puzzled.

"Yes. I dreamt about you too."

She smiles now. "Did you? What did you dream?"

I grin. "I'll show you later."

She giggles, and I let myself out onto the street, giving her a wave as I walk back past the window, thinking to myself, as I look out over the harbour, how wonderful life is. When I moved here, I wasn't too sure about this place, but now, I can't imagine ever leaving.

Gemma belongs here… and that means I do, too.

Chapter Thirteen

Gemma

How lucky am I?

I've somehow met the perfect man and have gone from being lonely and uncertain, to being filled with joy. I won't say I don't feel a little insecure sometimes… but that's mainly because I don't really know what's happening, and because I know I'm keeping a huge secret from Tom, when I shouldn't be.

Still, I'm trying very hard not to think about that at the moment… because I'm just so happy.

Thanks to Tom.

Making love with him is like heaven… like paradise. I couldn't wish to have a better man in my life. He's attentive and kind, and he takes care of me… and I can't wait until tonight, when I'm going to see him again, and he's going to show me what he dreamed about last night. That thought makes my body heat and my breath catch in my throat. I know how exciting my own dreams were, and he's got a much more vivid imagination than I have. It makes sense, given my lack of experience… not that I'm giving any time to thinking about what's gone before, for either of us. Because none of that matters to me. We're together and we're in love, and I really don't care about anything else.

Except, maybe that I would have quite liked to wake up beside him this morning. When he mentioned missing my kisses in his text, and then said he'd missed waking up next to me, I had to confess that I felt the same way. Obviously, it's not as easy for me as it is for him. I'd have to explain the situation to my father… and being as Dad doesn't even know I've got a serious boyfriend, let alone that my boyfriend is PC Tom Hughes, I have no idea how I'm going to go about doing that.

Still… I refuse to let any clouds darken my day, and as it's lunchtime, I think I'll just shut the shop for a little while and go upstairs to see Imelda.

"How's the morning been?" she asks, when I stick my head around the door to her living room.

"Not bad. Not as busy as I thought it might be, but it's quite cold again today."

She smiles. "I think there should be a law that all weekends should be warm and sunny and we should save the cold and windy days for the working week."

"Or that we should only have bad weather at night," I say and she nods her approval.

"That's even better. Still, you seem very happy, regardless of the weather."

"I am happy." I lean against the doorframe and fold my arms.

"And would your good cheer have anything to do with a certain young policeman?"

"It might." I can't help smiling.

"You wouldn't have spent the night with him, by any chance, would you?" She tilts her head to one side, raising her eyebrows at the same time.

"No." I let my arms fall to my sides, hoping to make myself seem less defensive, but I think there must have been sufficient unease in my voice, because Imelda sits up, using her arms for leverage and leans forward slightly.

"But you have slept with him, haven't you?" She narrows her eyes, as though that will help her see through me more clearly… which it obviously has, and I feel myself blush, despite my silence. "It's incredible, isn't it… when it's right," she says, smiling again.

"Is it ever wrong, then?" I ask, moving further into the room and sitting on the arm of the sofa she's currently lounging over.

"Oh yes. Sometimes it can be disastrous." She pulls a face, which makes me laugh. "I could tell you stories which would make your hair curl."

I'm not sure I want to hear any of Imelda's stories at the moment – good or bad. I'm too busy living through my own. Not that it feels like a story. It's all far too real.

"I'll go and make our sandwiches," I say, getting to my feet.

"You'll have trouble." Imelda shakes her head, looking guilty. "I forgot to tell you… I've run out of bread."

"Imelda…" I let out a sigh, because she could have warned me about this when I arrived, and I could have popped down to the baker's before we opened. As it is, there's bound to be a queue now, and I won't have time to make our sandwiches and eat them by the time I get back.

"Just nip down to Rachel's and pick us up some ready-made sandwiches for today." She forages through her handbag for her purse and then holds out a twenty-pound note from inside it. "You can get me a white loaf at the same time… and why don't we have some chocolate eclairs for this afternoon? I feel like a treat."

She smiles up at me, and I take the money.

"I doubt Rachel will have much choice in the way of sandwiches by this time of day."

"Oh... don't worry about that. I'll eat almost anything... except egg."

I chuckle, knowing that Imelda doesn't even like to be in the same room as an egg sandwich.

"Okay. I'll be as quick as I can."

I go back downstairs again and grab my jacket from the hook, shrugging it on, before I sling my handbag over my shoulder and head out of the door.

As I walk the few paces to Rachel's shop, I pull my phone from my bag and check it to see whether Tom's been in touch again. He hasn't, and while that's disappointing, it's also not surprising. It's only a couple of hours since he came into the shop, after all... and he is working, so I can't expect him to keep sending me messages. I need to learn to manage my expectations of him and our relationship.

'Relationship'... I smile to myself, because that sounds so very grown up, and I put my phone into my back pocket as I get to the baker's and join the short queue that's formed outside.

There's a small window at the front of the shop, where Rachel's mother used to display bread. Rachel doesn't. She uses the space to show off her own talent, which is creating special occasion cakes, beautifully decorated, with care and precision, to a very high standard. The one that's currently in the window looks like it's for a wedding and has pale pink handmade flowers tumbling down the side, as well as on top. I can't help staring, thinking to myself that it's just the sort of cake I'd like to have, if I were ever to get married... not that I'm thinking that far ahead. I'm managing my expectations. Or at least, I'm trying to. It's hard, though, because, when I think about it, I really like the idea of spending the rest of my life with Tom, and I certainly can't imagine every loving anyone else.

Still, things like marriage are a long way off... and they're out of my hands, really, because Tom would have to want them too.

And even though I think it's fair to say that we're in a 'relationship', I'm not sure he'd be prepared to go further than that at this stage. It's too soon.

So I need to stop thinking about it.

The queue moves forward quite quickly and I'm grateful when it's my turn, because I can have a conversation, rather than letting my imagination run away with me.

Rachel Pedrick is probably about ten years older than me. I'm not sure of her exact age, and she's just old enough that it's always felt rude to ask. The age gap between us has meant that we've never really socialised together, but I remember that, when Mum left, Rachel was especially kind. She wasn't interfering, she just made a point of always asking if I was okay, which I appreciated at the time… when I wasn't clinging to Dan Moyle for support, that is.

"How are you?" she asks, smiling at me from the other side of the counter.

I know Rachel only works in the shop when it's busy. The rest of the time, she's either running the business, or developing the cake decorating side of things, which is where she hopes her long-term future lies. I don't think she'll ever give up the bakery. She's proud of having inherited it from her mother, but she's made no secret of the fact that she thinks there's more to life than bread.

"I'm fine." I check out the sandwiches in the small refrigerated unit at the end of the cake display. "Can I have two chicken salad sandwiches, please?" I ask and she retrieves them for me.

"You're looking very pleased with yourself," she says.

"Am I?"

I wasn't aware I was looking any different to normal, but I suppose being in love can do that to a person.

"Yes." She smiles and I ask for the white loaf that Imelda wanted, and as she hands it over to me, she looks me in the eye. "Is there a reason for that?"

"There might be." My lips twist upwards and she leans forward. "You can't tell anyone, because it's early days…" *And I don't want my dad to find out…* "… but I've got a boyfriend."

Her smile becomes a grin. "Anyone I know?"

"No… probably not. He's new to the village." I stop myself from saying that he's joined our small police force, because while I trust Rachel to keep a secret, I daren't risk Dad hearing about me and Tom, from anyone but me.

"But he's nice?" she says, with genuine interest.

"Yes, he is. He's absolutely gorgeous, and he's kind. He looks after me, and he cooks for me… and he's just… perfect." I can't stop grinning as I'm speaking.

"He sounds like a keeper."

"He is."

I nod my head, only just remembering to buy the chocolate eclairs before I float back out of the shop, clutching my purchases in my arms.

There's a small part of me that can't help wondering whether I should have kept quiet about Tom. It's not as though I was the only customer in Rachel's shop. That said, I didn't recognise anyone who was in there, and I can't keep lying to everyone… even if I am lying to the two most important people in my life.

"I'm not going to think about that," I say to myself, under my breath, just as I feel a tugging on the strap of my bag, pulling at my shoulder, and I yelp, spinning around to see a man, wearing a hoodie, with dark eyes and pale skin, looking down at me.

"Give me the bag," he hisses.

"No!"

I clutch hold of the strap of my bag, letting the bread and sandwiches and the cream cakes fall to the ground. He tugs harder, though, yanking it from my shoulder and pulling me over. I hit the ground with a thud, landing on my left hand and elbow, crushing the sandwiches, as I hear the man's footsteps running away into the distance.

It takes a moment of strangely silent shock for realisation to dawn, and then a middle-aged woman steps up to me.

"Are you all right?" she asks and I shake my head, wondering why people ask such stupid questions, when the answer should be obvious. Of course I'm not all right.

I turn my hand over, only now noticing the cut, and as I do, the pain in my elbow becomes more pronounced.

"It hurts," I say, proving that my own powers of speech are less than intelligent.

"Do you want an ambulance?" she asks, as a couple of other people gather round, and then Rachel appears from nowhere.

"God... Gemma." She kneels beside me. "Has your bag been snatched? Are you hurt?"

I hold out my hand. "My elbow hurts too." I feel pathetic now, and as tears well in my eyes, I know there's only one person I want, and I struggle to my feet.

"I think you should stay where you are," Rachel says, but I shake my head.

"No... I need Tom."

"Is that your boyfriend?" she asks, looking closely at me.

"Yes."

"Okay. Why don't you come back inside the shop and we'll phone him?" There's quite a crowd gathering now, and I feel as though everyone is looking at me, so I agree, and let her lead me back inside the baker's shop.

A chair miraculously appears, courtesy of the woman who works with Rachel. Her name is Vicky Bligh, and she used to be a friend of my mum's – before she ran away to 'find herself', that is. I look up at her and smile my thanks. It's the best I can manage.

"Do you know Tom's number?" Rachel says, clasping her phone.

"No. It's on my contacts list."

"But I'm guessing your phone was in your bag." She crouches down in front of me as I shake my head.

"It's in my back pocket."

She smiles as I reach round, grateful that it's in my right-hand pocket, because my left arm is really hurting now, and I pull out my phone, unlocking it, before Rachel takes it from me.

"Here… I'll do it," she says. "It'll be quicker."

She's not wrong there. I think all I'll do when I hear Tom's voice is cry, and that won't help anyone.

I look up as she holds my phone to her ear, having pressed on the screen a few times first, and then finally she says, "Hello? This is Rachel, from the baker's on the harbour…" There's a brief pause and then she holds up her hand, as though he can see her, which he can't, of course. "I'm using Rachel's phone because she can't. She's been hurt, and her bag's been snatched…" She falls silent. "She's here, in my shop. I'll give you…" She stops talking again and then pulls the phone away from her ear.

"What did he say?" I ask, looking up at her.

"He hung up… before I could even give him the address. I think that means he's on his way, but if he's new to the village, I'm not sure he'll be able to find his way here."

"Oh, don't worry. He'll find me."

Chapter Fourteen

Tom

So far, today has been one of those days which, despite being quite good, has still felt bad. I know why that is, though. It's because I just want the working part of the day to be over, so I can see Gemma again. The thought of another evening with her and all the things we can do together has proved extremely distracting. So much so, that I've spent most of my day out on patrol, simply so that no-one at the station notices that I keep staring into space, my mind drifting off to where it would rather be…

I'm just walking down Church Lane. The garage is behind me and the police station a few yards ahead, and I'm wondering if I ought to go back and show my face when my phone rings. It's my personal phone and I pull it from the side pocket in my trousers, grateful now that I'm still out on patrol, because I doubt Sergeant Quick would be very pleased to know I'm taking personal calls while on duty.

I glance down at the screen, fully expecting to see my mother's name come up. Of all the people I know, she's the one with the most shocking sense of timing, and I actually frown to myself when I see Gemma's name instead. Why on earth would she be calling me? She knows I'm at work…

"Hi." I do my best to disguise my surprise.

"Hello?" What the hell… that's not Gemma's voice, and I stop walking instantly, every nerve in my body on edge. Before I get the chance to say anything though, the female voice on the end of the line says, "This is Rachel, from the baker's on the harbour…"

I'm half tempted to say that I already know where the baker's is, but that doesn't feel even remotely important at the moment, so instead I just say, "Okay. But why are you using Gemma's phone?"

"I'm using Gemma's phone because she can't." My whole body stiffens with fear. "She's been hurt, and her bag's been snatched…"

"Where is she?" I don't care about being polite. I just care about the fact that Gemma's hurt and I need to be with her. Now.

"She's here, in my shop…" I can hear her muttering something, but I'm already lowering my phone, hanging up at the same time as I take off, running the rest of the way down Church Lane and out onto the harbour, turning to my left. Up ahead, I can see a small group of people, gathered outside the baker's shop, and I tear along the pavement, dodging the few pedestrians who don't seem to be interested in this latest incident, and the signs that some shopkeepers have placed outside their premises, reaching the baker's in less than two minutes.

"Excuse me!" I raise my voice, pushing through the small gathering of people at the door, and they step aside, noting my uniform.

Rachel looks up and frowns before she smiles. "You're Tom?" she says.

"Yes." She appears confused, but I couldn't care less, as my eyes drift down to Gemma, who's sitting on a chair beside her, and I move forward, dropping to my knees. "Where are you hurt?" I ask, and she looks up at me and blinks, two tears falling onto her cheeks.

"You're here," she says, ignoring my question and gazing into my eyes.

"Of course I'm here." I smile at her. "Now, tell me where you're hurt."

"My hand." She holds it up, and I look down at the cut on her palm. "And my elbow."

I nod my head. "Okay. Anywhere else?"

"No."

I long to hold her, but I'm still a police officer and there are things I need to do first. I look around at the few people inside the shop and those standing in the doorway. "Does anyone know where the doctor lives?" I ask.

"Yes." The woman who's standing next to Rachel holds up her hand and steps forward slightly.

I nod my head at her. "Can you fetch him, please?"

"Of course."

She makes her way out through the back of the shop, which I'm hoping is a quicker way of getting to Bell Road. Or at least, it's one that will avoid the crowds of people.

"We could have phoned him," Rachel says, and I look up to see her frowning at me.

"We could have done, yes. But in the short time I've lived here, I've noticed that a lot of offices close at lunchtime. I'm guessing the doctor's might be one of them, and while he could ignore a ringing phone, he's hardly likely to turn a blind eye to someone hammering on his door."

Her frown clears, and she smiles at me. "I see," she says, and I return my gaze to Gemma.

"You're sure nothing else hurts?"

"Not that I'm aware of." She leans closer to me. "It was such a shock."

"I know." I don't. Nothing like this has ever happened to me, but I can't think what else to say.

"I'm so glad you're here. I hope you didn't mind us phoning, but I just wanted you…"

"I don't mind in the slightest. I'm glad you phoned… and I'm even more glad that you wanted me."

She manages a very slight smile and blinks a few times, to stop her tears. "I wish you could hold me," she says, glancing at all the people by the door.

"So do I." I shake my head. "But if we're ever going to catch this… this…" I can't think of a name that I can use in civilised company, so I don't say anything, except, "I need to do my job, and if I hold you now, I'm never going to want to let you go. So, just let me get this over and done with, and I'll be back."

"You won't go far, will you?" Gemma says, a look of fear crossing her eyes.

"No, of course not." I nod towards the door. "I'm just going to speak to those people out there to find out who might have seen something. In the meantime, you try to remember whatever you can about what happened, and we can talk it through later. All right?"

"Shall I make her some tea?" Rachel says, and I turn, remembering that she's still standing there.

"Probably best not. Not until the doctor's seen her."

She nods her head and, once I get up, giving Gemma's uninjured hand a quick squeeze, Rachel takes my place.

I turn and walk over to the door, where I find about eight or ten people still there, watching.

"Did anyone here actually see what happened?" I ask, raising my voice.

"I saw the young lady fall over, and the man run off," a woman says from my left.

"I saw him running too," says a man, nodding his head. Everyone else shakes theirs, looking disappointed.

"Okay. If I can ask the two of you to step aside, the rest of you can leave." I keep my eyes on the woman who spoke and the man who's now moved next to her, and wait while everyone else disperses, with some reluctance.

Once we're alone, I turn to the man. "If you'll just wait out here. I'll talk to this lady first?"

He nods his head. "Of course, Constable."

I step aside for the woman to enter the shop, and I turn, pulling my notebook from my pocket. "Can I ask your name?"

She nods her head, moving a little closer to me. "Jennifer Stephenson," she says, quietly, and I write that down.

"And where do you live?"

She gives me an address in Norfolk, explaining in great detail that she's not from around here, which was already rather obvious. She adds that she's come to visit her sister, who lives in St. Mary's Road, which I know from my patrols, is one of the half a dozen streets that lead off of Church Lane.

At my request, she gives me her sister's name and address, and then I turn the page in my notebook, looking up at her again. "And what exactly did you see?" I ask her.

"Not very much, I'm afraid." She shakes her head. "I'd just come out of the chemist's, and I was still putting my purse back into my handbag, when I heard the young lady cry out, just as she fell to the ground, and then I saw the man run off."

"In which direction?" I ask.

"Away from me, towards…" She hesitates, because I'm guessing she's not very familiar with the village. "Towards the fish and chip shop."

"Did you see where he went?"

"No. I went to see if I could help the young lady. There weren't very many people about, and she took quite a tumble."

I take a deep breath, trying to imagine how scared Gemma must have been, and then trying to ignore that feeling because it won't help.

"Did you see the man at all?" I ask. "Did you notice what he was wearing?"

"He had on a grey top and dark trousers. Jeans, maybe?"

I nod my head, jotting down everything she says, even though I doubt it will be of much use.

"You didn't see his face?"

"No. He had his back to me."

"Okay. Is there anything else you can think of that might be relevant?"

"No," she says, her brow furrowing, as though she's giving my question serious thought.

"Right. Well, thank you for your time. If you remember anything else, please call us at the station here in the village."

"Of course." She smiles, nodding her head at me, and she looks over my shoulder to where Gemma is sitting still. "I hope you'll be all right," she says, raising her voice.

"Thank you." On hearing Gemma's reply, I turn to look at her, noticing how pale she is, and I wonder whether I should have said 'yes' to Rachel's suggestion of tea, because the doctor seems to be taking an awfully long time.

The woman smiles again and moves towards the door, just as a tall, athletic-looking man comes through it, wearing a dark grey suit and carrying a black bag in one hand and a set of keys in the other.

"Mrs Bligh said someone had been hurt?" he says, looking at me.

"You're Doctor Carew?"

"Yes." He pockets his keys and holds out his hand. "Call me Robson, for heaven's sake. Or better still, Rob. You must be the new man… from London. My father's been talking about you."

"Nothing good, I'm sure," I say, joking, and he smiles.

"Oh, I don't know."

I step aside, so he can get to Gemma, right at the moment that Rachel's assistant returns to the scene through the back of the shop, slightly out of breath, and my radio sparks into life, the sound of Sergeant Quick's voice, echoing around the confined space.

"Excuse me a minute," I say, feeling frustrated. I could do without the interruption right now, and I step outside the shop, pressing the button at the side of the device. "Yes, sir?" It's impossible to keep the impatience out of my voice.

"Where the hell are you?" He's being even more curt than I am, for some reason.

"I'm just outside the baker's shop. There's been another bag snatching incident."

"That call's only just come in," he says, sounding confused, as well as crackly and slightly garbled. "How did you know about it?"

I don't want to tell him I only know about it because my girlfriend got Rachel Pedrick to phone me, using my personal number, which I answered while on duty, so I skirt around the issue. "The victim's been injured this time, sir." I add a note of urgency to my voice, which is far from faked. "The doctor's just arrived and I'm waiting to see what he's got to say, before we decide whether she needs to go to the hospital."

"Oh heck," he says, although I imagine he'd rather say something much more explicit. "Is it a holidaymaker?"

"No, sir." I know he's concerned about the reputation of the village, so I'm keen to set his mind at rest. "It's the young lady from the florist's."

"You mean Gemma?" His voice is suddenly louder, more urgent.

"Yes, sir."

"Keep her there. I'm on my way."

The radio goes silent and I stand, my finger still poised over the button, wondering what on earth can have made Sergeant Quick react like that, and why he feels it necessary to come running when I've already got the situation under control.

My mind's a blank, but there's no point in wasting time thinking it through. I'm sure all will become clear soon enough, and in the meantime, I turn to find the other witness still standing by the door to the baker's, looking at me expectantly.

"Would you mind waiting just a little longer?" I ask him.

"No, not at all." He's very obliging and I smile at him before going back into the shop, where Robson Carew is crouching down in front of Gemma, examining her arm.

"What's the verdict?" I say, going over to them, and kneeling myself, so I'm on Gemma's level and can give her a smile and a slight wink without anyone noticing.

"It's not broken," the doctor says, lowering her arm again. "But it's going to hurt for a few days and I have no doubt it will bruise very nicely."

"And the cut?" I ask, using my question as an excuse to hold Gemma's hand in mine.

"It's not too bad. It doesn't need stitches, so I'll clean it up and dress it." Robson looks closely at Gemma. "And then I think you need to go home for the rest of the day, and put your feet up."

"I'm sure I..." Gemma says, but her voice is cut off by Sergeant Quick, who stumbles through the door with a clatter, dragging air into his lungs as he stands there, gazing down at her.

"Gemma?" he says, with a voice as soft as any I've ever heard and I stand, looking from him to her, my heart constricting in my chest as I notice her expression, which is one of pure terror. I step forward to get between them, but Quick pushes me out of the way.

"Sir... I..." I fumble over my words, wondering what to say, and how to say it, when he turns to me.

"I know you're going to tell me that there are procedures to follow and that you know what you're doing," he says, his eyes fixing on mine, with something like contempt. "But I don't care about procedures when my daughter's involved."

I stare at him, the thoughts in my brain turning over a lot more slowly than usual, like they're being processed through treacle, as I take in the words he's just uttered. "Y—Your daughter?" I say through the closing gap in my windpipe.

"Yes." He nods over my shoulder. "Gemma's my daughter."

It's the strangest sensation, when two worlds collide, but that's exactly what it feels like, to discover that the woman I'm in love with... the woman I've shared every secret and thought with, over the last few weeks... the woman who I took to my bed last night, and who is no longer a virgin, because of me... is the daughter of the man I work for. She has to have been aware of that, ever since she found out who I am, what I do, and where I do it, and yet she's chosen to say nothing. She's chosen to lie to me.

"What do we know?" Sergeant Quick says, and I startle back to reality.

Not very much, it seems, I muse to myself. "Just that your daughter's handbag was snatched approximately twenty minutes ago."

He nods his head. "Have you taken Gemma's statement yet?" he asks.

"No. I only spoke to her to ascertain her injuries." And to tell her I was glad she wanted me enough to call me, even if she has been lying to me all along. I think I might also have said I wanted to hold her and never let her go… but I'm not so sure now. I don't feel like I know who she is anymore.

"And then you got the doctor out?" He sounds impatient, like he's fed up with having to press me for information, rather than me offering it. That would be because I'm in shock. My life is disintegrating around me as I'm standing here, and I can't even react. I can't say a word, or move a muscle.

"Yes, sir. I've taken one witness statement, and I still need to talk to that gentleman over there." I nod towards the man who's still waiting just outside the door.

"Okay, you'd better get on with that then." He dismisses me, moving aside to let me pass.

I step forward, towards the door, but as I do, I turn back, hoping for some kind of sign from Gemma… something I can cling on to. She's staring down at the floor by her feet, and even though I wait a full twenty or thirty seconds for her to look up, she doesn't. She sits like a statue, avoiding my gaze, and I guess that tells me everything I need to know.

I turn my back on her, and go outside, looking down at the man and trying to focus on anything other than the last couple of weeks, and all the things I've done with Gemma… all the things we've said. She's known for all that time that her father is my boss… a man who I've told her I don't get on with at all, on more than one occasion. Why didn't she tell me? She had plenty of chances…

"Do you want to take my statement now?" the man asks, interrupting my train of thought.

"Yes. Sorry." I take out my notebook again and run through my questions with him, discovering that he saw even less than

Jennifer Stephenson, and has nothing to add to the evidence we already have… if what we have can be called 'evidence'.

Once I've finished with him, I thank him and let him go, standing rooted to the spot for a while. Duty dictates I ought to go back into the shop, but I don't think I want to. I'm not ready to look upon the reality of Gemma's deceit. I'm not ready to face her.

Instead, I turn around and pick up all the rubbish from the pavement… the rubbish that I presume was going to be Gemma's lunch. There's a squashed loaf of bread and two crushed cream cakes, their contents oozing from the bag they were obviously being carried in. Beside them is what appears to be the contents of a sandwich, or maybe two. There's some chicken and lettuce, and a few slices of cucumber and tomato, and crouching down, I gather it all up and put it into the bin that's on the other side of the road, by the harbour wall.

As I finish, Rachel comes out of her shop, carrying a pack of wipes, which she offers to me.

"I was just coming out to do that," she says, as I remove the worst of the mess from my hands. "Gemma and I were only talking about you earlier."

"Oh?"

"Yes. She was telling me you're… together."

"Oh. Was she? She told you about us then, did she?"

She frowns at me, in an understandable reaction to my harsh response. "Sorry… have I spoken out of turn? Was it meant to be a secret?"

"No." I shake my head. "Not as far as I was concerned, it wasn't."

"Is that supposed to make sense?" she says. "Because I'm afraid you've lost me."

"Sorry. I'm a bit confused at the moment. Making sense is beyond me."

"What are you confused about?"

"The fact that I've only just this minute found out who my girlfriend is."

"No. I'm sorry. I'm still lost."

"Nowhere near as lost as I am." I turn and stare out over the harbour. "I imagine you knew that Gemma is Sergeant Quick's daughter?"

"Of course." She turns to me. "Oh. You mean, you didn't? Is that what you're saying?"

"Yes. Until just now, when he told me, I had no idea they were even related."

"She didn't tell you herself?"

"No… she didn't."

"And you didn't work it out for yourself, considering they share the same surname?"

"I didn't know her surname. I'm guessing that was intentional on her part, but it wasn't on mine. We've just been… otherwise occupied." I shake my head, drowning in memories. "She obviously didn't tell her father about me, either. But she let me fall in love with her." I lower my voice, whispering to myself now. "She let me share every single part of my life with her, including how hard I was finding it to settle here with the sergeant and his ways, even though she knew he was her father. She never said a word. She just let me… she let me…" I swallow the lump in my throat, and I feel Rachel's hand settle on my arm, as I turn to look at her, recalling her presence, and I realise she'll have heard everything I've just said. Not that I really care right now. I've got more important things to think about.

"Maybe she didn't know how to tell you," she says.

"I get that I'm new here, and you don't know me from the next stranger, but believe me, I'm really not that unapproachable."

"I'm sure you're not." She removes her hand. "But maybe she… maybe it was…" Her voice fades.

"It's a tough one, isn't it?" I say. "But I tell you what… you see if you can think up an excuse for what she's done, and if you do, can you let me know? Because I'm damned if I can come up with one."

I step away, moving back towards the baker's shop, right at the moment that Robson Carew comes out, closely followed by Sergeant Quick and then Gemma. My heart stills at the sight of her, so small beside her father, and so pale. She's close enough that I could reach out and touch her, if I wanted to… and I want to. Even now.

"It's been nice to meet you." Robson Carew steps forward, smiling. "Obviously it would have been nicer still in different circumstances, but maybe we can go out for a drink sometime?"

I nod my head. "Sure. Why not?"

I imagine I'll have some free time now…

I'm aware of a prickling over my skin and, as the doctor moves away, I look up to find Gemma staring at me, her eyes boring into mine with a depth of fear like I've never seen in her before, or in anyone else for that matter. I know what she's trying to tell me, or rather, what she's asking. Or maybe begging would be a better word. As I said to Rachel, it's clear to me that her father knows as little of me and my role in Gemma's life as I did of him and his. The look on her face says she wants it kept that way, and as much as I ache to pull her into my arms and ask her what on earth is going on here… as much as I need to know the truth, and to hear it from her lips, I won't betray her. I know how it feels. It's what I'm going through right now… and I won't do that to her. I love her too much.

"I'm going to take Gemma home," Sergeant Quick says, linking his arm through hers.

"Very good, sir. I'll go back to the station and type up the statements, and I'll handle everything there for the rest of the day."

"I'm sure *Geoff* will handle everything." He shakes his head, not missing the opportunity to put me in my place in front of Gemma, who glances up at him, but doesn't say a word.

"Fine," I reply, not bothering with the 'sir' this time. "I'm sure you or Geoff can handle taking your daughter's statement too."

Quick frowns, although I don't know why. He's just made it plain that he doesn't trust me in the slightest, so I'd have thought he'd prefer to deal with things himself from here on… or at least get someone he does trust to deal with them. He doesn't comment though and instead he just nods his head.

"Are you ready?" he says, looking down at Gemma.

"Yes." Her voice is a barely audible whisper, and without another word, they turn and start walking.

They've only gone a few paces though, when they stop and Gemma leans up, whispering something to her father, who looks down at her, and then turns to face me. For a moment, I wonder if I'm about to be publicly hauled over the coals for sleeping with my boss's daughter, but then Quick calls me over, with a wave of his hand.

My feet seem reluctant to work, but I put one of them in front of the other and walk towards the two of them.

"Yes… sir." The salutation is an afterthought again. A very deliberate one.

"Gemma's just remembered that Imelda doesn't know what's happened. Could you tell her before you go back to the station?"

"You'll have to go around the back," Gemma says, addressing me directly for the first time since her father arrived, although she still won't look at me.

"Yes, she's laid up with a broken ankle," Quick says, offering an explanation. He looks down at Gemma. "Is the back door open?" he asks.

Gemma thinks for a moment. "I'm not sure."

Quick shakes his head before turning back to me. "Well, if it isn't, I've got no idea how you're going to get inside, because the stairs are beyond Imelda at the moment. Still, a small matter like that shouldn't prove too hard for a man like you." His voice is thick with sarcasm.

"I'm sure I'll work it out." I can't be bothered to bite. Not that it would matter if I did… not anymore. It isn't as though I've got anything to stay here for now, is it?

I glance at Gemma and notice the disappointment in her eyes as she looks up at her father, and just for a second, I let myself hope…

Tell him! The voice in my head is shouting at her. *You don't have to defend me, but at least tell him about us. Tell him who I am and what we mean to each other… we can still make this work, if you just tell him the truth…*

She sighs, shaking her head and looks down at the ground, and I feel the weight of that rejection, bearing heavily on my shoulders as I turn. I'm just about to move away, when in the reflection of the shop window, I notice Gemma leaning up and whispering something to her father again.

"Hughes?" Sergeant Quick calls and I turn back.

"Yes?"

"Thank you," Gemma says, speaking instead of her father.

I don't reply to her, because I can't. Instead, I just nod my head and walk away towards the florist's.

As far as I'm concerned, it's too late for 'thank you'.

It feels more like time for 'goodbye'.

Chapter Fifteen

Gemma

Dad's done nothing but fuss ever since we got home, and while I know he means well, I wish he'd stop. In fact, I wish he'd just leave me alone. I need to think. Although I'm not sure I *want* to think, because thinking hurts… especially when I'm thinking about Tom.

"You need a bath," Dad says, and I look at him from my place on the sofa, where I've been sitting for the last half an hour. When we first got home, he took me into the kitchen and made me phone my bank to cancel my card and order a new one. Luckily I don't have any credit cards, but I had to wait for ages while the man at the bank went through everything. I was grateful to get in here and sit down, and the prospect of getting up again doesn't appeal. "It'll help with the bruising… and the shock."

He thinks the constant tears I've been crying since he put his arm around me and steered me away from Tom are all about the attack. I know he thinks I'm upset because a stranger stole my bag and pushed me to the ground. I know he thinks this is all 'shock'. But it isn't. This is fear… fear that Tom will never be able to forgive me; that our relationship is over before it's even begun. This is heartbreak… heartbreak that I've hurt Tom. I might have felt too ashamed of myself to make eye contact with him, once the truth had come out, but the few times I caught a glimpse of him made it clear that he was hurt… and angry. His face was hard to read, but it certainly didn't look like he loved me anymore. That's why I had to get Dad to call him back when I wanted to thank him. I wasn't sure whether Tom would come back for me, but I knew he'd obey my father… and he did. Not that he acknowledged my thanks, or even understood them. He didn't realise I was thanking him for coming when I called, or for being so kind and attentive, or for passing on the message to Imelda… and most especially for not giving me away to my father in front of the entire village.

He could easily have done that, but he didn't… and I'm grateful. Because while I know I've got to tell Dad the truth – even if I am very late in doing so – I want to talk to Tom first. I want to explain to him how we ended up in this position. I need to know whether he can forgive me and if there's anything worth explaining to my dad before I bother to take the plunge.

"I'm not sure I want a bath," I say, sniffling into a tissue at the thought of what Tom must think of me, and then adding it to the pile that's building on the coffee table, beside my phone.

"It'll do you good, and you'll feel better afterwards." Dad's trying to help. I know he is, and I look up and see him smiling down at me, even though he can't disguise the worry in his eyes.

"Okay." I relent, and he holds out his hand, pulling me carefully to my feet.

"You'll need to keep your injured hand dry," he says, looking down at the neat dressing that Doctor Carew put on for me. "Do you think you'll be able to manage by yourself?"

I look up again. "You're not helping me in the bath, Dad." His smile widens.

"No. I suppose not."

I wouldn't mind Tom helping me if it meant he'd forgiven me. But we're not at that stage yet. And before we are, I need to talk to him… and then to Dad.

God… this is such a mess.

"Come on then," Dad says, "I can at least run the bath for you, while you get undressed."

I can't argue with him, so I let him lead the way upstairs and while he goes into the bathroom, I walk into my bedroom and sit on the edge of my bed, wishing now that I'd thought to bring my phone up here with me. I might not have been able to phone Tom – not with Dad just next door – but at least I could have sent him a text message. It wouldn't have been the same as hearing his voice, but I'd have been able to say 'sorry'.

"Are you ready yet?" Dad's voice breaks into my thoughts, and I startle, standing up and undoing my jeans.

"No. I won't be a minute."

"Okay. I'll just pop down and put the kettle on."

"All right." I listen as he trots down the stairs. Somehow I know he won't stay down there though, so I quickly undress, putting on my robe, before I make my way into the bathroom and close the door behind me.

I've only just climbed into the bath, careful to keep my bandaged hand out of the water, when I hear Dad's voice outside the door.

"Are you all right, love?"

"Yes, Dad. I'm fine."

"You haven't locked the door, have you?"

"No." Something told me he'd want it left unlocked 'just in case'.

"Good. I've got some clothes to put away in my bedroom, so I won't be far away if you need anything."

"Okay." I lie back, tears still rolling down my cheeks, and in the end, I only stay in the bath for about twenty minutes, because I really am struggling, and I need to talk to Tom… and I can't do that in here. Not only that, I'm finding it harder than I'd thought to keep my hand dry.

So, I climb out and pull the plug, wrapping myself in a towel and sitting on the edge of the bath. My leg's hurting now, which it wasn't before, and I pull back the towel to have a look at it. There don't seem to be any cuts that I can see, but it might be bruised, I suppose.

"Is everything okay?" Dad's voice comes through the door.

"Yes. I've just got out. I was struggling to keep my hand out of the water," I explain, although that's only a small part of the reason I've ended my bath so soon.

"Okay. I'll finish making the tea while you get dressed… unless you need some help."

"Hardly, Dad." I shake my head, ignoring the fact that he can't see me through the closed door.

I wait until I hear his footsteps on the stairs and then leave the bathroom, still wrapped in the towel, going back into my bedroom, where I pull some underwear out of my chest of drawers. I suppose I could just put on my pyjamas. It might only be the middle of the afternoon, but what would it matter? Except… I suppose, if I managed to get hold of Tom, and he wanted to meet up, it would be easier if I was already dressed. I nod my head, deciding to put some clothes on, and I find a pair of clean jeans and a jumper before going over to the bed and getting dressed.

Downstairs, Dad greets me with a cup of tea and a plate of digestive biscuits, helping me to get comfortable on the sofa, before he sits in the chair by the window.

"Does that feel better?" he asks.

"Yes, thank you." That's a lie… another one. I don't feel better at all, but it's what Dad wants to hear.

He smiles. "I knew a bath would do you good."

"My leg's hurting now." His smile fades, becoming a frown.

"In what way?"

"I don't know. I think it's just bruised."

He nods. "We'll keep an eye on it over the next day or so, and if it gets any worse, I'll make you an appointment to see the doctor."

"Okay."

He takes a sip of tea, wincing slightly because it's hot, and then takes a digestive from the plate, dunking it into his cup.

"Doctor Carew was very kind today," I say, making conversation.

"He's a good man… like his father." Dad's reply doesn't surprise me. He's fond of Geoff Carew and I look across at him, only now noticing that he's still in uniform.

"You don't have to sit here with me, you know? If you need to go back to work…" I let my voice fade and he shakes his head.

"I wouldn't dream of it. I was just going to drink this, and then I'll go upstairs and change." He takes another digestive, not bothering to dunk this one. "Besides, I'm sure Geoff can cope without me… and if he can't, I have absolutely no doubt that Tom Hughes will." He rolls his eyes, and I note that his voice has that same derisive tone he used earlier, when he was talking directly to Tom.

"You weren't very nice to him," I say, frowning.

He glances up at me. "Who? Tom Hughes?" I nod my head. "Well, in case you didn't gather, he's the man from the Met I've been telling you about… the one who's so full of big ideas."

"Is he?" I say, tilting my head to one side. That's not the version I've heard from Tom. "I mean, is he so full of big ideas?"

"He can be… sometimes," he says, adding the last word, rather grudgingly.

"So it's not that you're being harsh on him because you expect him to fail… or because you want him to?"

"They all fail eventually, Gemma. There's no point in pretending otherwise."

"That's very negative, Dad."

"It's very realistic," he says, and then shrugs. "Still, I'm grateful to him for looking after you when you needed him."

I want to say that he was only there because I called him. I want to explain that, when I was in trouble, the person I needed most in all the world was Tom… and not my dad. Except I can't hurt his feelings like that.

I can still remember the look on Tom's face when Dad was talking down to him. I could tell he was struggling not to react… to blurt out the truth of the situation… to score points over the man who'd made his professional life a misery. He didn't though, and that must have been hard for him, because it meant he had to lie – or at least be economic with the truth – and I know that's something that doesn't sit well with Tom. For as long as I've known him, he's made a big deal about honesty… little knowing that I've been deceiving him the whole time.

"What happened?" Dad says, his voice a little softer, and I look up at him.

"When?"

He frowns. "This lunchtime, outside the baker's." I half expect him to say 'when else?' because he doesn't realise my mind is all over the place.

"I don't remember very much about it… just the man standing in front of me, tugging at my bag, telling me to give it to him, when I wouldn't, and then pulling me over as he yanked it from my shoulder."

"You shouldn't have tried to fight him off," Dad says, shaking his head. "Nothing in your bag is worth getting hurt for."

"I know that now, Dad, but I was just acting on instinct. And my instinct was to be absolutely furious with him for thinking he had the right to take my bag from me."

Dad smiles. "Well, at least you're okay. Your bruises will mend, and nothing's broken."

Except my heart... and maybe Tom's, too.

If he even cares about me anymore.

Dad finishes his tea, and I take a few sips of mine, declining a biscuit when he offers me the plate, and once he's put his cup down on the table, he sits forward in the chair, looking over at me.

"Will you be all right on your own down here for a few minutes while I take a quick shower and change out of my uniform?"

He's going to leave me alone? Thank God.

I try not to appear too enthusiastic at the prospect, and just smile at him. "I'll be fine, Dad."

"Do you want me to put the television on?" he asks, getting to his feet.

"No, thanks." I look at the clock on the mantlepiece and see that it's five o'clock already. "I doubt there will be much on at this time on a Saturday, other than sport."

He chuckles, because I know he probably wouldn't mind watching some sport himself, and picking up his cup to take out to the kitchen, he leaves the room.

I wait a few minutes to give him time to go upstairs and get into the shower, and once I hear the water running, I lean over and grab my phone from the table. Going to my contacts list, I connect a call to Tom, holding the phone to my ear as it rings, and rings, and then his voicemail kicks in. I hope that's because he's busy working, and not because he's checked his phone and decided he doesn't want to talk to me. I can't think about that now. Instead, I listen to the automated voice, telling me I've reached Tom's number, but that he's not available. I'm almost tempted to smile, because the concept of recording his own message will have been beyond Tom. The problem is, I'm too scared to smile. So, I take a breath and say, "Hi. It's me. Gemma." I decide to clarify that. I know he can't have removed my name from his contacts. He doesn't know how to. But I suppose he might have asked someone else to do it for him, in his desperation to strike me out of his life. "I'm sorry. Really, I am. I know you probably hate me right now, but can you call me when you get this, so we can talk, and I can explain things to you? I—I know we arranged to meet up later, but I don't know if you still want me… if you still love me, so I won't come unless I hear from you. Please call. I—I love you, Tom. And I'm so sorry." I can't think of anything else to say, and I can hear the cracks in my voice as my tears fall again, so I hang up, keeping my phone right beside me in the hope he'll call back.

I tell myself he'll still be at work. That's why he can't talk. But he'll call later, when he gets home. I hope…

"Everything all right?" Dad says, coming back into the room, wearing jeans and a shirt, and I glance at the clock, realising that I've been sitting staring at my phone for half an hour, and that Tom hasn't called.

"Yes." He comes and perches on the edge of the sofa. I shift back slightly to make room for him, and he looks down at my phone, which has fallen between the cushions, picking it up and handing it to me.

"Did you want to call that boyfriend of yours?" he asks, tilting his head to one side. "I'm assuming you were going to meet him tonight, but if I'm being honest, I don't think you should. I think you should stay here and get some rest, and have an early night."

I blink back my tears. "It's fine... we didn't make any arrangements for tonight." It seems I'm good at lying. I know perfectly well that Tom and I have very firm arrangements for this evening. He was going to show me his dreams...

Instead of which, my life has turned into a total nightmare.

Dad frowns slightly. "Are things cooling off between the two of you?" he asks. "I mean... I know it wasn't serious, but..." He lets his sentence hang, and I struggle not to burst into tears.

"I'm not sure," I say, with complete honesty, for once.

"Well, you weren't convinced he was your type, were you? So I shouldn't worry about it." He puts his hand on my arm and gives me a gentle squeeze. "There are plenty more fish in the sea. And at least neither of us is working tomorrow, so we can spend the day together, if you like?"

I nod my head, trying not to think about all the lies I've told, or the fact that, if Tom can't forgive me, I'm going to be spending a lot more time at home in the future.

"Shall we get some fish and chips for dinner tonight?" Dad says. "I'm not really in the mood for cooking, and I'm not sure you're up to it." He grins, nodding towards my damaged hand.

"No, I'm not."

Somehow I doubt I'm going to hear from Tom, either. I'm not sure I'm going to hear from him ever again. Tears prick my eyes, but I hide them, looking down at my hands.

"Good." Dad stands up again, picking up my cup and the plate of half eaten digestives. "We'll give it until just after six and wander down to the fish and chip shop together, shall we?"

I glance up at him, my tears falling as I blink and a wave of fear washes through me at the thought of going back out onto the harbour, where it happened, where that man stood in front of me and threatened me... and hurt me. "I—I could stay here, couldn't I?" My voice sounds pathetic, and I want to shake myself for being so weak. All afternoon, I've been so wound up about Tom and what's going to happen to us, it hasn't dawned on me until now that I'm actually frightened.

Dad puts the cup and plate back down and sits beside me once more.

"Don't cry, Gem. I know you're scared," he says, seeing right through me, at least to the parts that I'm willing to show him. "But you've got to face it. Otherwise, you're going to find it harder and harder as time wears on. I'll be with you, so you'll be perfectly safe."

I suck in a breath, reasoning with myself that he's right. I can't hide away, fearful of leaving the house. Porthgarrion is my home. I've lived here all my life, and even though the thought of walking along the harbour fills me with dread, I know Dad's right. I have to do it, and I have to do it sooner rather than later, because if I don't, it'll become even more fearful.

"Okay," I whisper, and he leans over and kisses my forehead.

"That's my girl," he says, and gives me a smile.

Chapter Sixteen

Tom

I try around the back of the florist's shop first, Gemma's 'thank you' still ringing in my ears and the sight of her tear-laden eyes still filling my head. Unfortunately, the door's locked. So, I go around to the front again, and knock, doing my best to ignore the fact that the last time I was here, I was kissing Gemma and looking forward to spending another evening with her.

There's no reply, so I knock again… and again. And eventually I hear a window opening above my head.

"Hello?" A female voice sounds from above me and I step back out onto the pavement and look up to see a middle-aged woman, with dark blonde hair piled up rather haphazardly on her head, peering down at me.

"Hello. Are you Imelda?"

"Yes," she says, her brow furrowing.

"I'm sorry to get you up, but I've got a message for you, from Gemma."

"Ahh…" She smiles, as though she knows something I don't. "I was getting worried about her."

"Yes... I'm afraid she's been involved in an incident." That's the official way of putting things, and I can't think of a better one at the moment.

"Oh, dear God... what's happened?"

"Her bag was snatched. She..."

"This is ridiculous." She shakes her head. "We can't have this conversation with you in the street and me leaning out of the window."

"I know, but you can't get down the stairs."

"If you go around to the back of the shop, there's a key underneath the pot of tulips." She stares at me for a moment and then says, "You know what tulips look like, don't you?"

"Yes." I nod my head and she returns the gesture, before disappearing back inside the room and closing the window, giving me no choice other than to obey her instructions.

I make my way around to the back of the shop again, going through the gate that I discovered earlier, and down the path which leads to the back door. Sure enough, among many pots of flowers and plants, is one filled with purple and yellow tulips. My first thought is how insecure this arrangement is, but as I bend to lift the pot and retrieve the key, I can't help but remember my very first conversation with Gemma, when she explained to me what this flower actually means. I straighten up again, surprised by the pain that fills my chest, and I look up at the clouding sky, shaking my head, because I can't think about loving her right now. It hurts too much.

Instead, I let myself in, the door opening straight into the back area of the shop. It's a large space, with a wooden workbench occupying most of one side, and shelves on which there are all kinds of ribbons, as well as rolls of clear and coloured wrapping, in dispensers, mounted on the wall. I can imagine Gemma working here, and picture her standing by the bench, her beautiful head bowed as she concentrates on her job.

"Stop it," I mutter to myself, and I wander through towards the front of the shop, which doesn't help at all. I don't have to use my imagination in here. I've seen her at work in this part of the shop. It was where we first met, after all.

"Come up the stairs..." Imelda's voice drifts down to me and, taking care of the potted plants that sit to one side of each of the first few treads, I make my way up the spiral staircase, grateful to be going into truly unfamiliar territory. "I'm in the front room." Her directions are a little unnecessarily. I've just been looking up at her from the outside of her own shop, but I make my way towards the sound of her voice anyway, into a large living room, which is so brightly coloured it almost takes my breath away. There are two sofas and two chairs, but none of them match each other, and all of them are covered in throws and cushions of various shades. The rug on the floor is also vibrant, as are the paintings, a couple of which look like they might be originals.

I turn around and glance down at Imelda herself, who's now lying along the length of one sofa, her hair still looking like it could fall from its precarious position, with just a mild gust of wind. She dresses in a similar style to her decor... with a varied colour palette, and is of slim build with a kindly, smiling face.

"Take a seat," she says, waving her hand in the vague direction of the rest of her furniture, and I sit on the edge of one of the chairs. "You said there was an incident?"

"Yes. Gemma's handbag was snatched, and she was injured."

Imelda sits forward now, suddenly a lot more concerned. "You didn't say she'd been injured."

"You didn't give me the chance."

She nods her head, as though accepting my statement, and then says, "Is she all right?"

"Her injuries aren't serious. The man who snatched her bag either pulled or pushed her to the ground. I'm not sure which way round it was. Gemma cut her hand and bruised her elbow, and she's a bit shaken up." Although whether that's because of the attack, or because her lies have been found out, I'm not sure.

"Oh... the poor thing." There's genuine sympathy in Imelda's voice. "I take it she's gone home."

"Yes."

She smiles and settles back again into the sofa. "You must be Tom," she says, surprising me.

"I am. How did you know?"

Her smile widens. "Oh... I've heard all about you."

"You have?"

"Yes. Gemma tells me all sorts of things," she says, enigmatically, and stares up at me. "I take it you know her mother left about five years ago?"

"I do, yes." *At least she didn't lie about that.*

Imelda nods her head. "Her father's done his best for her, and he's done a fantastic job, but I'm sure you understand, there are things a young woman doesn't necessarily want to talk to her father about."

"There are things Gemma doesn't necessarily want to talk to anyone about," I say. "Like who she is."

Imelda frowns now and tilts her head to one side. "Can I assume from that comment you've found out that Rory is her father?"

"Yes, you can." I sit forward a little. "And I'll assume from your remark that you're aware Gemma hasn't been entirely honest with me."

"I am aware of that, yes," she says, sighing. "I told her it was a mistake."

"It's a shame she didn't listen to you then." I can't help my harsh reply or the slight rise in my voice.

"You're angry," Imelda says. She could hardly fail to pick up on that.

"Yes, I am. Do you blame me?"

"No."

"She lied... so many times." I lower my voice, but I can't disguise the pain behind it.

"Did she?" she says, challenging me. "Did she actually lie to you? And before you answer, think about it."

I do as she says, recalling my conversations with Gemma, since the moment I told her what I do for a living, and where I do it. I think about the times when I've told her how difficult I've been finding it to work with Sergeant Quick... her father. And I think about all the chances she's had to tell me the truth... chances she hasn't taken. While I'm remembering, I have to admit to myself that she didn't actually lie. She just failed to tell the truth.

"Okay," I say eventually. "Maybe she didn't lie... but she wasn't entirely honest either."

"I told her once that lying and keeping secrets are essentially the same thing. If you care about someone, that is... if you're serious about them."

"We were serious," I say, that pain returning to my chest as I think about putting our relationship into the past, where it feels like we don't belong. "She said she loved me."

"What about you? Do you love her?"

"Yes."

There's no point in pretending otherwise, or putting my love for Gemma in the past. Not when it hurts this much.

"Then forgive her," she says simply.

"Just like that?" I shake my head.

"No. Not 'just like that'. Forgiveness is hard. Especially when you've been hurt, and you don't understand why."

"She had so many chances to tell me." I voice my thoughts, feeling the need to justify my pain, and Imelda nods her head encouragingly. "Right from the start, I was honest with her. I told her I'm a police officer, and that was an enormous risk to take, as far as I was concerned. I've gone out with women in the past, who've failed to return my calls, or even changed their numbers, once they've found out what I do for a living."

"More fool them," Imelda says, and I look up to see her smiling.

"If you say so. But that's not the point. I knew right from the moment I first saw Gemma that she was different, and I'll admit my first instinct had been to conceal my occupation from her. I didn't want it to get in the way… to spoil things. But after just a couple of hours with her, I knew I couldn't deceive her… so I admitted the fact that I'd been trying to hide it from her, and I told her the truth. Then, the very next day, I came into the shop to visit her, in uniform, and apologised for not making it clear that I'm actually working here… in the village. She could have told me then who her father is, but she didn't say a word. Since then, I've told her countless stories of the trouble I've been having with Sergeant Quick, and she's listened attentively… and said nothing."

"That's the trouble with lies… or with keeping secrets," she says. "Once they get started, they're almost impossible to stop. At least, not without hurting someone."

"You think this doesn't hurt?" My words come out in a rush, and I wish I could take them back. This woman is a stranger to me. I shouldn't be talking to her like this. "I'm sorry." I stand as she looks up at me.

"Please don't make any hasty decisions," she says, clearly understanding that our conversation is over; that I've said too much already. "Bitter experience has taught me you almost always regret them."

"I'm not at the decision-making stage yet. Hasty or otherwise. I'm still thinking."

She smiles. "Thinking's good," she says, and she shifts, trying to get comfortable, I presume. In doing so, her long dress moves slightly, revealing the brace she's wearing on her ankle, which I'd temporarily forgotten about.

"Can I get you anything?" I feel guilty now for not asking earlier.

"No... I'm fine. I can hobble around up here. It's just the stairs that have me a bit flummoxed at the moment."

"Will you be all right? You're sure there's nothing I can do?"

She shakes her head. "No... but thank you for offering."

I move towards the door. "I'll put your key back under the tulips for now, but you really should find a more secure way of storing it, and you certainly shouldn't shout its whereabouts out of the window."

She chuckles. "You're not in London now," she says. "There are plenty of people here who still leave their back doors open... even at night."

"Dear God..." I mutter and she laughs out loud.

"I hope to see you again soon, Tom." I turn to her, and see her pale blue eyes, filled with sympathy, although I can't reply, because I've got no idea what the future holds.

Back at the station, Geoff's standing on the other side of the counter and looks up as I enter.

"I was thinking you'd got lost," he says. "How's Gemma?"

"She's fine." I don't know if that's true, but I let myself in through the side door.

"That's a relief," he says, sighing. "I've known Rory Quick for donkey's years, and I've never seen him panic like that before. Still, I suppose that's what fathers do for their daughters, isn't it?"

"I suppose." I sit down at my desk, pulling out my notebook, so I can get on… or at least appear to be getting on.

Fortunately, at that moment, someone comes in through the front door, and Geoff turns around to greet them, so I'm not obliged to make conversation, and I look down at my notes, wishing we had something more to go on than such vague descriptions. I turn the page, just as my phone rings… my personal phone. I know I should leave it, but I can't help myself, and I pull it from my trouser pocket and check the screen, my chest constricting when I read the word 'Gemma' on the screen.

My finger hovers over the green button, and although I want to talk to her, although I want to ask her why she's lied – or at least neglected to tell the truth – I can't bring myself to press it. I can't be sure how I'll respond. Until I'm certain about that, I think it's best to be silent… for both of our sakes.

Geoff's still busy, so when my phone beeps, letting me know I've got a message, I play it, turning away in my seat as I listen to Gemma's voice…

"Hi. It's me. Gemma." *Did she think I wouldn't know that?* "I'm sorry. Really, I am. I know you probably hate me right now, but can you call me when you get this, so we can talk, and I can explain things to you? I—I know we arranged to meet up later, but I don't know if you still want me… if you still love me, so I won't come unless I hear from you. Please call. I—I love you, Tom. And I'm so sorry."

I can hear her voice breaking up through her words, and I'm almost certain she's crying by the end of her message. I'm struggling too, if I'm being honest.

How could she possibly think I'd hate her? I'm angry with her. I'm really bloody angry with her. But I could never hate her… no matter what.

I know I should let her explain, but I'm not ready yet. I need a bit more time first, because no matter how angry I am, hearing her voice has confirmed that I love her more than ever. Before I talk to her, though, it seems wise to calm down, and think things through… and I need to do that by myself.

I've made it to the end of the shift, thank goodness, and I leave Geoff to lock up, while I head home, strolling to the end of Church Lane. I'm not in any rush, because even though I need to think and I need to be alone, I'm not sure that home is the best place for me right now. There are going to be too many reminders of Gemma there… of Gemma and last night, and I think that's just going to confuse me even more. I think it's going to be really hard to be angry with her, when I'm faced with the memories of making love to her, of her body beneath mine, of her cries and our caresses… and our love.

And her lies.

No, her secrets.

And her lies.

I look up as I round the corner onto the harbour and my heart stops, because coming out of the fish and chip shop, is Gemma… followed by the man I now know to be her father. Sergeant Quick. It's the first time I've seen him out of uniform, and he looks remarkably human. I stand, rooted to spot and watch as he links her arm through his. He's carrying a bag, which I presume contains their supper, and they slowly set off towards home, on the other side of the harbour. Gemma seems to be limping slightly and I wonder if she's sustained another injury; something that wasn't obvious at the time… and while I'm tempted to run up to her and ask, I know I can't. It's fairly obvious to me she still hasn't told her father about me. If she had, I doubt Sergeant Quick would have kept the news to himself, and his silence means the lies – or the secrets – are still continuing. And that doesn't feel too good to me.

If she'd only told me the truth at the beginning, it wouldn't have made that much difference. Okay, so it might have made things even more awkward for me at work, but I'm sure Sergeant Quick and I could have ironed out our differences, and it would certainly have been a lot better than where we are now… because where we are now, is just a bloody mess.

I keep my eyes fixed on the back of Gemma's head, even as I start to walk again. She doesn't appear to be talking, although Sergeant Quick does. He's looking out at the harbour now, and saying something, just as Gemma stops suddenly and pulls him back with her. He turns and looks down at her, and even from here, I can see the stiffness in her body, the change in her demeanour. Something's wrong…

I keep moving forward, more slowly, as Quick looks around, first in my direction, although he doesn't seem to notice me, and then to his right, towards Bell Road, before he turns back to Gemma, who's now shaking. He's talking quickly, although Gemma remains silent, and then she points and I follow the direction of her hand, and see a man, standing on the corner, wearing a grey hoodie and leaning against the wall.

Instinctively, I know this is the man who robbed Gemma of her bag earlier, and I take off, running as fast as I can in his direction.

As I pass Gemma and her father, she glances up, noticing me, a look of shock crossing her face.

"Is that him?" I call out.

"Yes," she says, nodding her head, and without breaking my stride, I carry on, just as the man looks up and spots me, turning on his heels and starting off up Bell Road.

I take the corner, hoping there are no cars coming, as I cross over the road. That puts me on the same side as the man, who I can see is nearing the art gallery, so I pick up the pace, and catch up to him, just before the entrance to the hotel, tackling him to the ground.

He struggles, kicking out against me and hitting home at least once with a wayward fist against my ribcage, until I bring him under control and use my full height and weight against him, turning him onto his front and pinning him down. Then I take a breath before I reach for my cuffs and clip them on his wrists, with a more than usually satisfying snap.

"Get up." I stand myself and haul him to his feet, not giving him any choice in the matter. He's still struggling, and I notice a few people approach from the end of Bell Road, walking towards me. Among them are them Sergeant Quick and Gemma, who's still clutching her father's arm, while staring at me.

She tilts her head as they approach, and manages a smile, which I can't return, so instead I look at her father... my boss.

"I'll take him back to the station, sir," I say. "It's all locked up, but I'll do the paperwork and let him stew in a cell until the morning."

"I think you mean 'the' cell, Constable." He never misses an opportunity, it seems, even when I've just captured the man who's not only been causing havoc in the village for the last few weeks, but who also assaulted his daughter. "We only have the one."

I don't reply, and instead I push the man forward, keeping a firm grip on his arm, as we pass through the crowd.

"Thank you..."

"Well done..."

The words echo around me, and I feel the odd tap on my shoulder, and then I hear my name, in the sergeant's familiar voice, and I turn to face him, wondering what's coming next as he walks towards me, Gemma still by his side.

"I think I might have misjudged you," he says, shocking the hell out of me, although I can tell he's having trouble making his speech, just from the pained expression on his face. "It seems you might be a useful man to have around, after all."

I wonder how much it hurt him to say that. In my experience, compliments seem to be fairly thin on the ground with Sergeant Quick. He's only ever paid me one before. It was when he and Geoff were arguing over whether a daughter ought to let her father meet her new boyfriend…

My mouth dries and my skin prickles, as I recall the full extent of that discussion, while I watch the sergeant lead Gemma away, not waiting for my response. That's just as well, because I don't have one. He's still clutching their fish and chips, and makes a remark about going home before it gets cold, in a moment that to them, and everyone else, must seem very ordinary. It's a moment that, to me, feels like the complete opposite of ordinary. It feels like the devastation of every minute hope I've allowed myself to cling onto, ever since this lunchtime, when I discovered that the woman I love isn't who I thought she was…

I've just remembered that conversation between myself, the sergeant and Geoff, when they'd asked for my opinion – or at least Geoff did – about whether a father was entitled to meet his daughter's boyfriend. The daughter in question was the sergeant's, and I remember him mentioning her age, and saying she'd only just turned twenty. That must mean they were talking about Gemma. By extension, it's easy to work out that the 'boyfriend' must have been me. Sergeant Quick praised me at the time for my mature attitude, in explaining to him that, if his daughter wasn't serious about her boyfriend, then I didn't think he had the right to demand a meeting between them. And now, standing here, watching them walk away together, I'm reminded of his reply… which was that his daughter had told him that her relationship wasn't serious at all.

I felt bad before. I felt hurt and angry, and confused. But now I feel betrayed as well. Not only did Gemma lie about who she is, and about her father's identity, but now it appears she lied about loving me too.

I walk the hooded man back to the police station so I can formally charge him, my mind in a whirl of bewildered thoughts.

I know Gemma left me that message, begging me to talk to her, but how can I? How can I trust her to tell me the truth about anything, knowing what I know? And even if I listened to her, and she could somehow explain this complicated web of deceit she's woven around us all, what kind of future would the two of us have? None at all, I imagine, once Sergeant Quick found out that the man he's made a point of despising until now, has bedded his daughter and taken her virginity, in this evidently trivial relationship of hers.

Chapter Seventeen

Gemma

Tom was simply magnificent.

I don't even know exactly what happened, because the whole thing is still a bit of a blur. I just remember seeing the man... the man who snatched my bag, and feeling as though my legs were going to give way. My heart was beating fast, and my palms were sweating, and even though Dad clearly noticed something was wrong, I couldn't put words to my fear, because it had swallowed them down... whole.

I pointed, but couldn't get him to understand what I was pointing at. I could hear him talking, but I couldn't get him to see that conversation was beyond me.

That was when I saw him. I saw Tom, running past. Our eyes met, and he called out, "Is that him?" and I knew he understood. He understood completely.

I said, "Yes," with a nod of my head, and he carried on, sprinting around the corner of Bell Road, making my breath catch in my throat, because if a car had been coming down the hill, it would have run him over. He seemed oblivious, though, and as Dad finally seemed to understand, and he and I followed, we caught sight of Tom tackling the robber to the ground.

It was like something out of a film. Except it wasn't. It was real… and it was happening right here in Porthgarrion.

The man struggled and I winced as he punched Tom in the side. Not that he seemed to notice. He just turned the man over onto his front and pinned him to the pavement before handcuffing his wrists together.

A small crowd of locals and holidaymakers had gathered around us by that stage, and as Tom pulled to man to his feet, he seemed to notice his audience. I saw him blush slightly, even as he held on to the man, who was still trying to break free, and then his eyes fixed on mine, just for a second. I smiled, partly because I was grateful to him, but also because I needed to know we were okay. He didn't smile back, though, and I struggled not to cry as he looked away, turning his gaze on Dad instead.

I think I heard them talking about what Tom was going to do with the robber… about the fact that he was going to take him back to the police station. Dad said something about them only having one cell, which I thought was very sarcastic of him. Tom had just captured the man, single-handed, and had possibly been injured himself, and I wanted to tell Dad not to be so petty. How was I going to do that, though, without giving myself away to him?

So I stood in silence and watched as Tom led the man away, listening as the people around me congratulated him, and wishing he'd look my way and give me a crumb of hope. He didn't. He just kept on walking… at least until Dad called him back and praised him. That surprised me, given Dad's earlier comments, and I could tell by the look on his face that Tom was shocked, too. He still didn't look in my direction, though. He acted like I didn't exist, and before I could swallow my pride and go to him, Dad pulled me away, reminding me that our fish and chips would get cold. Did he think that mattered when my life was falling apart... when I was walking away from the man I love, having denied him... yet again?

Dear God... what's wrong with me?

As if it isn't bad enough that I lied in the first place... as if it isn't unforgivable that I've deceived Tom about who I am and what my father is in his life... I've compounded all of that by pretending to my father that our relationship doesn't exist, in front of Tom. And I've done that twice now. I did it earlier today, when Dad came to Rachel's after I was assaulted, and I looked at Tom and begged him with my eyes not to give me away... and now I've just done it again. I could have taken my chances – either of them – and told Dad about Tom. So why didn't I?

I wish I knew...

We got home, and I nibbled at the fish and chips Dad had bought, using shock and tiredness as an excuse for my lack of appetite... because it seems I'm no good with the truth. Fortunately, Dad had decided we'd eat in the living room, on our laps, so he'd put the television on and that provided a distraction from conversation. Somehow, I don't think he wanted to talk about Tom any more than I did, although our reasoning was very different. I don't think he wanted to admit he'd been wrong about the man he'd been casting aspersions on for the last few weeks. So, we watched a movie instead, and then I went to bed.

It was only when I was lying by myself, in my room, staring out of the window at the clear night sky, that I tried calling Tom again. It wasn't late... only about nine-thirty or a quarter to ten. I didn't think he'd be in bed yet, and while he hadn't returned my earlier call, I was getting a little desperate. The thought that I'd destroyed our happiness was eating away at me, and my hands shook as I clicked on his name and waited for the call to connect.

Except it didn't. It went straight to his voicemail. And I knew then that he didn't want to talk to me. I wanted to talk to him though, so I swallowed hard, and said, "Hello… it's me." I didn't bother saying my name that time, hoping he'd know it was me. "You've obviously turned your phone off, and I'm guessing that means you don't want to talk to me. I—I'm sorry, Tom. I'm sorry I've hurt you and I'm sorry I lied to you. If I could turn the clock back, I would, but I can't. I—I don't know what else to say to you…" I genuinely didn't, so I just hung up and let my tears fall.

I couldn't blame him for not wanting to speak to me. It was perfectly understandable. I'd lied to him… as well as to my father. I just wished Tom would give me the chance to explain, because his silence was too enormous to contemplate.

I don't know how, but I fell asleep eventually. That probably was the shock and tiredness, not to mention the silent tears I cried for a while, until sleep claimed me.

I kept my phone clutched in my hand though, on the off-chance that I'd misinterpreted Tom's silence. I clung to the hope that he might not be too hurt or angry to speak, that he might not have turned his phone off at all. Maybe the battery had died, or he'd been talking to his mother when I called. It was possible…

Except it wasn't, of course. Or at least they weren't the reasons he didn't call me. Because my phone was still in my hand when I woke up yesterday morning, feeling despondent that I still hadn't heard a word from him.

Lying in bed in the cold light of day and thinking about all the things we'd never done together – like waking up in the same bed – the reality of what I'd done hit me harder than ever, and I placed another call to him.

This time, it rang, and I allowed myself to hope, my heart beating hard in my chest, until the woman's voice sounded in my ear, telling me Tom wasn't available.

I thought about hanging up and not bothering to leave a message, but I didn't want him to think I didn't care, so I whispered, "It's me. Again. Please talk to me. Please, Tom." I felt my voice break and hung up, wondering if I was being desperate, needy, clinging... whether I should just leave him to come round in his own time. Then I realised he might not want to come round... ever... and I buried my head in the pillow and cried.

"Is everything all right, Gem?" My dad's voice and the sound of him knocking on the door made me jump and I sat up, wiping my cheeks with the back of my hand and trying not to sniff too loudly.

"Yes," I said through my tears, clearing my throat to make my voice sound as normal as possible.

"Good." I could hear him smiling, even though I couldn't see him. "I'm just going for a shower, but I was wondering how you'd feel about having brunch at the café this morning."

I let out a sigh, because I'd rather have just stayed shut up in my room, hiding away from life and my own mistakes. But Dad was making an effort, so I had to as well... otherwise it was only going to arouse his suspicions.

"If you like." I did my best to sound enthusiastic.

"Excellent. I won't be long in the bathroom, and then you can go through and we can be out by about ten?" He phrased his statement like a question, but I knew he was telling me he wanted to be out by ten... and it wasn't really an option.

"Okay, Dad."

I heard his footsteps move away from the door and relaxed back onto my pillows, glancing down at my phone, which was still mocking me with its blank screen, and while I kept wishing it would ring, and I'd see Tom's name on the screen, I also wondered how it was possible for someone I'd known for such a comparatively short time, to leave such a huge void in my life.

Our Sunday wasn't too bad in the end… as long as I ignored the fear that crept over me every time I thought about Tom, and the fact that I hadn't heard from him.

Brunch at the café was nice, and Dad spent most of his time speculating about Carter Edwards, the man who owns it, and about whom he seems unable to glean any information. He's lived in the village for years, since just a few months after my mother left, and while he's friendly enough, he keeps himself to himself. No-one seems to know where he came from, and he doesn't even have much of an accent to give anything away. As far as I know, there's never been anyone in his life… certainly not since he's lived here, because nothing escapes the village gossips. Although even as I was thinking that, while watching him clear the table beside ours, it occurred to me that Tom and I kept our relationship quiet for weeks. Dad was none the wiser, was he? And he lives with me, and works with Tom… so who knows what's going on with Carter.

After we'd finished our brunch, we went for a walk along the harbour, and I veered between hope that we'd run into Tom, and fear about what I'd do if we did. Of course, meeting him would have left me with the same quandary I'd had on Saturday… namely, how to tell my father about us, and that I need to talk to Tom before I do. In the end, of course, it didn't matter, because we didn't see him.

Instead, we went back home, and after Dad had changed the dressing on my hand, which was looking a lot better, I buried myself in a book. I hoped that might provide a suitable distraction, and it did for a while. Dad spent the afternoon in the garden, tidying up, and then came in and made us a roast dinner.

It was while he was peeling the potatoes that I took my chance and went upstairs to the bathroom, where I connected a call to Tom again, sitting on the edge of the bath while it rang…

and rang… and rang. And finally, I heard the familiar computerised tones of the woman's voice again, telling me to leave a message. So I did, my tears falling, even as I spoke.

"Please, Tom. What do I have to do? I've said I'm sorry, and I am. I've begged, and I've pleaded, but I'll do it all again." I sucked in a breath. "Please… just let me explain. That's all I'm asking." Tears dripped onto my cheeks and I sniffled, wiping them away with my fingers. "I hate this. I hate not seeing you… not being with you. Even if you can't forgive me, can you just tell me that? Because the silence is killing me."

I lowered the phone and let my finger hover over the red button, wondering whether to end the call, or add 'I love you'. I ended the call. What was the point in telling him I love him when he wouldn't even acknowledge my existence?

I cried myself to sleep again last night. I still hadn't heard from Tom and that meant one of two things… either he'd listened to my messages and didn't want to speak to me. Or he hadn't listened to my messages, because he knew it was me who'd left them, and didn't want to hear what I have to say. Either way, his silence was deafening… and it hurt.

"What are you doing out of bed so early?" Dad looks up as I walk into the kitchen and my breath catches in my throat as I look at his uniform. I see him in uniform every single day, but today it means so much more, because I know he's going to be seeing Tom… the man who doesn't care about me anymore.

"I'm going to work." I move forward into the room and make my way over to the kettle.

"Why?" I can hear the disbelief in his voice, even though I've got my back to him. "I'm sure Imelda won't have a problem with you taking a few days off."

"Probably not. But I can't sit around here feeling sorry for myself." I need to keep busy. I need something to do… or I'm going to go mad.

"Are you even sure you can work?" he says, and I hear his chair scrape against the floor as he stands. He comes over, leaning against the work surface beside me. "Your hand is still quite sore, and I've seen the way you're nursing that elbow."

"I can deal with a few flowers," I say, putting some coffee into a cup.

"It's not a matter of dealing with a few flowers though, is it?" He leans closer. "You usually have a delivery on a Monday, don't you?"

"Yes. Which is why I have to go in."

"Maybe… maybe not. It's Imelda's business, not yours. It's not really your problem. Besides, I have a vague idea of what you get up to, and I know that delivery days are hard work."

"Which I'll manage."

He huffs, because he knows when he's beaten. At least sometimes. "All right. But I want your promise that you'll come home if it gets too much for you. Imelda will understand."

"I know she will, but I'm sure I'll be fine."

He pushes himself off the work surface, although I can feel his disappointment. I'm not going to rise to it though, because I don't want to give him the chance to talk me out of going into work.

Fortunately, Dad has to leave, and although he takes his time over it, he eventually makes it out of the door. He stops on the threshold though, letting the breeze blow through the house and looks back at me as I stand in the doorway to the kitchen.

"You are all right, aren't you, Gemma?" he says, with a deep concern in his voice.

"Yes. I'm fine."

He frowns and stares at me for a moment, and then, with a slight shake of his head, he steps outside and closes the door behind him, which gives me half an hour to myself, to finish my coffee and get ready for work. I can't be bothered with breakfast, but I remember to get some sausages out of the freezer for dinner, swallowing down the lump in my throat as I do, because even as I try to decide whether to have mashed potatoes or chips with them, I can't help but remember that most of my evenings over the last few weeks have revolved around Tom… and not the mundanities of dinner at home with my dad.

Still, I suppose that's all over now…

It might be breezy, but it's actually quite warm, so I don't bother with a jacket and just pull a cardigan on over my blouse, before I grab my handbag and head off for work. I try very hard to capture that feeling of gratitude that I used to have, just because I live in such a wonderful place, but it seems to have abandoned me, and all I can feel is a sense of desolation, like a dark cloud descending over me, even though it's a beautiful sunny day.

I really need to pull myself together, to acknowledge that whatever I had with Tom is over… and that I've got no-one to blame but myself.

It's just that I'm not ready yet.

I need some time to lick my wounds, and to feel sorry for myself, even if it was my fault it ended the way it did.

I let myself into the shop and glance around, trying very hard not to remember that this was the place where I first saw him, where he first asked me out… and where it first became clear to me he works with my father, and that I should have told him the truth then, when I had the chance. If I had, none of this would have happened.

"Gemma? Is that you?"

I hear Imelda's voice from upstairs and move further into the shop, hanging my bag on the hook behind the counter and stepping over to the stairs, looking up them.

"Yes, it's me."

"What on earth are you doing here?"

I can't see her, but it's clear that she's in the living room, from the direction of her voice, and I slowly climb up the stairs, going straight in to her.

She's sitting up on the sofa, with her feet on the floor, as though she'd been about to get up.

"Stay where you are," I say and she looks up at me.

"I didn't expect you to come in today." She glances at my bandaged hand, her face a picture of concern and pity. "Are you all right?"

"I'm fine. I couldn't sit at home… and there's the delivery to deal with. Anyway, I'm not that badly injured. It's just a cut, that's all."

"And that's all that's wrong?"

"Well… no, I've got a bruised elbow, and my leg hurts a bit, but…"

She shakes her head. "You should be at home, resting," she says, narrowing her eyes at me.

"I—I can't." My voice catches, and without warning, I burst into tears.

"Oh, my dear." She moves down the sofa a little, and pats the space beside her. "Come and sit." I obey, crossing the room, and sitting down, my whole body shaking as I sob, and sob. "Is this about Tom?" she asks, and I look up at her, startled.

"Yes, but how…?"

She smiles, which in itself stops me from talking, and she takes advantage and hands me a tissue to dry my tears. "He came to see me on Saturday afternoon," she says, and I remember asking my dad to ask Tom to call on Imelda and let her know what had happened.

"Oh, yes…"

"He told me you'd been injured, and that it had all come to light, about your father being his boss."

"It was awful," I wail, a fresh wave of tears washing over me.

"I'm sure it was," she says calmly. "But if you'd told him the truth in the first place, it wouldn't have had to be, would it?"

I shake my head, because as much as I don't need her wisdom after the event, I can't deny the truth of what she's saying.

"Did he say anything else?" I ask, between sniffles, as she hands me another tissue and I wipe my eyes.

"He made it very clear that he's hurt." My heart constricts in my chest. "He's angry too."

"Did he say that?"

"He didn't need to. It was obvious."

"He must hate me."

"No. He doesn't hate you." There's such a certainty to her voice, I have to look up at her.

"How do you know?"

"Because if he hated you, he wouldn't care about what you'd done," she says, shrugging her shoulders. "And he cares."

"In that case, why hasn't he returned my calls?"

"I imagine, because he's been doing what he said he'd be doing…"

"What's that?" I ask, leaning forward, urgency marking my intrigue.

"Thinking."

"Thinking?" What does that mean?

"Yes. I told him not to make any hasty decisions about you, and he said he wasn't going to. He said he wasn't ready to make decisions yet. He was still thinking."

"I wish he was talking, rather than thinking." I need to hear his voice. Regardless of everything Imelda has said, I need to hear it from him, not her.

"You need to give him time," she says. "Look at it from his point of view. It's bad enough that you didn't tell him the truth about who you are, but finding out the way he did... it was a tremendous shock for him."

"I don't suppose it helped that I didn't come clean, even then," I say, unable to raise my voice above an embarrassed whisper.

"No, it probably didn't. But he struck me as a good man, Gemma. Be patient. Allow for the fact that you've hurt him and let him work it out for himself."

I nod my head slowly, feeling the weight of guilt hanging heavily on my shoulders as I get to my feet.

"You should take things easy today," Imelda says, with a warning note to her voice. "Just get the driver to stack the new flowers in the preparation room. You don't have to unpack them today."

"I'll do what I can," I say, and she frowns. "I—I need to keep busy."

Her frown fades, and she nods her head. "I understand," she whispers, with a half smile, and before I start crying again, I go back down the stairs.

I spend the morning thinking about what Imelda said, trying not to read too much into it, even though she seems so sure that Tom doesn't hate me, that it isn't over, and that I just need to give him time. Because if that's the case, then I'll do it. He can have as long as he needs. I owe him that much. I just wish he'd tell me himself that there's a chance for us, rather than leaving me wondering... in silence.

I suppose it must be about half-past eleven, and I'm tying up a bouquet for a telephone order. It's a bit of a struggle with my bandaged hand, and I'm just thinking about taking a break from it and making a cup of coffee, when I feel my skin prickle, and look up to see Tom striding past the shop.

He looks as gorgeous as ever, but he doesn't even glance in my direction, keeping his eyes fixed ahead and although I feel my shoulders drop in defeat, there's a part of me that simply won't let go, not after the conversation I had with Imelda this morning.

I drop the flowers and run to the front door, yanking it open and stepping out onto the pavement.

"Tom!" I shout his name, but he doesn't stop. He doesn't even break his stride. He keeps on walking. "Tom!" I call again, a little louder. He ignores me again, and I wonder whether Imelda was making things up, whether she was trying to be kind... giving me hope where there is none.

I'm about to step back into the shop when Rachel comes out of the baker's and Tom stops. He turns and looks down at her, and they talk. She steps closer to him, smiling as she speaks and he smiles back. I feel a strange, stabbing pain in my chest, which hurts so much, I can't stand there anymore. I can't watch him being him, knowing I'll never be me again.

As the first tear hits my cheek, I go back inside the shop and turn the sign to 'closed', because I don't want anyone to come in and see me crying.

He might have told Imelda he was thinking, but he's obviously not thinking about me anymore.

Chapter Eighteen

Tom

"Tom!"

I hear Gemma calling out my name for the second time, and I'm so tempted to stop. I'm so tempted to turn around and go to her, even if only to shout at her for messing around with other people's feelings. Except I can't. I know that if I turn around and go to her, I won't shout at her. I'll take her in my arms and kiss her, because I miss her so much, it hurts.

I think missing her hurts more than her lies… or her absence of truth.

That hasn't helped with the whole thinking process I told Imelda I was going through. It's just confused me even more. Wanting her, needing her, loving her… they're not conducive to thinking straight… and I need to think straight.

I've been trying to do just that all weekend, and I've been failing dismally.

I think the problem was that, when I got home on Saturday evening, even though I was still feeling hurt and angry and confused by Gemma's multiple betrayals, I made the mistake of replaying her message… the one she'd sent me earlier in the day, when she'd said she thought I must hate her. I sat on the sofa, with my phone in my hand, listening to her voice, and I tried to envisage the concept of hating her. It was impossible, of course, because I love her.

Knowing that, and feeling that didn't help very much… not when it came to the hurt and anger and confusion. It just amplified everything.

So I opened a bottle of wine, and drank it, while I replayed Gemma's message, over and over. I needed to hear her voice, not her words. After a while, though, as the wine turned my brain and everything around me into a haze, I switched my phone off. Hearing Gemma's voice had become too hard, and I needed to avoid the temptation of continually listening to her… besides, I was in danger of opening a second bottle.

So instead, I took myself off to bed, and woke up yesterday morning, feeling a bit the worse for wear. I wasn't exactly hungover, just fragile. I stumbled down the stairs and made myself a pot of coffee, which I sat at the table and drank, before I remembered my phone was still lying on the sofa and was still turned off.

Switching it back on, I discovered a text message from my mother, asking if I wanted to visit her for lunch next weekend, and a missed call… from Gemma, timed at just before ten o'clock the previous night. There was also a voicemail, which I assumed would be from her too, and I sat down before I let it play.

"Hello… it's me." I heard the hesitation in her voice and wondered whether she'd thought twice about giving her name again. "You've obviously turned your phone off, and I'm guessing that means you don't want to talk to me." That wasn't the reason I'd turned my phone off, but I couldn't deny she was right. I didn't want to talk to her. Not yet. "I—I'm sorry, Tom," she continued, stuttering through her emotions. "I'm sorry I've hurt you and I'm sorry I lied to you. If I could turn the clock back, I would, but I can't. I—I don't know what else to say to you…"

I heard her sob, and then the female voice asked me if I wanted to save or delete the message. That was when I realised Gemma had stopped talking, mid-sentence. I selected 'save', although I wasn't sure why, and then put the phone on charge in the kitchen before I went upstairs and put on a pair of shorts and a t-shirt. I've found in the past that a good way of thinking things through is to work out, and that was what I intended doing. So I made my way down to the garage, via the back garden, and I did just that.

I spent the entire morning down there, until I was hot and tired and no further forward, because thinking about Gemma and our relationship just sent me round in never-ending circles. In the end, it was exhaustion that got the better of me and just before lunch, I returned to the house and dragged my body up the stairs to shower.

I felt slightly more human once I was dressed, and I managed to eat something for lunch, but I still couldn't think straight, and was thrown into turmoil when my phone rang, just as I was pouring myself a cup of tea, in the middle of the afternoon. Checking the screen, I saw the word 'Mum', and then remembered her message from that morning, and wanted to kick myself for not replying to her. A simple text message would have sufficed, and would have avoided the need for conversation. I could have ignored her – obviously – but that's never worked for me in the past, so I unplugged my phone from the charger, pressed the green button and connected the call.

"Hi, Mum." I tried to sound as cheerful as possible.

"Hello." She sounded concerned. "Is everything all right?"

"Yes. Sorry I didn't reply to your message. I overslept and then my phone died." I felt bad for lying to her, but it was only a white lie. If I'd told her the truth, I'd never have heard the last of it.

"Oh, I see. I just wanted to check about next weekend, because I haven't seen you for a couple of weeks, and I wasn't sure if you were planning on coming for a visit. It doesn't matter if you're busy, it's just..." She hesitated in the middle of her lengthy and somewhat garbled explanation, and if I hadn't known better, I'd have sworn she was embarrassed.

"It's just what?"

"If you must know, I've met someone."

"As in, a man?"

"Yes. His name's Neil and it's very early days. We only met just over a week ago, but we've been seeing quite a lot of each other and he wants to take me out to lunch on Sunday. I didn't want to say yes to him if you had plans to come over here."

"Well, I didn't." Although I felt guilty, then, that I hadn't been to see her since the weekend Gemma and I first got together. I also felt uncomfortable. She was telling me about her relationship and yet she knew nothing about mine. It wasn't that I was keeping secrets. I just hadn't had time to talk to Mum, and I'd wanted to take Gemma there so I could introduce them to each other. Of course, I'd seen that as a way of getting Gemma to let me meet her father, too... before I realised I'd already met him. "I could come over the weekend after," I said, choosing not to mention Gemma for the time being. I didn't feel like explaining how much of a mess everything was... or why.

"Okay." She sounded brighter, and I wondered if that was because she'd be able to have lunch with Neil, or whether she was looking forward to seeing me soon... or possibly both.

"What's he like?" I asked. I felt intrigued that she'd finally decided to dip her toe in the water again, after so long.

"He's very nice. Don't laugh, but he's a retired police officer."

"Dear God. What rank was he? Am I going to have to salute every time he comes into the room?" I wondered if I was destined to be surrounded by superior officers at every turn.

"He was a detective inspector. But you don't have to worry. He's not at all stuffy. He's good fun."

"I'm not sure I want to know any more, Mum." I shook my head, even though she couldn't see me. There are limits to what a son needs to hear about his mother.

"No, you probably don't," she said, with an air of mystery to her voice, and I smiled to myself.

"I'll call you about coming down to see you," I said, still wondering about whether I'd be able to introduce Gemma to my mother by then, or whether we'd even be talking again.

We ended our call, and I was about to put the phone down when I noticed another voicemail. I checked my missed calls and saw that there had been one from Gemma, while I'd been working out, timed at eight-thirty, and I held the phone to my ear as I listened to her saying, "It's me. Again. Please talk to me. Please, Tom."

That was it. That was all she said. She sounded desperate though, and that cut through me. I leant back against the work surface, trying to decide whether to call her back… or, better still, go round there. Almost at once, I wished I hadn't even contemplated that last idea, because I still didn't know if she'd told her father about us, so me turning up on the doorstep and asking to discuss our relationship with her was likely to end in disaster. Therein lay the problem, really, didn't it? The thing I knew, deep down, was holding me back. I still didn't know where I stood. I had no idea who knew what, or why any of it had happened in the first place… and just thinking that was enough to make me put my phone back down, and take my tea into the living room, where I sat and read a book for a few hours.

I guess it was around six o'clock when my stomach growled and I realised I was hungry. I put the book down, wondering what to eat, just as my phone rang again. A sixth sense told me it would be Gemma, although I still got up and went to the kitchen, to see for myself, and I stared at her name on the screen, my finger poised over the green button as it stopped ringing. I knew I could have made it if I'd wanted to. I could have run, or I could have kept the phone beside me... and that told me everything I needed to know.

I still wasn't ready to talk.

The beeping told me she had more to say to me though, so I listened...

"Please, Tom. What do I have to do?" She was actually crying this time. "I've said I'm sorry, and I am." That much was true. She'd apologised over and over. "I've begged, and I've pleaded, but I'll do it all again." I heard a stuttering breath. "Please... just let me explain. That's all I'm asking." There was a pause, during which she sniffed and then took a breath. "I hate this. I hate not seeing you... not being with you. Even if you can't forgive me, can you just tell me that? Because the silence is killing me."

My heart ached for her. It ached for us. She didn't seem to understand, though... she still doesn't. We were in love... at least we were supposed to be. I'm in love with her, without a doubt, and she told me she was in love with me, even if she told her father we're not serious. On Friday night, we made love for the first time, and it was momentous. It was magical. Then yesterday, I discovered she'd been lying to me all along. It's a lot to take in. And while I know we need to talk – and we will – I'm not ready yet. She might think the silence is killing her, but her deceit is doing exactly the same thing to me.

Only none of this is of my making.

That's why, when I walked past the flower shop just now, I didn't glance inside, even though I was desperate for a glimpse of her. It's also why, when she calls my name – twice – I don't turn around.

I want her back, more than anything. Not being with her hurts me, too. But if we're going to have a chance, then I need for my head to be in the right place, before I talk to her. My heart already is. I've never stopped loving her and I never will. It's just that my head's got some catching up to do… otherwise, when I'm done kissing her, I might still yell at her for messing with other people's feelings. And I don't ever want to yell at her.

I keep walking, trying to pretend I didn't hear her, and as I'm making my way past the baker's, Rachel comes out through the door and stops me.

"Everyone's talking about you," she says with a smile.

"They are?"

"Yes." She nods her head, coming a little closer. "We'll have to get you fitted with a cape, so you can look the part of a superhero."

I shake my head, smiling slightly. "I'm not a superhero."

"Try telling that to the locals. I've heard all about your exploits, catching the robber on Saturday evening."

"I was just doing my job," I say, and she smiles again.

"Well, I very much doubt Geoff Carew could have caught up with the man and tackled him like that."

I can't help laughing at the suggestion and she giggles too, and I'm about to move on when a thought occurs, and I turn back.

"Do you remember me talking to you on Saturday afternoon, about Gemma and me?"

"Yes." She frowns slightly.

"Do you think you could forget I ever said anything?"

Her frown disappears and her lips twitch upwards. "Why? Have the two of you worked it all out then?"

"No. But I don't want anyone to think badly of her for not telling the truth… you included."

She tilts her head slightly. "I told Gemma you were a keeper," she says, and then sighs. "And I didn't think badly of her. She made a mistake, that's all." I wish it were that simple. "Do you think you'll be able to work things out?"

"To be honest, I don't know yet. But I hope so." I step away. "I just wanted to ask if you could forget my little outburst."

"What little outburst?" she says, grinning, and I smile back at her before I move on.

As I turn the corner into Church Lane, on my way back to the station, I can't help thinking how ironic it is that while one part of my life is in pieces, the other part – namely my job – is actually working out.

"Where is everyone?" I say to Geoff as I go through the door beside the counter, in to a deserted office.

"Justin's taking an early lunch break," he replies. "And the sergeant has gone with Kenneth to check out the bag snatcher's home address."

"He actually admitted to having one, did he?" I ask. "He wasn't exactly forthcoming with personal details on Saturday evening."

Geoff shrugs. "He gave an address. Whether it turns out to be legitimate, I suppose only time will tell."

It clearly doesn't take that much time, and before long, Sergeant Quick comes in through the front entrance, carrying a large box, followed by Kenneth, who's weighed down by two heavy-looking bags… one in each hand.

"Open the door, will you?" Quick says to Geoff, who obliges, and I get to my feet as well.

"Looks like you struck gold," Geoff says, as I clear some space and Quick deposits his box on my desk.

"Judging from the number of bags we found, I'd say chummy in there has been up to his tricks for a lot longer than we thought. We've found enough evidence to pass the whole thing over to CID… all nicely wrapped up." Quick smiles, and I get the impression that he'd have been a lot less satisfied if he'd had to hand over the suspect without the evidence to back up the arrest. I can't say I blame him for that. I'd feel the same.

"Are we going to just pass it over, or catalogue it first?" I ask, and he turns to me.

"Catalogue it first," he says, but without his usual sarcastic tone, which makes a pleasant change. He takes a deep breath and stretches his back. "The thing is, we don't have long. I've arranged to transfer the prisoner at five o'clock." We all glance at the clock and see that it's already half-past twelve.

"Well, if we work together…" Geoff says, not bothering to finish his sentence, because it really isn't necessary, and while Kenneth puts the kettle on, the rest of us set about unloading the individual evidence bags and laying their contents out on the desks, and then on the floor, when we run out of space.

We have to work hard and meticulously, because not only do the handbags themselves have to be described and documented, but so does everything that's inside them, so when Justin gets back from lunch, we leave Geoff at the front desk and divide into two teams, one person on each writing up the notes, while the other goes through the bags.

We've found addresses inside the bags, in the form of driver's licenses and letters, suggesting our robber has been operating in several local villages, not just Porthgarrion, which makes sense of the quantity of bags we're having to wade through. I'm working with the sergeant, much to my surprise. I'd half expected him to avoid having too much to do with me, but he seemed quite keen. When we're about halfway through our pile of evidence bags, he chuckles to himself, and holds up the next one. I look up from my notes, recognising Gemma's handbag, as he opens it.

"I'm not sure I should be doing this," the sergeant says, even though it's obvious he's got no intention of letting anyone else go through his daughter's belongings.

No-one answers, and slowly but surely, he rifles through her things, describing them for me to note down. It's quite a small bag, and because it was only taken recently, it still contains everything I imagine it always did. We can't return it to her yet though, because it will have to be retained as evidence for the time being.

We finish with ten minutes to spare and get everything bagged up again just before the two CID officers arrive from St Austell to take away our prisoner.

Sergeant Quick deals with them and the required paperwork, and the rest of us heave a sigh of relief while Geoff makes a well-earned cup of tea.

When the sergeant comes back in, he looks over at Geoff, and then at me.

"I was going to suggest that we go out for a drink," he says, surprising me. "You've done well, Hughes, and I think it would be good to clear the air, don't you?"

"Yes, sir." Ordinarily, I'd be thrilled at him finally accepting me, but as it is, I can't think of anything I want to do less than have a drink with Gemma's father. He's got no idea who I am in her life, so we'd hardly be clearing the air, would we? I'd be keeping Gemma's secret from him, and if he ever found out, I can't imagine he'd be best pleased. What can I say, though?

"The thing is," he says, sounding doubtful now, "Gemma's still not quite herself, and she insisted on going into work today… against my better judgement, I might add." Those final few words are said with a definite warning, even though she's not here, and I wonder for a moment what the atmosphere must have been like in their house this morning.

"You should probably get home to her then, sir," I say, trying my best not to sound relieved.

"You don't mind?" I can't believe the change in the man, but I shake my head, anyway.

"Not in the slightest."

"Maybe we can catch up at the end of the week?" he says, surprising me still further by persevering with his invitation.

"Yes, sir."

He smiles and goes into his office and I wonder why I didn't take the chance to ask to see him privately… to tell him who I am. To tell him I'm his daughter's 'not serious' boyfriend. If I can even call myself her boyfriend now.

I know why I didn't though, and it has nothing to do with my job, or with my newfound status at the station, as something of a hero in Sergeant Quick's eyes. It's that I feel Gemma should be the one to tell him. He's her father, after all.

If I told the sergeant who I am, not only would it be bound to cause problems here at work, but it might also cause problems for Gemma. I know nothing of their relationship, but I imagine he'd be very disappointed to hear the news from a third party… especially from the man who, just a few days ago, shared a bed with his daughter.

So, I say nothing, and I do nothing. And when the time comes, we all make our way home.

I take the walk slowly, wondering how I'm going to react if I see Gemma. She'll probably be closing up the shop by now, unless she's got some late customers. Obviously, I ignored her earlier, but will I be able to do the same thing again tonight? I'm not sure. It's hard to say when I miss her so much. I wouldn't have believed it was possible to miss someone as much as I miss Gemma, especially not when she's only been in my life for such a short time, but it feels as though a part of me is missing... and it's the part that matters the most.

The problem is, all the while her father knows nothing about us – which I'm absolutely certain he doesn't – I'm not sure I can talk to her. The deceit is still ongoing, and it feels too much for me. She has to own up to how she feels about me.

It's all or nothing.

Although the thought of 'nothing' is terrifying.

I suck in a breath, steeling myself for facing her, for how I'll react, but as I walk past the window, I notice the shop is already in darkness.

She's gone home.

I've still got no idea where I stand.

My only saving grace is that I won't have to face either of them tomorrow, because I've got the day off.

My kitchen cupboard and garden furniture are being delivered, and once that had been confirmed, I arranged with the sergeant to take the time off. When I made the request, he was less than impressed and let me know in no uncertain terms that I should have arranged the delivery for a day when I wasn't rostered on to work. Now I'm a hero, he seems less bothered and even told me to have a good day when we were leaving the station.

I let myself into my house, wishing I could look forward to Gemma coming over for dinner.

Except I don't feel like I can look forward to anything. Not while we're living in this no-man's-land of uncertainty. I could phone her, I suppose. I could ask her to come round… have it out with her. But what would she tell her father? Would she lie about where she was going? Would she tell him she was going to see her 'not serious' boyfriend?

I shake my head, that feeling of despondency overshadowing me again.

Why the hell did she have to lie?

I throw my keys and phone onto the sofa and make my way upstairs, where I undress and go through to the bathroom, taking a shower… and taking my time over it. I'm not hungry, and I know if I go downstairs, I'll only open another bottle of wine… and I'm not sure that's a good idea.

Eventually, boredom gets the better of me, and I climb out of the shower, wrapping a towel around my hips, and I pad out into the bedroom and down the stairs, not bothering to get dressed. I've got a couple of ready meals in the fridge and I pull one out and microwave it. Then, pushing my phone and keys to one side, I sit on the sofa, eating but not tasting anything. I turn on the television and watch a movie, not seeing it at all.

As much as I don't understand Gemma, or what she's done, and as much as I'm still confused, hurt and angry… without her, nothing works. It's all broken… and so am I.

Chapter Nineteen

Gemma

In the end, by about twenty past five, I'm exhausted, and although I don't want to admit defeat, I really have to, and I call up the stairs to Imelda that I'm going to lock up the shop and go home.

"Are you all right?" she calls back down.

"I'm just tired." I don't want her to fuss. After all, I'm only closing forty minutes early, and she doesn't need to make a big deal out of it.

"Then get some rest," she says. "And if you're still tired tomorrow, don't come in. It won't hurt for the shop to be closed for a day or two."

"I'll see how I feel."

I won't. I'll do my level best to make it in. Not because I'm worried about the shop being closed, but because I need the distraction of coming here. Obviously, being here means I'm more likely to see Tom, like I did this morning. I haven't forgotten how it felt when he ignored me, or the pain in my chest when I saw him talking to Rachel, but it's better than sitting at home, wondering if I'll ever hear from him again… if I'll ever be happy again.

I close up the shop and grab my bag, calling out, "Goodnight," to Imelda as I leave. She reiterates that I shouldn't come in tomorrow, unless I'm feeling better, and then I lock up and slowly head for home, my leg aching almost as much as my heart.

It's windy, and not as warm as it was this morning, and by the time I get home, I'm absolutely freezing. So, after I've let myself into the house and hooked up my bag, I go upstairs and run a hot bath, soaking in it for a while, before I climb out and put on some long pyjamas and thick socks. For a moment or two, I contemplate my dressing gown, but acknowledge that's a bit too much, and then come back downstairs, going through to the living room. I'm going to leave Dad to make the dinner when he gets in. I really am that tired.

Before I sit, though, I go back out into the hallway and grab my phone from my bag, checking to see whether I've got any messages. I know I won't have, and as I come back into the living room and flop down on the couch, I let out a sigh. Why hasn't he returned a single call? Does he hate me that much? Can love turn to hate that fast?

Instinctively, I connect a call to him, even though I'm already crying, and I wait while it rings until his voicemail tells me to leave a message. I can't though, because I can't get any words out through my tears, and after a few seconds, I hang up, just as I hear the key turning in the lock.

"Gemma?" Dad calls, and I sit up, searching the room for tissues… except there aren't any. "Are you home?"

"I—In here," I mumble.

He appears in the doorway and looks down at me.

"What's wrong?" He comes straight over, crouching down beside me, and I know I'm going to have to tell him.

"Everything."

"That's a bit broad, Gemma. Can you narrow it down for me? Are you in pain?"

"Not the kind of pain you mean, no."

He frowns and joins me on the sofa, both of us sitting back.

"I'm too old to crouch down like that," he says, although we both know that's not true. "Now, tell me what's wrong?"

"I've made such a mess of everything," I say, my tears falling again.

He reaches out and takes my hands in his. "Gem, you've got to be a bit more precise than that. What exactly is it you've messed up?"

"Everything. I've hurt him, and now he won't talk to me."

"Hurt who?" He shakes his head, frowning in confusion.

"Tom."

He leans back. "Tom? Tom who?"

"Tom Hughes."

There's a moment's silence and then he says, "You mean the same Tom Hughes who works with me?" I nod my head.

"Yes. He's the man I've been seeing for the last few weeks."

Dad stands now, staring down at me, his brow furrowed, as he folds his arms across his chest.

"Are you telling me he's been seeing you behind my back all this time? He's been lying to me?"

"No." I sit up, edging forward on the sofa again. "It's not like that. It's not Tom's fault, Dad."

He huffs, moving around the other side of the coffee table, his head shaking. "Wait a minute... you said you weren't serious about the man you were seeing. If that's the case, why are you sitting here crying, worrying about the fact that he won't talk to you?"

"Because I lied about that. I was serious about him. I am serious..."

"And when you said he wasn't your type?"

"That was a lie, too. I love him, Dad."

He stands completely still and then pushes his fingers back through his hair. "And what about him? Is he stringing you along?"

"No. Will you please stop seeing the worst in him? He says he loves me too… or at least he did, before I hurt him."

Dad pauses for a moment, as though he's thinking, and then lets out a sigh, before he comes back over and sits beside me again. "How exactly did you do that?" he says, his voice much calmer and softer now.

"Because I didn't tell him the truth about you… any more than I told you the truth about him. He explained right at the very beginning exactly who he is, and what he does… and that he works with you."

"Right… so, why didn't you just admit to being my daughter?" he asks, frowning again and looking down at me.

"Because I didn't want there being any issues between us. You'd already said you expected him to fail, and you clearly had such a negative attitude towards him, I thought the very last thing you'd want to hear was that I was going out with him. Tom would never have agreed to keeping our relationship a secret from you, so that made it impossible for me to tell him who you are to me. Don't you see?"

"Not really. My attitude to Tom – negative or otherwise – was to do with work. I'm still unclear why you decided it was better to keep us both in the dark about something personal."

"It wasn't a long-term plan. It wasn't really a plan at all. I was going to tell you both eventually… and it seemed like a good idea at the time."

"Why? Secrets and lies are always a bad idea in relationships. I should know." He mumbles out those last few words and then stops talking.

"What does that mean?"

He sighs. "If you must know, it means your mother didn't leave me because she wanted to 'find herself'."

"Then why did she leave?"

"Because she fell in love with another man."

I can't disguise my gasp of surprise. "Another man? Why didn't you tell me?"

"Shock, I think. I'd just found out your mother had been having an affair for months, and I hadn't suspected a thing. I'd been blind to it all, and I couldn't take it in... and I suppose I didn't want you to think badly of her. So I just said the first thing that came into my head."

"Did you hope she'd come back?"

"No, I don't think so." He shakes his head. "I don't think I could have forgiven her, Gem. And it's not like she asked for my forgiveness, did she? She asked me to divorce her."

"But I always thought she divorced you." I'll admit it's not something Dad and I talked about very much, so it's not that he lied... I just made the assumption.

"No. She didn't have grounds. If she was going to file for divorce, she'd have had to wait at least two years. But because of her affair, I could divorce her on the grounds of her adultery."

"And you did?"

"Yes."

"So, why didn't you tell me then, about why she'd really left?"

"Because I didn't want to upset you. She'd left us both behind so she could start a new life. She'd made it very clear she wanted a clean break, and it seemed more important to me that we should just get on with our lives... without her. Besides, it was hard enough for me to admit my marriage was over after sixteen years. I didn't want to tell you I hadn't been enough for her."

"Oh, Dad…" I lean in to him and put my arms around his waist.

"It's not a great feeling, you know… to be left for someone else."

I pull back slightly and look up at him. "Did you know the man?" I ask.

"Yes. You probably don't remember, but the year before your mother left, we had a PC transfer down here from somewhere in North London. I can't remember the station now, but his name was Mike Wells. He wasn't anything special as coppers go, but he was all right and he fitted in. He arrived not long before Christmas, and I took him out for a drink and made the mistake – as it turned out – of introducing him to your mother."

"You introduced them?" I can only imagine how that must have made Dad feel, when Mum ran off with the man.

"Yes. He was quite a bit younger than her, so I suppose I didn't see it coming…" He lets his voice fade.

"Is that why you've had such a negative attitude towards every other man who's come here from London ever since?" I ask after a brief pause. He shrugs his answer, refusing to speak, but staring at the floor in front of us. "You're being very immature, Dad." He opens his mouth, but then closes it again and I shake my head. "You can't argue with me. Just because Mum ran off with a man from London, doesn't mean they're all inherently bad."

He sucks in a breath and lets it out slowly. "I know. It was a stupid attitude to take, and I'm sorry for not telling you about her."

"I'm sorry too."

"I think you're saying that to the wrong person, don't you? Surely you had to realise this would come back and bite you eventually. Porthgarrion is far too small a village to keep a secret like that."

"I know. Like I said, I didn't plan this. I kept meaning to tell Tom... and you, obviously. I just never found the right moment. And then that man snatched my bag, and I was hurt and upset and I wanted Tom."

He frowns, and I can see a shadow behind his eyes. "You... you wanted Tom?"

"Yes. I'm sorry, but I wanted him." There's no point in lying. Not now. "I phoned him. Or at least, I got Rachel to phone him. I was in too much of a state to do anything myself, so I gave her my phone and asked her to call him for me."

"So he didn't just happen to be there?" Dad says, tipping his head slightly to his right.

"No. I called, and he came running, and he helped me. Then you called him on the radio, and you came running too... and my whole world came crumbling down."

"You've made a real mess of things, haven't you?" He doesn't bother to sugar-coat anything for me.

"Yes, I have."

"I'll give Tom one thing though," he says unexpectedly. "He didn't give you away. There have been several opportunities since Saturday afternoon for him to let the cat out of the bag to me, and he hasn't taken one of them. He could have tried to score points over me, especially given the way I've treated him since he arrived here... and he didn't."

I can hear something that sounds like admiration in his voice, but I'm not sure there's any point in it now.

"I'm sorry." What else can I say? "I know this is going to make things awkward for you at work."

"Is it?" he says. "I don't see why. Not really. Although I have to say, you could have made things much simpler, if you'd just told us both the truth from the beginning."

"I know, but it wasn't that simple."

"Why not? It was just a matter of being honest."

"You make it sound so easy… but it wasn't. I was scared, Dad."

"What of?"

"That you wouldn't let me keep seeing Tom if you found out."

He smiles and says, "Seriously? It's the twenty-first century, Gem. I can hardly lock you up in a tower because I don't approve of your suitors. Besides, you're twenty years old. I can't stop you from doing anything… as long as it's legal." He reaches out and takes my hand. "Tom makes you happy – at least, he seemed to be, before all this blew up – so why would I want to stop you from seeing him?"

I suddenly burst into tears at the thought of how things were before I messed up.

"Hey…" Dad moves closer and pulls me into a hug. "Why are you crying?"

"Because he won't talk to me," I mumble into his chest. "Imelda says Tom's angry and hurt, but he won't take my calls or return any of my messages, so how can I explain any of it to him? I love him so much, Dad… and he can't even bear the sound of my voice."

Chapter Twenty

Tom

The noise of something hammering in my head wakes me up, and for just a second or two I wonder how much I drank last night… until I remember I didn't drink anything. I avoided opening that bottle of wine altogether, and I realise that the hammering is someone at the front door, as I leap out of bed and rush down the stairs, almost falling over my own feet.

Outside, is a man, standing behind a large box, looking a bit fed up.

"Wake you up, did I?" he says sarcastically, looking me up and down.

"Yes."

I'm only wearing a pair of shorts, and I imagine my hair is all over the place, so I can't see any reason to pretend that I've been up for hours.

He shakes his head. "Where do you want this?" he asks, bending to lift the box.

"Just inside the door will be fine."

I daren't ask him to move it any further into the house. He's already disapproving enough. That wouldn't normally bother me, but I think the shock of waking up like that, coupled with the fact that I've had very little sleep, has left me rather ill-prepared for the day. Of course, what sleep I have had has been punctuated with dreams of Gemma, but I can't think about that now.

He hands me a clipboard, pointing to where I'm supposed to sign on the slip of paper, and then leaves, without another word, and I stare down at the box that contains my new kitchen cupboard.

I hadn't expected it to arrive quite this early, but I'm not complaining and I drag the box through to the kitchen, leaving it against the wall for now. I put on some coffee, and then jump out of my skin as someone else knocks on my door… or at least I assume it's someone else, and not the same delivery man, come back to check I'm still up.

I open the door again, and this time I find a man wearing green overalls, staring back at me.

"You're expecting an order from Green Leaves Garden Centre?" he says, with much less interest in my attire, or the fact that I've so clearly just got out of bed, than my previous visitor.

"Yes." I think for a moment, because I don't particularly want to have it delivered inside the house. "Can you put it in the garage for me?"

"I can put it anywhere you want, mate," he says. "I'll just need to offload the van."

"Okay. Give me a minute and I'll meet you out the front."

He disappears and I run up the stairs, where I strip off my shorts and quickly pull on a pair of jeans and a t-shirt, before returning to the front door, where I slip on some shoes and grab my keys from the sofa, where I threw them last night. Outside, the man has already removed two boxes from the back of his green lorry, and has propped them up against the steps, so I open the garage and start moving them inside.

Between us, we make light work of the task, and as soon as I've signed for the delivery, the man drives off, leaving me to rearrange my garage, stacking the boxes carefully at the back, so I can at least get my car out safely.

Once I'm inside the house again, I go into the kitchen and pour myself a coffee, trying to decide what to do with the rest of my day. I hadn't expected that the deliveries would be over and done with quite this early, but at least I can take my time getting dressed, and reorganise my kitchen, now that the cupboard is here. I think the garden furniture can wait until the weekend. It's not as though I'm going to be using it yet.

I'm about to start up the stairs, taking my coffee with me, when my phone rings. I left it on the sofa last night and I go over and pick it up, seeing an unknown number come up on the screen. Of course, I could leave it, but I decide against that, and connect the call.

"Hello?"

"Hughes?"

I recognise the voice of Sergeant Quick, and even if I didn't, he's the only person I know who addresses me by my surname.

"Yes, sir?"

"I know it's your day off, but something important has come up and I need to see you here, at the station."

"Now, sir?"

"Yes. Now, sir."

He sounds like the sarcastic man I thought I'd left behind, the man who was quick to judge and slow to apologise, and I wonder for a moment what I can have done wrong now.

"I'm not dressed yet," I say, although I don't know why I'm bothering to explain myself to him.

"You're not?" He sounds surprised.

"No. I've had a… a busy morning."

"Doing what?" He sound suspicious now, bordering on angry. What's the matter with him, for heaven's sake?

"My deliveries came earlier than I expected," I say, not that it's any of his business what I do with my free time. "But I can be there in half an hour." I don't want to stay on the phone being berated for my poor habits.

"Fine."

I'm about to ask him what's happened, just so I have a clue how much of a roasting I'm about to receive, when I realise the line is dead. He's already gone.

"Fabulous," I say to myself and look down at my phone, shaking my head. It's only as I'm about to put it down that I notice the little red dot beside the telephone symbol, telling me I've got a voicemail. I click on it and make the connection, holding the phone to my ear again as I listen to the automated female voice telling me that the message I'm about to listen to was left by a number I know to be Gemma's at eight minutes past six yesterday evening. I wait, expecting to hear her voice, but instead, I just hear a few seconds of sobbing before the message cuts out and I'm being asked if I want to save or delete it.

I disconnect the call, knowing the message will save by default and I wonder… did Gemma phone just to cry at me? Or did she call meaning to say something, and find she couldn't talk? Either way, the sound of her weeping echoes around my head as I put the phone down again and make my way up the stairs.

I decided against wearing my uniform for my visit to the station. It's just a visit, after all. I'm still officially on my day off.

Even so, I check my watch as I leave the house, and roll my eyes, noting that I'm already five minutes late for my appointment. Ordinarily, I probably wouldn't care that much, but I don't want to cause any more friction between the sergeant and myself. He's bound to be more than a bit irate when Gemma finally tells him the truth about us... assuming she ever does, of course.

God, that's a depressing thought... and as I walk past the florist's, I don't break my stride, although I take a quick glance inside. There are three customers blocking my view of the counter where I assume Gemma is working. I'm not sure whether to feel grateful for that, or sad that I haven't seen her in so long... but either way, I've got other things to think about for the moment, and I pick up my pace, because I don't want to be any later than I already am.

Inside the station, Geoff is sitting behind the counter, but the office is otherwise deserted and I let myself in through the door.

"I'm supposed to be seeing Sergeant Quick," I say, when he looks me up and down.

"He said you're to go straight in."

He nods towards the sergeant's office and I make my way over, knocking once and waiting to hear the words, "Come in," before I push the door inward and pass through, closing it behind me.

"You wanted to see me, sir?" I move across the room, standing in front of the sergeant's desk, which is quite modern, in a room filled with filing cabinets. The window behind him offers a view of nothing more grandiose than the back alleyway that leads from the rear of the building to the small car park for police vehicles.

"Yes." He sits back in his leather chair and gazes up at me, although he doesn't remark on my lack of uniform. Instead, he tilts his head slightly to one side and says, "Would you mind telling me what's going on?"

I feel a bit blindsided by that question. "With what?"

"With you and Gemma."

Well, that's thrown me completely and I take a half step back, before I say, "Can I assume she's told you about us?"

"Yes... but you could have told me before now, couldn't you?"

"Why?" I ask, moving forward again, emboldened by his accusatory tone. "I didn't even know you and Gemma were related until Saturday lunchtime. And before you tell me I could've said something between then and now, I'd like to remind you, you're not my father. You're Gemma's. The truth had to come from her, because she's the one who started the lies." His eyes narrow slightly, but I'm not flinching from him, even if he is my boss. "I was completely open with your daughter," I say, not giving him a chance to talk. "She's different. She's special, and I didn't want to lie to her. I couldn't. So I told her about my job, even though that hasn't always gone well for me in the past. She could have explained who you are, but she didn't. She kept it to herself... and she continued keeping it to herself, while letting me complain to her about how you've been treating me."

The sergeant stands, his chair rolling backwards and hitting the radiator beneath the window, with a loud clang.

"If you have any complaints about how you've been treated, you should have come to me, not discussed them with my daughter."

"I didn't know she was your daughter at the time," I remind him. "And, in any case, that's beside the point, isn't it, sir?"

"Is it?"

"Yes. I may have told Gemma how I felt about working here, but I'm big enough to fight my own professional battles with you, if I feel the need... which I don't."

He sighs, standing upright again. "In which case, what is the point?"

"Gemma," I say, stating the obvious. "And the fact that she omitted to tell either of us about the other, and that, in your case, she referred to her relationship with me as 'not serious', when in reality, as far as I'm concerned, it's very serious." I shrug my shoulders. "Still…" I lower my voice a little, "… it's nice to know how Gemma feels."

I turn to leave, because I've said everything that needs to be said, but before I've taken two steps, the sergeant calls me back, with a bite to his voice.

"I haven't finished with you yet."

I turn to face him. "With all due respect, sir, this has nothing to do with my work here. It's between Gemma and myself and while I appreciate that you're her father and you obviously care about her, she's an adult, and we'll work things out between ourselves."

"Will you?" he says, narrowing his eyes again. "Will you work it out? Or will you keep putting your pride ahead of doing what's right?"

"What does that mean?"

"It means I know she's been calling you. I know she's been leaving you messages, and that you've been ignoring her… and that's not a very nice thing to do."

I shake my head. "Maybe it isn't. But it's not very nice being lied to either… or knowing that she doesn't take our relationship seriously, despite telling me the polar opposite." I take a breath. "I'm in love with your daughter, and what she did… it hurts."

He's shocked to the point of silence and he takes a moment to recover before he says, "She regrets the lies," with a much softer tone of voice than before. "She regrets all of it, and I don't think she meant it when she told me your relationship wasn't serious. I think she just wanted to see you without me interfering." He pauses for a second, and then reaches behind him, straightening his chair, before he sits down again and looks up at me. "But you'd know all that for yourself, if you'd just take her calls. She'd be able to explain it, instead of crying herself to sleep."

I move forward, despite the pain in my chest that's threatening to take my breath away. "She's been crying herself to sleep?"

"Yes. I assumed it was to do with the assault, until last night, when I got home and found her crying her eyes out in the living room. She explained everything to me, about the lies and the secrets… and how much she loves you."

I pull back the chair in front of me and sit in it, uninvited, although the sergeant doesn't seem to object.

"I'd heard her crying in her messages," I murmur. "But I didn't realise she was crying herself to sleep."

"Well, she was… she still is. She thinks it's all over between you, and she's heartbroken, if you must know."

"She should try being me then," I say, and he shakes his head at me.

"You're hurt… I understand that. I even think you have a right to be… but you needn't think you're the only man in the world to go through something like this. I've been cheated on myself, so I know exactly what it feels like to be betrayed, but what doesn't make much sense to me at the moment is that you've just told me you're in love with Gemma, and yet you won't even talk to her."

"It's not that simple." I ignore his comment about being cheated on for now. This is neither the time nor the place to remark on that, and he raises his eyebrows in surprise. "Try looking at this from my point of view. Let's say I'd been able to put my own feelings one side and I'd called Gemma after her first phone message, and asked her to meet me. What would she have told you, do you think? Would she have said she was coming to meet me, Tom Hughes, or would she have made an excuse to leave the house... like seeing her 'not serious' boyfriend?"

He stares at me and then says, "I don't know."

"Don't you?" I gaze at him for a moment, but he doesn't say a word. "If we're being honest, I think we both know she'd have made up an excuse... and that's why I didn't call her. I didn't want to speak to her, or see her, until I was calm enough to accept another lie... and I wasn't. I wanted her to tell you first, so that everything would be out in the open, but it seemed more likely to me that she'd wait to tell you until after she knew where she stood with me. After all, why risk your wrath, if she didn't have to?"

"My wrath? What do you think I am? A monster?"

"Okay, maybe wrath is the wrong word, but she'd lied to you too, and I didn't imagine you were going to be too happy about that... or about the fact that she'd been seeing me. You didn't seem to like me very much, so I assumed the idea of me being your daughter's boyfriend would hardly fill you with joy."

He blushes and leans back in his seat. "I suppose I can understand that, but while you've been busy being logical and hurt, and making allowances for my feelings, you've forgotten about Gemma's."

"No, I haven't." I raise my voice, regardless of his rank... and mine. "I haven't, for one second, forgotten about Gemma, or how she'd be feeling."

"In that case, why can't you remember that you're the grown-up in this relationship? Gemma's a lot younger than you, and she's much less experienced, I would imagine. She knows she's made a mistake – well, several mistakes, really – but you could try giving her a break, couldn't you? She's called you over and over, but I don't think she knows how to make the next move..."

He lets his voice fade and I sit forward slightly.

"If I do it for her… if I make the next move for her, are you going to have a problem? With us being together, I mean? Because you're right, I am a grown-up, and I'm not playing at this. I never was."

"I'm glad to hear it," he says, and a smile twitches at the corners of his lips. "Especially as I thought you were more interested in Rachel Pedrick than anyone else."

"Rachel? At the baker's?"

"Yes."

I shake my head. "She's nice enough, I'm sure, but she's not Gemma," I say and he smiles, as a thought occurs to me. "Please tell me you haven't mentioned your suspicions to Gemma?"

"No. I'm not totally insensitive. And to get back to the point, if I had a problem with you and Gemma being together, don't you think I'd be filling her head with suggestions about you and Rachel… telling her she's well rid of you? If I had a problem, do you think I'd be sitting here, having this embarrassing conversation about my daughter's love life?" He sighs, shaking his head. "I know she's not a child anymore, Tom, but she's still very young, and I'd rather you made the next move for her than broke her heart."

I suck in a breath, reeling from the fact that he just called me by my first name, and from the thought of Gemma being hurt.

"I never intended to break her heart."

He holds up his hand. "I know. I'm not blaming you. Not really. You… you look like you could do with some fresh air. Why don't you go for a walk along the harbour… and see if that walk takes you past Imelda's place?"

I smile. I can't help myself, and I get to my feet. "Maybe I'll do that."

"Good." He stands too. "And we'll still have that drink on Friday, shall we?"

"Um... yes, sir."

He nods. "You should bring Gemma with you."

My smile widens. "Yes, sir."

He smiles himself. "I think you should stop calling me 'sir' when we're not at work." He holds out his hand for me to shake and as I do, he says, "My name's Rory." I nod my head, and he releases my hand, leaning in a little closer. "But if you call me that during working hours, I'll haul you over the coals."

"Very good, sir."

I chuckle, and so does he.

I pause on the threshold of the flower shop, feeling relieved that there are no customers inside now, although there's also no sign of Gemma, either. The sign on the door says 'open' though, so taking a breath, I push it and step inside. The bell above my head rings, and after just a few seconds, Gemma appears from the preparation room at the back of the shop. She's carrying a roll of ribbon, which she's winding and she doesn't look up straight away, which gives me a chance to study her for a moment... to take in her tight stonewashed jeans, that are clinging to her hips and thighs, and the pretty yellow blouse, that's undone sufficiently to reveal just a hint of cleavage... just a hint and no more. I stifle my groan, although my body responds to her in an instant, as she looks up and stops dead.

"Tom," she whispers, and I step forward to the counter as she drops the ribbon.

"Yes." Tears are already forming in her eyes, and while I'm tempted to walk around the counter and kiss her, I don't. I have to do this right. "I see you've got some tulips," I say, nodding towards the display near the front of the shop.

"Yes." She looks a bit confused. "Did you want some?"

"Yes, please. I'll take all of them."

Her eyes widen slightly, and she peers around me. "But there must be twenty bunches there. They're three pounds each."

"That's fine."

She hesitates for a moment, as though she wants to say something else, and then with a rather disappointed shrug, she moves around the counter, by-passing me and going over to the tulips, which are displayed in a couple of metal buckets. She gathers them in her arms, and while she's got her back turned, I take a pen from the pot on the counter, putting it into my back pocket. I'm not stealing it, I'm only borrowing it… and it's for a very good cause. By the time Gemma returns, bringing the tulips back with her, I'm standing exactly as I was.

"Do you want me to wrap them?" she asks, sounding sadder than I would have thought possible.

"Yes, please."

She nods her head and sets about wrapping the tulips, creating three large bunches in total.

"That's sixty pounds," she says, in a small whisper, once she's finished, and I give her my credit card, selecting a small greetings card from the display while she types the amount into the machine, before giving it to me to input my pin number. I'm careful not to touch her hand as I give it back, and then pick up the flowers from the counter, cradling them in my arms.

"Thank you," I say, with a nod of my head, and then I turn and leave the shop, closing the door behind me.

I don't look back. Instead, I walk across the street to the harbour wall, putting the flowers down for a moment, while I take out the pen and write the card. Then I tuck it inside its envelope, placing it between the flowers, before I gather them up again and retrace my steps.

The bell rings out for a second time, only now Gemma is standing at the counter, exactly where I left her and she looks up, slightly startled, as I enter and shut the door behind me, turning the sign around to say 'closed'. She doesn't say a word, but as I walk towards her, I can see the tears streaking her cheeks, so rather than handing the flowers across the counter, I go around to her side, standing only a foot from her, when I hold them out, waiting for her to take them.

"Th—They're for me?" She stares at me, blinking rapidly, and then reaches up and wipes her cheeks with the backs of her hands, before she takes the flowers, looking down at them as though she's never seen them before.

"Of course they're for you. Who else would they be for?"

She shrugs, looking back at me. "I don't know. I saw you with Rachel yesterday, and the thought crossed my mind that you might move on... with someone else." Her voice cracks and I step closer to her, recalling her father's suspicions and feeling even more grateful now that he kept them to himself.

"Rachel just came out to thank me for catching the bag snatcher. There's nothing going on between us, Gemma. I'd never do that to you... I'd never knowingly hurt you."

"I hurt you, though, didn't I?" she whispers.

"Yes, you did." Tears well in her eyes, and I lean in to her, nodding towards the flowers. "You need to read the card."

She blinks again a few times and then puts the flowers down on the counter, taking the card, and pulling it from its envelope, turning it around and looking down at it. I know what it says. I only wrote the words 'Can we start again?' a few minutes ago, and she nods her head, the card falling from her fingers as she bursts into tears.

I put my hands on her waist and pull her close to me, except that doesn't feel like quite enough, so I lift her and she instinctively wraps her arms and legs around me.

"I was going to buy you yellow roses," I say. "I know they're your favourite colour, and they stand for new beginnings, but it seemed more important to go for the tulips. So... are they enough of a declaration of my love? Or do you need me to say it?"

"Could you say it?"

I lean back slightly, so I can see her, so I can look into her eyes. "You're my one perfect love, Gemma. No matter what happens, I will always love you."

"Even though I hurt you?" She still sounds doubtful.

"Yes. Listen to me… I. Love. You."

"I love you too… and I'm sorry, Tom. I'm so sorry."

"I know you are, and I'm sorry too. I should've taken your calls."

"Why didn't you?" I sit her down on the counter, parting her legs a little wider and moving into the space between them. "You turned your phone off," she says, playing with the second button down on my shirt.

"You can open that, if you want to. I don't mind."

She looks up at me and bites her bottom lip, although she doesn't undo the button. She doesn't move her hand away either. "Did you turn your phone off because you didn't want to talk to me?" she says, after a moment's pause.

"No. I'd been replaying your first message over and over, and it hurt." She winces, but I continue, "It seemed wise to remove the temptation of hearing your voice by turning off the phone." I lean in so our lips are almost touching. Almost, but not quite. "I listened to all your messages though."

"So why didn't you call me back?" She stares up into my eyes, her own filled with confusion.

"Because I'm a man." She tilts her head. "Generally speaking, we're not great with being hurt. It does ridiculous things to our pride and we tend to over-react." She smiles, but it's still a little half-hearted. "And anyway, I didn't want to talk to you over the phone. I wanted to talk to you face-to-face."

"Then why did you ignore me yesterday, when I called out to you?"

I sigh, knowing I have to be honest, because that's what this is all about. "I knew if I turned around and came back to you, I'd end up kissing you." Her eyes widen and she licks her lips, which is very tempting. So tempting that I clasp her face between my hands, relishing the contact… the intimacy.

"Would that have been such a bad thing?"

"Ordinarily, no. But it was too soon for kissing."

"It was?"

"Yes. We needed to talk before we could kiss. Only I wasn't ready to talk. I—I was too angry. You'd messed with my head and my heart, and I wasn't ready to confront that." She blinks and two tears fall onto her cheeks. I wipe them away with my thumbs. "It wasn't just that," I say. "I had another reason for not taking your calls… for keeping my distance. It wasn't just about being a man, or wanting to see you face-to-face."

"What was it about then?"

"I wasn't sure what you'd do, if I asked you to meet me."

She swallows down her tears, frowning. "I'd have said yes, of course. I was desperate to see you."

"I know. But what would you have told your father? Would you have come clean and explained you were going to meet me, or would you have made up something about your 'not serious' boyfriend?"

"My what?" She pulls back, forcing me to release her.

"Your 'not serious' boyfriend." I step away, turning my back on her. "Not long after you and I started seeing each other, your dad and Geoff were having a debate about whether a father should feel entitled to meet his daughter's boyfriend. Geoff asked my opinion, which seemed to rile your dad, because the daughter in question was his own, and I guess he thought it was none of my business. Geoff pushed me for an answer, though, so

I said it depended on whether the relationship was serious… at which point your dad recalled his daughter saying that her relationship with her boyfriend wasn't serious at all. I thought nothing of it at the time, but once it became clear who you were, and who your father was… well, let's just say it wasn't a very pleasant thought."

I hear movement behind me and I turn, just as Gemma jumps down from the counter and comes over, standing right in front of me, looking up into my eyes.

"I'm sorry, Tom," she says. "It was just that I didn't want Dad to interfere. I—"

"I know. At least, I know now. At the time, when I realised I was your 'not serious' boyfriend, it hurt. It hurt a lot. I couldn't believe you'd lied about loving me."

"I didn't. I lied to Dad about us being serious, to throw him off the scent."

"I understand that now." I smile down at her. "But when I first put two and two together, I sort of came up with five, and thought it meant you didn't love me… not that you'd been deceiving your dad."

She steps forward, resting her hand on my chest. "I never meant for all of this to happen," she says. "I never meant to hurt you."

"I know you didn't."

"It was just that, at the beginning, Dad was so negative about you, and once I realised who you were and that you worked for him, I didn't know what to say… so I said nothing. Obviously, I kept on saying nothing, until it all spiralled out of control." She sighs. "If only he hadn't been so down on you, none of this would have happened."

"Hmm… well, he knows how I feel about that now."

"He does?" She's surprised.

"Yes. He and I have just had a long conversation. I told him that one of things that made this so difficult and complicated was that I'd opened up to you about my professional relationship with him, and you'd still said nothing about who he was. He wanted to know if I felt badly treated by him, so I told him I did."

"Gosh." Her eyes widen.

"It's the truth, Gemma. He was very quick to judge me… he can't deny it."

She sighs and shakes her head. "No… but I suppose I can't blame him for that," she whispers.

"Why not?"

She looks up and takes a deep breath. "Because of the reason my mother left him."

"To find herself, you mean?"

"No. That was just what he told me at the time. The reality was very different." She steps away and leans back on the counter. "My mother ran away with a younger policeman, who'd transferred down here from the Met."

I let my head rock back and gaze up at the ceiling. That makes sense of the cheating comment he made in his office… and so much more. "Oh, I see… and since then, he's assumed the worst of all of us, has he?" I look back down at her again.

"Yes. He knows his reactions have been silly, and a bit overboard… but it seems men are good at that."

She smiles and I step over to her, placing my hands on either side of her, pinning her to the counter, so I'm close enough to hear her gasp.

"What's wrong?" I ask.

"I—I've just realised," she says, blushing. "You said you had a long conversation with my dad… so I imagine he told you that I said you weren't my type…"

"No, he didn't." I lean back slightly. "When did you say that to him?"

"I can't remember. But I didn't mean it." She shakes her head. "I was trying to stop his constant questioning about us."

"I see."

"A—Are you cross?"

"No. As long as you promise you didn't mean it."

"I didn't. I promise."

"Okay. In that case, can we forget about it, and do as I suggested?" She tilts her head, looking confused. "Can we start again?"

"Oh. Yes please."

She gazes up into my eyes and I move closer, our bodies fused. "I think we'll start by agreeing that there aren't going to be any more secrets between us."

"Definitely not."

"And tonight, when you've finished here, I'm going to come back and pick you up. Then we'll walk round to your place, and you're going to pack a bag."

"Am I?" she breathes.

"You are. We've got a lot of talking to do, and I'd rather do that at my place. Then, when we're done talking, we're going to make up for spending the last few days apart, and I'm going to make love to you… all night long."

She blinks and sucks in a breath. "H—How on earth am I supposed to explain that to my father?"

I smile down at her. "That's the main reason I'm going to be picking you up from work and taking you home before we go round to my place… so we can explain things to him together. Although I don't think we'll tell him I'm planning on making love to you all night. I think we'll paraphrase that part… somehow."

She blushes and smiles and says, "I think that might be a good idea."

I lean down, letting my lips brush over hers, the intimate contact sending sparks to every nerve ending in my body. She sighs into me. "We will tell him you're going to be spending the night with me though," I murmur, between gentle kisses. "And we'll tell him we're going to work things out between us. He already knows I'm in love with you… so…"

"How does he know that?"

She leans back, but I put my hand behind her head and pull her close again, kissing her a little harder.

"Because I told him," I say, breaking the kiss and resting my forehead against hers. "We're in this together, Gemma… from now on."

"Always…" she says, in a soft dreamy voice, as I silence her with a kiss

The End

Thank you for reading *It Started with Flowers*. I hope you enjoyed it, and if you did, I hope you'll take the time to leave a short review.

The characters of Porthgarrion will return soon in *It Started with Hello*, in which we'll find out what happens when Rory Quick is brought out of his shell by village newcomer, Laura Clark.

Printed in Great Britain
by Amazon